The Wanderlings

THE CAT WHO WENT INTO THE WOODS

ALEXA MILNE

ENTWINED PUBLISHING

The Cat Who Went Into the Woods
ISBN # 978-1-80250-258-9
©Copyright Alexa Milne 2025
Cover Art by Kelly Martin ©Copyright August 2025
Interior text design by Entwined Publishing
Published by Eternal, an Entwined Publishing imprint

Published in 2025 by Entwined Publishing, United Kingdom.

Entwined Publishing is a division of Totally Entwined Group Limited.

THE CAT WHO WENT INTO THE WOODS

Dedication

This book is dedicated to my cats, all of whom came to me via the cat distribution service. My three boys, who are sadly no longer with us, came from the RSPCA — cat number one — and off the street — cats two and three. I truly believe cats decide where they want to be.

My current girl cat did not like her new owner's dog. I took her in. She was the first cat I had as a kitten. Now, she has reached the grand old age of thirteen.

All my cats have had differing personalities and musical tastes. They have kept me company and given me love in their own unique ways. Believe me, there are few things in life as amazing as being loved by a cat.

I'd also like to thank those who helped me along the way to produce this book.

Chapter One

Harry stared out of the kitchen window while his mother bustled around making breakfasts for the current batch of guests at the family B&B.

"Looks like summer's given up early this year," he said surveying the layer of flat grey cloud that covered the sky and the huge raindrops clattering on the window. A lack of visibility meant the mountains and hills of the Lake District, much of the reason tourists came to the area, could not be seen. He bit into his bacon sandwich and licked the corner of his mouth when the fat attempted to escape the bread.

"Don't you and Rich have a job today?" Lucy Katt asked.

"Yes, Mum. A wasps' nest in a roof space in Penrith. Rich said he'd knock on when he was ready to go." Harry yawned.

"Late night?" his mother asked.

Harry grinned. His cat-like tread meant he often got in without his mother hearing. "What can I say? I met some people."

"Human?"

Harry nodded. "Yes, they were."

"He's probably had all the shifters in Cumbria by now." Oona Katt entered the kitchen carrying used crockery and cutlery on a tray. She placed them in the dishwasher then sat at the table.

"Gran? Really? Is this the sort of language you should be using in front of your grandson?"

Oona shrugged. "Well it's true, isn't it?" She turned to her daughter. "The Clarkes are off to the pencil museum. This isn't the weather for wandering the hills."

Harry's phone sang out a tune. "Damn. It's Mountain Rescue. Please don't tell me some idiot has gone hiking in trainers, not in this weather."

"It wouldn't be the first time, laddie. There's some bloody barmpots around." Harry's grandmother has never lost her Scottish vocabulary. He connected the call.

"Hi, Bez."

"We need you, Harry. A couple have been reported missing overnight. No one noticed they hadn't returned until they didn't show up for breakfast this morning. The hotel owner wasn't sure what equipment they had with them but said one of the other guests mentioned the pair intended to walk the Fairfield Horseshoe."

"That route can be tricky even if you're experienced, and with the weather setting in like it has overnight, it's high enough to get caught in a cloud." Harry grabbed his bag.

"Yeah, and as we have no idea how far they got, we'll need more than one team. And we've no idea if either or even both are injured. Phone signal can be dodgy up there, too."

"Okay, I'll get ready," Harry said.

"Great. Malc will swing by with the dogs and pick you up. We've got some of their clothes which will help them find a scent."

Harry grimaced. As a cat shifter, dogs could be problematic, but these animals were well-trained. "It would have been beautiful when they set off yesterday, but people should check the forecasts. Right, son, I'll see you soon."

Harry picked up his pre-prepared bag and stashed his phone in his pocket. He'd need waterproofs and his best boots. "Can you let—"

"Rich know?" His mother nodded. "Be careful out there, won't you?"

Harry kissed his mother's head. "Of course I will."

He waited on the doorstep. The rain hadn't stopped. In fact, if anything, it was coming down harder. Malc arrived fifteen minutes later. Harry stowed his bag on the back seat and climbed in beside the older man. Malc was a legend in Mountain Rescue, having been a volunteer for thirty-five years. He knew every inch of the fells and mountains and still ran them regularly.

"We're meeting at the car park," Malc said.

"Makes sense, but it's still a decent walk from there." Harry pulled out his phone. "Conditions will be treacherous. It's not a route for those who aren't used to walking."

Malc nodded. "No, it isn't. Let's hope these two didn't set off in T-shirts, shorts, and trainers."

"Remember the bloke who broke his leg last year—nasty compound fracture. He was lucky we found him when we did."

At the car park, twenty volunteers were gathered. Harry knew most of them after a year in the service. He noted the stretchers and other equipment. Malc gathered them around and gave out instructions.

"Visibility won't be good up there, and watch your feet. We don't want one of you lot adding to our woes. Let's hope they haven't done much damage to themselves. It's a three-to-four-hour trek, and we'll get no air support in this weather."

Harry noticed a face he hadn't seen before in the other group. The man was short and stocky, built like a rugby prop forward, and he had an impressive auburn beard. For a second or two, their eyes met across the space. The man stared then turned away as if he'd seen a ghost. Harry nudged Malc.

"Who's the bloke over there in the yellow jacket—the one with the beard? I've not seen him before."

Malc turned to look. "His name's Ted Woodward. He moved into the area a few months ago. He's a countryside and forest ranger. He worked farther north before with Jacko Grimshaw. Says he's good but doesn't talk much. Not one for drinking with the lads, apparently. Right, we'd better get moving." He blew his whistle and everyone turned to wait for instructions.

The walk proved to be as difficult as expected with all of them slipping on the rocks at some point. No one talked much. Most kept their heads down, checking where they were putting their feet. In this weather, it was unlikely the dogs would pick up anything either. By the time they got to the paths along the tops, Harry wondered if they'd ever find the couple unless the weather improved. It would be so easy to put your foot in the wrong place and slide down the side of the valley. If one of them hit a rock, it would stop their fall but could cause other damage. Along the way, they shouted out names until, finally, they heard a faint reply. Harry's ears picked up the sound, then there was a sudden burst of light.

"At least they had the sense to bring a flare," Malc said. The other team appeared out of the mist.

"Right, Harry, get yourself roped up and we'll let you make your way down to them."

Known for being good at clambering on all surfaces, Harry secured the ropes and harness. The man he'd spotted before stepped up to hold him.

"Be careful, Harry." So this bloke, Ted, had taken time to find out his name, and, from his accent, was Scottish. What had brought him here?

Harry glanced up at him and shivered but not with cold—something tingled his senses. He composed himself. "Don't worry. I always land on my feet."

Harry and another of the volunteers found the couple in a small tent propped against one of the larger boulders.

"Hello in there. Mountain Rescue here. Are you all right?"

A head poked out. "Thank goodness. We wondered if anyone would find us in this weather. It's my husband. He slipped from the top of the ridge. I think he's broken his leg below his knee. The bone isn't sticking out, but he's in a lot of pain. I made the best splint I could—I'm a nurse." The man next to her groaned. She leant back and touched his face.

"It's all right, darling. People are here."

Harry and the others organised the stretcher and helped the pair back up the steep slope. It would take around another three hours of walking to get the injured man back to the car park then on to the hospital. All the volunteers munched on energy bars and drank coffee before they started back along the narrow path.

Halfway, carrying a heavy stretcher, Harry wished he hadn't been out so late and drunk so much the night before. He slipped, jerking his knee painfully.

"You all right there, son?" Malc said. Harry wasn't and he knew better than to endanger the person they were rescuing through false bravado. He shook his head and Malc nodded.

"Jimmy, take over from Harry, will you?" They exchanged quickly and Harry continued behind the group, limping slightly. He hoped he'd manage to walk it off.

The rain settled into a persistent drizzle that kept every surface wet. As an experienced member of the rescue team, Harry knew he'd need to take care with every step, especially the uneven stone staircase that wove its way down to the town.

Shit! The ground crumbled and slid from underneath him. He tried to grab hold of something but everything slipped through his fingers and he tumbled, rolling over and over down the slope. While trying to protect himself, he attempted to shout and heard various replies then pain shot through his temple. *Have I hit rock?* Everything turned to black.

For a few seconds he woke, tried to breathe, but only took in water. *Not good.* He had the vague impression of being manoeuvred and a body above him then everything went black again. *Is that someone kissing me?* He woke to find himself on his side, spluttering water from his lungs. His head ached.

"That's it, laddie, cough it up. You'll be all right, but I reckon you've used a few of those nine lives of yours. So much for always landing on your feet."

Harry tried to put the man's words together. There was something important he'd said. He wanted to speak but weariness overtook him.

"It's okay. Lie back but keep breathing. You've had a nasty knock."

The next time Harry opened his eyes, he closed them again quickly — the bright lights almost burnt his eyes. He stretched out a hand and touched sheets and blankets. He was in a bed. He tentatively opened his eyes again then lifted his hand to his head. He found that the area was swathed in bandages. He also had an oxygen tube.

"I fell off the ridge. Someone rescued me," he said, as much to himself as to anyone else.

A face he recognised appeared in front of him. "You're awake then?"

"Rich? Am I in hospital?"

"Yes, of course you are, yer idiot. You had a tumble and hit your head on the way to the bottom. You landed in a large puddle face down and swallowed water. Luckily for you, one of the other blokes managed to scramble down and gave you CPR. They had to carry you out on another stretcher."

Harry turned his head and pain shot through his temple. He groaned. "Hurts."

"You were lucky. They don't think you've fractured your skull or anything, just a nasty gash and probably concussion. They want to keep you in overnight for observation. Malc said he'd pop in later, and Mum and Gran are outside. I'll let them know you're conscious."

The curtain pulled back and a nurse appeared. "Good, you're awake." She pulled in a machine. "I need to do your obs, then we can let your mum and gran in. You gave everyone a scare, young man."

Harry attempted to smile. The nurse was pretty, but the salmon-pink uniform did nothing for her. "Thanks," he managed as she wrapped a blood pressure cuff around his arm and stuck a pulse and oxygen measure on his finger.

"Is the bloke we rescued all right?"

"He's got a nasty leg break, but he'll survive. Thankfully it wasn't too cold out there and they had a shelter." She shrugged. "I've never understood this desire to tramp around mountains and hills in all sorts of weather. Much better to sit with a drink and admire them from afar in my view. There you are. Your oxygen levels have improved and your blood pressure and pulse are almost back to normal. We need to keep an eye on your lungs, so we'll maintain the oxygen for a while. You inhaled water and that's not good. Right. The doctor will be along sometime. For now, you need to get some rest."

His mother and grandmother appeared less than a minute later. "I thought you were supposed to be doing the rescuing," his gran said. Her smile didn't reduce the worry in her eyes.

"Sorry, I slipped."

His mum took hold of his hand. "Take no notice. Malc told me conditions were bad up there. It could have happened to anyone. Thom sends his love from Los Angeles."

"You didn't need to bother him. He's got that audition for the big movie."

"He would have been mad if we didn't."

Harry yawned. His eyelids wanted to close. "Sorry. Tired."

Lucy Katt leaned over and kissed his cheek. "We'll leave you to rest and call in the morning to see if they'll let you out. Do what the medics tell you."

"Yes, Mum." He closed his eyes and was asleep before they left the room.

A few hours later, he woke again. Before he opened his eyes, he sensed a presence beside the bed. Slowly, he squinted through one eye."

"So you're awake then, laddie."

Harry searched his brain for a name. "Ted," he said. "You saved me." His memory kicked in and he smiled. "You kissed me."

A blush of red spread across what Harry could see of the man's face. "Aye, I did, sort of while saving your life. I'm told you landed on your head. You were lucky not to damage anything else. You took a nasty tumble."

Harry tampered down his desire to tease. This man had saved him, after all. "Thank you. I appreciate it, the rescuing and…" *No good. I can't resist.* "…the kissing."

"Think nothing of it. In fact, forget it ever happened. You'd have done the same for me or anyone out there."

Harry tried to focus. There was something about the solid, bearded man in the plaid shirt and blue jeans that made him sit up and take notice.

"Well, I'll be off now. I just wanted to check you were all right and hadn't done too much damage to your pretty face."

Confused, Harry found he had no reply.

Ted bent over, nearer to him. "And I'm glad you didn't use all those nine lives of yours either."

Harry spluttered attempting to speak. *Does he know?* Before he could say anything else, Ted had disappeared out of the door, leaving him wondering.

Chapter Two

Ted loved these late summer mornings when he was up with the dawn and the sun was already shining. After the rain of the last couple of days, it was a relief to be able do the repairs to the paths. Tourists were vital to the area, but they did leave damage in their wake.

He took his bowl of porridge and mug of tea and sat out on the wooden veranda at the front of his cabin. From there he could see the sun rising over the hills and mountains. He couldn't imagine living somewhere flat. It wasn't Scotland, but it was still beautiful. The forest floor was still damp, and here and there, where the sun broke through the trees, steam escaped from the ground. He grinned as a rabbit appeared out of the nearby burrow. They stared at each other, then the rabbit continued with its day.

After filling his bird feeders and putting something out for the hedgehogs, Ted returned indoors and checked his list of jobs for the day. As he scrolled through local news, a photo of Harry Katt appeared along with a story about what had happened, which thankfully didn't contain his name, not that it would matter if it did. Ted Woodward had all the history and documentation he needed to prove his new identity.

He stared at the photograph. Harry Katt was undoubtedly attractive with that white streak though his dark hair and his stubble shaped and trimmed, unlike Ted's own extensive beard. His foster parents had provided him with information about the shifter population of the area. The Katt triplets were renowned for being a small fraction of a group of cat shifters fathered by the same man. Thom was now a well-known actor while Rich and Harry ran a thriving local pest control firm.

I shouldn't have said what I did to him. Did I give too much away?

The sound of Ted's phone disturbed his thoughts. He swiped the green button. "Hi, Dad. Everything okay? It's early, even for you."

"Just thought I'd catch up with you — see how things are going. You know how your mother worries."

He'd been in Cumbria for several months, but his parents worried. Both knew keeping secrets was hard. "I'm fine, Dad. The house is great, much better than staying in the rented place I had before. The people I'm working with don't appear to be too inquisitive. Oh, and I had a mountain rescue yesterday — the weather was dreich. We've had so much rain." He explained what had happened.

"So this lad is one of the Katt family. We were told about them."

"Yes, Dad. I know, but it turns out he's also on the rescue team." Of the Katt brothers, Harry had come with a specific warning that made him all the more interesting on paper. In the flesh, he was something to see even when he was puking up water or lying in a hospital bed covered in bruises and bandages.

"He didn't notice anything about you?"

"No. It's been so long since I transformed, I doubt anyone could tell. I'm much more human than beaver, which is what everyone wanted me to be, isn't it? I have Otis to keep an eye on me. I wouldn't be surprised if this place was bugged either, though I didn't find anything when I checked."

"Son."

"I wanted to see how far they'd go. I have to know, Dad. Being the sole beaver shifter in the world is a huge burden to carry, but I know my instructions."

"Good. The council has its reasons, laddie. You know how any branch of shifters believed to be extinct is supposed to remain that way, and ours is not to reason why. Your appearance all those years ago shocked the whole shifter society."

Ted shrugged. "I know, Dad, and I've followed every rule to the letter until...well, you know. Other than work, I keep to myself, and it's not like I'm going to get some girl pregnant, now, is it? Me being gay works for them too."

His father sighed. "I know you get lonely, son, but we couldn't risk you being found out. Dougie seemed like a good bloke, but he turned out to be a wrong 'un. It was best to get him away before things got too difficult."

"I know, Dad. It won't happen again. It's easier not to get involved with anyone, not just pure humans. How many times do I have to say that the rules are carved into my brain."

Before he'd left Scotland, he been interrogated by someone from the Shifter Secret Service. He'd chuckled when his father had explained who the man represented.

"Really. There's a secret service. Does he dress like James Bond?" He'd found it hard to take the whole thing seriously at first, unlike the operative who came to see him. The man had been built like a brick outhouse and Ted had doubted that a smile had ever crossed his lips. He'd been told to sit and listen because his life might depend on following the rules. The reality of his situation had smacked him right between the eyes.

He glanced at his watch. "Sorry, Dad. I've got to go. We're repairing paths today. Give Mum my love."

"I will, and take care out there."

Ted slipped the phone into his pocket, grabbed his coat and backpack, secured the door behind him, then climbed into his Land Rover. This morning they were meeting at the depot in Ambleside to collect a truck full of gravel.

Lenny and Stu were already there when Ted arrived. The truck was loaded and ready to go.

"Sorry, traffic," Ted said.

Stu grinned at him. "Just because you're a bloody hero doesn't mean you get special treatment, you know."

Under his beard, heat rushed into Ted's cheeks. "Don't. Anyone would have done the same. I was just in the right place at the right time."

"It was the main topic of gossip in the pub last night," Lenny added.

This was the last thing Ted wanted to hear. He was supposed to keep a low profile, not become the talk of the bar. "I couldn't leave him there, could I? Right. Enough. We've got work to do. I hope you've brought your muscles. Shifting this lot in barrows to the path isn't going to be easy."

Stu flexed his arms. "I've got ten years or more on you two. I bet I manage to lift more."

Ted said nothing. This was one of those occasions when he had to be careful about how strong he could be. Beavers could drag huge branches and he had more than the power of a man at his disposal.

"Come on, then, laddie. You get paid to work not to be a bloody hero." Lenny's mocking of Ted's accent brought him out of his thoughts. "Shift yourself into this truck." Ted grinned at Lenny's choice of words.

They spent the rest of the morning shovelling gravel over a pre-prepared surface. These paths had to be flat to allow wheelchair users access as well as walkers, cyclists and horse riders. Footfall and weather gradually eroded all surfaces over time. This year they'd be installing wooden pathways and several bridges as well. Since he'd started this job Ted had discovered his favourite task was working in the forest. Here they planted with a new tree for every diseased one they removed. He could tell what variety it was by examining its bark, its shape, and its leaves.

"Did you find out how Harry Katt was doing?" Stu asked, while they trundled the wheelbarrows along. "That could have been nasty, landing face down in the water. And it's not like him to be so careless. Have you ever seen him climb? I swear he could compete on those artificial walls. He's so fast and finds hand holes and foot holes all over the place."

Ted wasn't surprised. He'd realised who Harry was as soon as he'd seen him with the white streak in his hair. Katt by name and cat by nature. "Anyone can be unlucky. And it was so wet up there. I asked at the hospital and he's got a concussion and a few bruises."

"The Katts have a reputation for always landing on their feet. As kids they climbed up trees and onto roofs, and, being identical, they drove the teachers crazy, didn't they, Stu?" Lenny said. "There are three of them, you know. Identical, though the eldest, Thom, dyes his hair now he's a star of stage and screen."

Ted had no idea about Thom Katt, never having seen his show, only Rich and Harry, but curiosity got the better of him. "Should I know him? I don't watch much television, and I've never been to the theatre."

Lenny stared at him. "Sandy, my wife, adores him and his co-star in *Within Bow Bells*—the soap. You know, it's set in London. He plays one half of a gay couple with John Ballantyne. You must have heard of him."

"Oh, aye. From the Marvel films," he said. Those he did know.

"That's right. I suppose the broadband isn't great where you are, or up in the Highlands."

"It's patchy." In truth, his reception at the cabin was excellent. He'd had cable brought from the main road. "And I'm just not good at sitting for a long time just watching something. I like to keep active. And the other brother?"

"Rich," Lenny said. "The sensible one. He runs the pest control firm with Harry. Unlike Harry, who'll shag anything that stands still long enough, Rich is married and settled down. His wife is expecting, too."

Ted wondered if she was a shifter, or had Rich managed to get away with marrying a human like his brother? And as for Harry, he knew toms were renowned for putting themselves about, but surely Harry had to be careful.

"Sounds like an interesting family," Ted said.

"Oh, they are. The Katts have farmed in this part of the Lake District for years, but they sold off the land when Oona's husband died and now she runs a B&B with Lucy, who's the boys' mother. It's popular with visitors. And now I think it's time for some lunch."

By the time five p.m. came around, all three men were ready to stop. Ted ached to his bones, but there was satisfaction in a job well done.

Stu stretched. "I don't know about you two, but I intend to have a long bath, then a few drinks, and hope I sleep. Tomorrow is my day off."

Lenny chuckled. "These youngsters—no staying power. You and me, Ted, are on the tree survey tomorrow. Lots of walking but not so much lifting. Let's get this lot loaded and back to the depot. There's a chicken pie with my name on made by the fair hands of my gorgeous wife waiting for me at home. Then it's feet up and watching the footie. What about you, Ted? Any plans?"

"No. Nothing in particular. Food and rest, that's all."

"Doesn't it get lonely out there?" Stu asked. Ted was fed up with answering this question but he'd been taught to be polite and give everyone the same answer.

"I'm used to it," Ted said. "I was lucky they let me renovate the old cabin and update it. It's well-placed—near enough to the road to get in utilities, but far enough away people don't know it's there. Remember I used to live in the Scottish Highlands, miles away from a town. I'm much nearer civilisation here, and I love getting up in the morning to the sound of birds."

"Each to their own, I suppose," Stu said. "It's always bedlam in our house with me being the eldest of five."

Ted grinned. "You're hardly living in the middle of a huge metropolis yourself, Stu. It's a town with a population under three thousand. And over winter about a third of them will disappear."

"Yes, but at least I can get a decent pint and takeaway within a few yards. These things matter."

An hour later, Ted was indeed sat on his sofa with his feet up thinking about the man he'd rescued the day before. A knock at the door disturbed his thoughts, but he had a good idea who it would be.

"It's open," he called out.

"Only me," Otis said, striding across the room.

"Help yourself to some clothes."

The tall, slim, naked man reached into a cupboard and pulled out a pair of jeans and jumper. He dressed then sat in the armchair opposite.

"You've been having adventures and being the hero, I hear."

Ted shrugged. "Was I supposed to leave him face down in the water?"

"No, I suppose not, but you do know who and what he is."

"I do," Ted conceded. "I've learnt quite a lot about the Katts today."

"Exactly. And you know what cats are like — endlessly bloody curious. And Harry Katt is well-known around here."

"So I've heard. I'm not likely to cross paths with him again unless we're called out on a rescue. Have you met them?"

"Not Harry, but Rich plays darts on a local team. He knows I'm an otter shifter but it's not something we've talked about because there are always others with us."

"And yet you swam all the way here and walked naked from the river. You could have been seen."

"I was careful. And I know I have clothing here. Anyway, we're talking about you, not me. Those who need to know are aware of my existence but not yours. The rules are different for you because of the decisions made by your ancestors. You know the Grand Council doesn't want any problems."

"And for the umpteenth time, I don't intend to give them any. I doubt someone as good-looking as Harry Katt would have any interest in a short, stocky specimen like me, despite his reputation."

Otis leant forward. "Yes, but you're a hero, and he's a tom cat."

"Has he divulged information about our society to anyone? Is that it? Is he a liability?"

"No, I don't think so, but the family has connections — problematic connections. I don't know the details. I'd better get back now. I'll leave the clothes in the usual place. You should come over for dinner one night soon."

Ted followed Otis outside. The sun was setting over the hills sending pink and yellow streaks across the sky. He sat on the wooden chair to watch as birds flitted to and fro on the feeders. Whoever the Katts were connected to was clearly an issue. What made Harry so special? Did Otis know more than he was saying? Ted couldn't see that it mattered anyway, because Ted doubted handsome Harry would have any interest in him.

Chapter Three

"Mum, please stop fussing. The hospital said I needed to rest for ten days and I have. I'm fine. I haven't had a headache since Sunday." Harry sipped the coffee his mother had put in front of him.

Lucy Katt picked up his empty bowl from the table and placed it in the dishwasher. "Now, listen here, young man, I'm the one who gave birth to you and your brothers. Don't you forget that."

Harry fought the need to smile at the familiar words of rebuke.

"Fussing is in my job description. So, what *do* you intend to do with your day?"

"I thought I might visit the bloke who saved me — you know, to say thank you, and maybe take him something."

Her penetrating stare hit Harry so hard he turned his attention to his mug of tea then composed himself enough to meet her gaze.

"I thanked him at the time. There's no need for you to go. From what I've heard, except for work, he keeps himself to himself, and I know what your thanks can consist of."

Harry frowned. In cat form, his tail would have bristled. "I don't intend to offer him my body, Mum. I was thinking more along the lines of a decent bottle of whisky, with him being Scottish, or some sort of food hamper. Can't I even be nice now? After all, he did rescue me."

Lucy clutched the back of a chair. "Okay, but don't go over the top. Maybe he doesn't drink, and he could be a vegan for all you know. You could ring first, or have something delivered. He seemed shy when I met him — not one to blow his own trumpet. You turning up might embarrass him."

She had a point. "Okay. I hear you, but I'd still like to thank him. I can't help being curious, can I? It's in my DNA. But I do need to get out of here for a while. Maybe I'll go fishing. That's quiet."

His mother smiled, knowing his version of fishing wasn't always the same as most. "Just use a rod and stay out of the water. You're not a bloody tiger, you know." Unlike his brothers, Harry enjoyed swimming.

"I will. After landing face down in the stuff, I'm not keen on getting into a stream or mere."

"And make sure you're somewhere with a phone signal or I'll worry you've fainted or something."

Harry stood and hugged his mother. "You worry too much."

She stared at him. "Well, you three give me a lot to worry about. Thom's in LA with John Ballantyne today auditioning, and Rich is about to become a father. I need you to behave yourself."

"I will." *If I cross my fingers, a little lie doesn't count, does it?* "Now, where did I leave my fishing gear?"

Harry headed out of the town travelling north. His contacts in Mountain Rescue had told him what little they knew of Ted Woodward, and that wasn't much beyond the fact that he was Scottish, had arrived several months ago, kept himself to himself, and lived in a wooden cabin surrounded by trees somewhere along the river Rothay. It had taken a few more bribes to get someone to give him a more accurate location — Len did love a single malt. Even so, he almost missed the turn onto the narrow track through the trees. Only the marker at the side of the road Len had warned him about gave him any indication and he signalled, glad there was no car too close behind him. He regretted attempting the track in his Mini when he hit the first bump. He stopped and stepped out of the car to do the rest on foot. He'd be quicker in cat form, but transforming created the inconvenient problem of no clothing.

Strolling along the track, he could see work had been done in places to clear the area and allow more growth on the forest floor. Some of these woodlands were ancient, but fir trees had been introduced to fill spaces. Lack of light getting through the canopy meant nothing survived below and the seeds of the deciduous trees didn't get enough sunlight to grow. Clearing helped, but you had to know which trees to fell. Every forest was much more managed than people suspected.

All at once, the path opened up and before him stood the cutest cabin. It looked like something out of a nursery rhyme, though this one was made of wood, not gingerbread. To one side were two smaller buildings — a garage and probably somewhere Ted used as a shed. A sturdy 4x4 stood parked at the side of the house, suggesting the man was in.

He paused and considered his choice. His stomach swirled and released a few thousand butterflies. Harry had no idea why this man affected him so — why he had this strange desire to see him again. Gathering himself, he strode to the front door and knocked — no answer. He tried again — still no answer. Maybe he was around the other side. Harry took in the outside of the house and attempted to drive thoughts of lying to his mother out of his mind. It wouldn't be the first time he'd been economical with the truth.

Walking to the back, he noted the solar panels on the roof and the signs of a generator in the shed. No doubt Ted had an oil supply stored somewhere, like many others in more rural areas. He checked his phone. At least the place had a signal. Glancing through a window, he saw a well-equipped country-style kitchen but no sign of any movement.

Around the corner, Harry came face-to-face with a magnificent view. He stopped to take in the sight. Birds flitted across a garden filled with growing vegetables in raised beds. Fragrant flowers filled the air with scent, including a climbing rose making its way over the building. The land in front of him swept away down a manageable slope towards the river below. He noted the wooden seats and table on the veranda at the back of the house and guessed Ted would spend time there staring at the local wildlife and the changing colours of land and sky. However, despite the beauty of the surroundings, Harry knew he'd miss the hustle and bustle of the B&B. He glanced back at the river. *May as well, as I'm here. It looks like a good place to fish.* He had all the permits he needed. The whisky he carried for Ted wouldn't come to any harm.

Back at the Mini, he checked and found a small car park farther along the Rothay. It appeared the river contained trout, a fish he was fond of cooked or raw. Once there, he gathered his fishing gear, his book, and the basket of goodies his mum had made up for him and strolled along the bank until he found the perfect spot. Maybe he'd catch sight of an otter. He knew otter shifters existed in the area, but he hadn't met one in person. Maybe today would be the day. He unfolded his chair, baited his rod with a wriggly maggot and sent the line out over the water. He wasn't sure he'd catch anything — the season was nearly over — but it gave him a few hours away from his mother's care. Today, the weather had been kind and he lay back with his face to the sun absorbing the vitamin D. He was woken by a splash.

Instinctively, he grabbed the fishing line, but it wasn't moving. Farther along, he saw a body swimming in the water. Piled branches had created a small pond. If he didn't know better, he'd have suspected beavers, but there weren't any in this area, unless they'd sneaked in like they had at Longleat Park. At least here they wouldn't find themselves swimming on a lake with hippos and sealions. However, this body was human and also, from what Harry could tell, naked. Although he knew he should look away — he didn't. Whoever it was in the water was enjoying themselves splashing around, swimming on their front and lying on their back until he — Harry was pretty sure the person was a he — dived under and disappeared. He waited for the swimmer to emerge again. Minutes passed — five minutes, ten minutes.

After twelve minutes, Harry reeled in his line and stood, shielding his eyes against the sun. There was no sign of the man. Maybe he'd swum off and emerged from the water out of his line of sight. Harry left his belongings and wandered along the bank. He found a bag full of clothes around a hundred metres farther on. The man wouldn't have gone far. Maybe he'd got caught somewhere — people threw all sorts into rivers. Harry stripped to his underwear. He was about to wade in when a naked body emerged from the water. He wasn't sure which of them was more shocked as they stared at each other.

"What the hell are you doing here?" an angry-looking Ted Woodward asked as he strode nearer.

"I thought you'd drowned or got into trouble. You've been under for ages."

"So you decided to jump in after me even though mere days ago you had concussion and I had to rescue *you*."

"I'm fine now." Harry couldn't help staring. He also couldn't think when he'd last seen a man with so much body hair — legs, arms, chest, as well as head and face, but the water just seemed to slide right off him. Harry dragged his gaze away from an impressively sized cock nestled in its own area of chestnut-brown foliage. Ted didn't seem to care. He grabbed his bag, took out the towel and rubbed himself dry. Harry looked away while Ted pulled on jeans and a jumper then sat to put on his boots.

"You can turn around now."

Harry spun on the spot to find Ted glaring at him.

"I'm trained," he said, staring up at him from his sitting position on the grass. "I did a course back in Scotland. I can hold my breath a long while."

"Like pearl fishers," Harry replied finding his voice.

"Yes, like pearl fishers. In Scotland people often get into trouble in lochs, and they can be deep. We all get trained in how to rescue someone in trouble. I also like to swim." His gaze took in Harry from head to toe, who, glancing down, realised he'd forgotten he was standing in just his rather small briefs.

"I wouldn't have pinned you down as a swimmer." Ted paused and frowned for a second. "I mean, after what happened on the mountain."

"I like water. They took us to the local pool at school to learn to swim and do life-saving training, though I prefer natural water to chlorinated stuff. I had to get out of the house so I came here to catch trout, but I guess you've scared them all away now."

A splash from the river made them both turn. A brown head disappeared into the distance and dived. "Was that an otter?" Harry asked. "I know they live along the Rothay."

"Perhaps," Ted said. "Now, I think you should get dressed. I don't know about you, but I could do with a warm drink and something to eat. Get your stuff. My cabin is up the hill."

Harry pointed along to where his car was parked. "I can give you a lift up if you like." Ted nodded. Fifteen minutes later, after a short drive and a stroll through the forest from the road, they reached the cabin.

"You have a beautiful place here," Harry said as if seeing it for the first time. "No one would find it if they didn't know it was here or stumbled on it by accident." He followed Ted up the couple of steps into the small hallway.

"Could you take off your boots?" Ted asked. "You can leave them here."

"Of course. Mum makes me remove them too. She says she has enough to do with the visitors trampling dirt into her carpets without me doing the same."

"She runs a B&B, doesn't she? I only got to speak to her briefly when we met."

"Yes, on the outskirts of Ambleside."

"And I believe you're one of triplets." He gestured for Harry to go through the door. "That must be interesting, especially if you're identical. And your brother is in the movies."

Ted had clearly done his homework. "Yes, we are identical. Even Mum dressed us in different colours." He gazed around the open space which contained both living room and kitchen. "This is well organised with everything in its place." He strode across the wooden floor to the French doors. "And you have an amazing view. I bet you sit out there all the time."

"Coffee or hot chocolate?" Ted asked.

"Oh, chocolate, please. So, did you do this place up?"

"I helped. Trees are my speciality, though I turn my hand to most things as a ranger. It's as eco-friendly as I could make it. Take a seat on the sofa. Can I make you a sandwich? I've cheese and coleslaw, is that all right for you?"

Once again, Harry thought he was being tested. Ted couldn't know about him, could he? "Cheese is fine. Are you a vegetarian or vegan?" Two could play at this game of twenty questions, and his spider-senses were trying to tell him something, but he wasn't sure what. Could he be one of those humans who were able to detect shifters? Thom had met such a person in London so there must be others, and some of Ted's comments about nine lives, falling on his feet, and now about swimming gave him cause to wonder.

"Vegetarian. As a young boy I was taken on a shoot. I hated all the killing." He gazed directly at Harry. "I can't understand why people hunt other creatures for fun."

Harry touched his chest as if he'd been punched and the wind knocked out of him. Shame washed over him.

Ted placed the mug of hot chocolate on the table and sat in the armchair.

"I love meat and fish," Harry said, sticking out his chin. "I don't think I could ever give them up."

"Each to their own. We all have to make our own choices. And you help run a pest control firm."

Harry had the feeling he'd been judged and found guilty. "I do, with my brother, Rich. There's a lot of demand and the work varies. Have you always been a ranger?" Harry sipped at the chocolate. He couldn't help noticing how, despite his criticisms of Harry's eating habits, Ted watched him lick his lips. *Interesting.*

"Yes. As I said, trees are my speciality. We check on them, make sure they're healthy, fell the diseased ones, and advise people about protected trees. But I do other things. Last week, I helped to repair a gravel path, and we also finished building a new wooden bridge which we need to put into place next week. There's a lot to do in a National Park. I also go into schools sometimes, to talk about guarding the landscape."

"It must be so quiet out here on your own. It's always busy at home. I'm still getting used to not sharing a room."

Ted shrugged. "I have the internet, and I read a lot."

Harry glanced around the room and recognised an author's name on a few books. "You certainly do. My brother Thom knows Raven St Clair. I met her a while back. She writes shapeshifter books, doesn't she?" He asked the question carefully but got no obvious response.

"She does. I like gothic horror and fantasy stories. They take me out of real life."

Harry chuckled. "We all need that at times. I'm more of a fan of the psychological thriller myself." He finished his sandwich. "Thank you for the food. I think I'd better get off now. Maybe I'll see you around.

"You know where to find me," Ted said.

"I do."

It wasn't until he was driving away that Harry realised he hadn't given Ted the whisky.

Chapter Four

"The things you drag me to. I thought I was supposed to stay out of the way of others unless absolutely necessary." Ted stared out of the windscreen of Otis' car. "And I'm hopeless at darts."

"You'll be fine. It's only this once. We need a team of four or we have to forfeit the match, and it's a cup game. Jim's got food poisoning and is reported to be open at both ends."

Ted pulled a face. "I didn't need the details. How many games do we have to play?"

"We each play one match with all members of the other team. A match is best of three. Just do your best."

"Who else is on our team? Do I know them? Are they like us?"

"No, they're not shifters. They all work for the local council like me. George works in highway maintenance and Jason is a refuse collector. They're ordinary blokes who like a drink and a night out. I've known them for years. I know you've been told to keep a low profile, but, let's face it, I can't tell from looking at you. Why would anyone even suspect?"

"I suppose you have a point. It's been over thirty years since I transformed. They say the longer you don't, the harder it is to remember how, which is why the beavers died out. Also, the longer between shifting, the more it hurts. What's the longest you've gone?"

Otis shrugged. "Three months. I'd miss the water too much. Do you miss anything?"

Little spots of rain hit the windscreen and Otis turned on the wipers.

Do I miss anything?

"I get urges," Ted said. "I find myself wanting to demolish trees with my teeth. I created a little damn on the river after chopping down a few damaged trees. Not too much to cause anyone to notice, though. I can't have them thinking beavers have strayed into the area. At least cold-water swimming isn't seen as peculiar anymore, so if someone finds me in the water it's not that strange." *I haven't told him about Harry Katt seeing me yet.* "And I love the water, like you."

"We all have our likes and dislikes—what we do, what we eat. I remember having frogs' legs on a school trip to France. They were delicious." Otis turned into the car park of The Golden Lion. "Here we are. Before we go in, I should mention, Richard Katt is on the other team. He won't say anything about me, but he's known I exist for a while."

"Now you tell me. I shouldn't be here."

"It'll be fine. No one will know, and you need to have some fun for your own good. Let's get in."

Despite Ted's concerns that the evening would not be fun or benefit him in any way, they hurried into the pub, not wanting to get too wet. Ted glanced around while Otis waved at two blokes stood at the bar then pulled Ted over towards his friends. "George, Jason, this is Ted, who's volunteered to play."

Both men held out a hand and Ted shook them in turn. "Strong grip," George said. "Are you any good with arrows?"

"I can hit the board," Ted said.

"That's better than nothing. Only the top three scores count so you'll need to be on form, Otis. Now, what are you drinking?"

"Just fizzy water for me, please."

Otis ordered the same. He didn't drink and drive.

"So, which team are we playing?" Ted asked.

The doors opened and in walked Harry Katt, someone who was clearly his brother Rich, and two others. Ted tensed like Otis next to him.

"Did you know?" he whispered.

"No, I wasn't expecting Harry, only his brother. He's never been with them before."

"You were the one who warned me about him. You're supposed to be keeping me on the straight and narrow, not leading me into temptation." The words slipped out before Ted's brain had got into gear.

Otis smirked. "Can't be helped. Harry'll know about me from Rich, anyway, and he has no suspicions about you. So, are you tempted, then? You wouldn't be the first or the fiftieth."

Ted punched his arm. "No, of course not. Regardless of my situation, relationships across species can be difficult. And he is a cat, as you've pointed out, with a reputation. I doubt he'd be interested in me."

Ted gazed across the room and caught Harry's eye. Harry grinned, then waved and hurried through the busy bar towards them.

"Ted. This is a surprise," Harry said, ignoring Otis and the others. "This is my brother, Rich. This handsome bloke is our captain, Jack Hopkins. And the young one is Alfie, our landlord's son. I didn't know you knew Otis?"

"We met at work," Otis said. "Jim's gone down with food poisoning. And, of course, I know you two know each other after he brought you back to life."

Under his beard, Ted blushed. "We do. I should point out darts is not my game. How's your head doing?"

"He's fine," Rich said. "Thick-skulled like all our family. I'll get us some drinks, then shall we get started?"

The pub had a games bar off the main one. The dartboard hung in one corner, while a full-sized snooker table took up most of the floor space. A door led to the skittle alley. Photographs of winning teams in all the local leagues for everything from dominos to football lined the walls.

Jack pulled the names out of the hat, and Ted found himself drawn against Harry in the first game. Harry threw his first three darts to score one hundred and forty. He high-fived the rest of his team and Ted sighed. Cats could see better at certain distances. Ted took out his glasses. Although his hearing and sense of smell were good, his eyesight was poor. He usually managed without, but he didn't want to be completely shown up. Harry stared at him.

"What? You've never seen a man in glasses?" he asked, stepping up to the oche.

"They suit you," Harry said. "You look like a hippie professor."

Ted threw his darts. Forty-five was not the best of starts. The match continued in similar fashion and he lost three games to nil.

"Never mind," Otis said. "You just didn't get your eye in. Leave the winning to us."

Harry put his arm around Ted's shoulder. "No one can be good at everything. The snooker table is free. Fancy a frame while this lot throw?"

"Why not?" Ted replied. He picked up a cue and reached an opening score of over sixty before Harry got to the table.

"So you're not totally useless, then," Harry said nudging him.

"I've played since I was tall enough to see over the table. The laird of our estate had a snooker room. I played with his son."

Harry missed the next black, and Ted cleared the table.

"I'll get us a drink." Harry said. "Fizzy water for you?"

"Yes, please, and a bag of cheese and onion." He sat at a table in the corner. Otis had won the second match, and Jack the third. Otis had got close in one of his other games but now, the outcome was down to the two youngsters, Jason and Alfie.

Harry and Ted returned to the snooker table. "What part of Scotland are you from?" Harry asked.

Ted was vague with his answers to detailed questions, as he'd been told to be no more specific than 'the Highlands'. He lined up another red and potted it in the top corner, leaving the white positioned on the black. "I lived on an estate. I swear there are more deer there than people. My dad was a gamekeeper and Mum a housekeeper. It was a fun place to grow up. I bet you and your brothers had a great time here, too. As I mentioned before, lots of scope for practical jokes when you're identical."

"We did. The area is a great place to grow up in. We roamed the hills near the village all the time. I think we climbed every tree. And we drove our teachers mad."

"I bet you've some stories."

"A few. Maybe I'll tell you a couple another time." He blinked slowly and Ted found himself staring at Harry's green eyes.

"How did you get into pest control?" Ted asked, changing the subject.

"A friend of our grandmother owned the firm but he wanted to retire to Spain so he trained us up. Thom wasn't interested, but Rich and I found our niche. We go all over now and tackle all sorts from rats, to cockroaches, to fleas, to wasps' nests. You'd be surprised at the infestations places can have. We're a local firm and we don't charge silly call-out prices like some of the nationals. We've built our reputation."

"Not only for pest control," Ted murmured.

Harry smirked at him. "Have you been listening to gossip, Ted? The locals say a lot about me. I take people as I find them. Can I help it if I'm popular and devastatingly attractive? I like to have a good time and have no regrets. I don't offer anything I can't give. Love is for my brothers. Me—I like to share with no strings."

"I see," Ted said. Well, at least he was upfront about his intentions.

Harry potted three colours in quick succession then sipped his pint. "What about you? What are your interests outside of work and fantasy books? What do you love?"

Ted panicked. "Um, I need the loo. You've won this frame. I'll be back in a minute." He hurried through the bar. In the gents, he stared in the mirror. *Love?* Love had only caused him problems. Dougie had fooled him into believing they were in a relationship. Ted had revealed all of himself, including the one aspect of beaver form he retained as a human—his webbed feet. Dougie had asked so many questions and pressed for answers enough to scare Ted. His worst fears had been realised when he'd found notes for a story exposing the existence of shifters. When Dougie disappeared, Ted had asked no questions. His parents had said it was for the best, and Ted had been sent to a new life in England. He threw water on his face then used the loo.

Pull yourself together. Harry has his own secrets, so it's not as if he'd be selling anyone's story to the papers.

Ted zipped himself up, washed his hands, then stepped back into the corridor where he found Harry waiting for him.

"I thought you might have run off," he said. "I didn't mean to worry you, asking a personal question. I know what no means, if you don't like men."

Ted's mouth dried and he coughed when he tried to speak. "It's not that. You're a good-looking bloke, and yes, I am gay." He shrugged. "It's complicated is all. My life is complicated."

Harry took one step nearer. "Someone hurt you, didn't they? Is that why you left home? I'm also a good listener, if you need one."

Ted couldn't deny the truth of those words but he couldn't trust Harry either—he couldn't trust anyone. He stepped past Harry. "We'd better get back to the game or people will talk."

The match had finished and the others were back in the bar. Jason had secured victory for them. Ted and Harry pulled over chairs and sat.

"Thought we'd lost you," Otis said, raising his eyebrows.

"No, I just needed to use the facilities. Losers provide the drinks, then."

"I'll get a round in," Harry said.

Otis glanced at this watch. "Only the one. I have to drop Ted off and get home. Olivia doesn't like me being out for too long."

"I could take Ted home, if you like," Harry offered.

"No, it's out of your way, and he's got an early call tomorrow to fit a bridge, haven't you?" Something in Otis' tone annoyed Ted. He hated being treated like a child by someone younger than him.

"I have," Ted replied through gritted teeth. So much of him wanted to take Harry's offer.

"And we've got a hornets' nest to deal with in the morning," Rich added.

A little while later, they stood saying their goodbyes in the car park. Harry sidled up next to Ted. "You know things don't have to be complicated, don't you? I'm all for the simple life — no strings and all the fun."

"Simple doesn't work for everyone," Ted said. He climbed in next to Otis, leaving Harry staring after him. Otis drove the car out onto the road.

"So, did Harry Katt turn on his famous charm?" he asked.

Ted attempted a chuckle. "He did offer to show me a good time with no strings."

"Well, there you are then. Perhaps you should get it out of your system. Rich says Harry rarely visits the same place twice. If you give in, he'll lose interest. Could be better that way."

Ted stared out into the dark lit only by the headlights of Otis' car. *Would it hurt if I had a brief fling with the man to scratch an itch?* He had no doubt Harry would offer a good time between the sheets, but he'd never been the sort of person who indulged in sex for the sake of getting off—not that he'd had much opportunity. Beavers tended to stay with their partners and families, unlike tom cats. Clearly, the triplets' father hadn't hung around. Had their mother known the person she was sleeping with was a shifter? He guessed not, therefore giving birth to babies who turned into kittens must have been a shock to say the least.

"I can hear you thinking from here," Otis said.

"Look. It's simpler to avoid entanglements. I can live without sex. And I might not live up to Harry's standards. I've no idea why he'd ask, anyway. He must be running out of fresh options. No. I have my work. It's enough."

"Your decision. I won't say anything."

Ted unfurled his hands. He wasn't so naïve as to think Otis didn't report to someone about Ted's activities.

Otis indicated and turned onto the path. "I'll drop you here, if that's all right. You're okay in the dark, aren't you?"

"Yes," Ted said. "I can find my way back." He waited while Otis reversed then made his way along the path. He could smell each type of tree and hear every noise. The only things bigger in these woods than him were the deer and they wouldn't approach. The cabin, with its security lights now on, appeared out of the darkness.

As he made himself a sandwich and mug of tea, Ted thought about Harry Katt. The man was not lacking in charm and he moved with the grace and style you'd expect in a feline. He took his food to the sofa and chewed while bringing up pictures from the Katt Brothers Pest Control Service and the B&B on his laptop. He also found many pictures of Thom Katt with his off- and on-screen partners. He couldn't help wondering how the Grand Council of Great Britain had viewed these particular developments, especially now there were rumours of a Hollywood career. Were other shifters up there on the silver screen? Shifters could only recognise each other in person and he'd never been anywhere to meet anyone famous.

He finished his food and drink, stripped off his clothes in the bedroom and threw them in the wash basket, then took himself to the bathroom for a shower. He let the hot water run over his body and lathered himself with gel. His hand strayed to his cock and, unbidden, the face of Harry Katt appeared in his mind. He let the spray wash off the soapy water while he stroked himself. Would Harry get on his knees for him? Ted could imagine the feel of those lips, the rasp of his tongue, and the suction, taking him in all the way to orgasm. He'd lay odds Harry had trained his gag reflex. He built up speed and steadied himself against the wall. His climax hit quickly and he breathed hard until he opened his eyes and Harry's grinning face disappeared.

Chapter Five

"I didn't expect to find you sitting at the kitchen table," Rich said, after stepping through the back door. "I thought you might have organised a secret rendezvous anyway, and that I might get a text telling me to pick you up from the house of a certain forest ranger this morning. It's not like you to strike out. Losing your touch, bro." Rich squeezed Harry's shoulder then sat between him and their grandmother.

"Richard," Oona Katt said, the warning obvious in her tone. "Leave the boy alone. Just because you and Thom have settled down. You know it takes some people longer to find the right person. This bloke might not be interested in men or casual sex. Not everyone is, you know." She ruffled Harry's hair then poured Rich a coffee.

"How's Suki doing, laddie?" Oona continued. "Can't be long now. I'll be ready to help with the birth, in case there are *complications*." She made punctuation marks in the air. "And Maggie has offered to help like she did with your births. Being a shifter herself, she knows what to do. At least Suki's only having twins. It could be neither of them transforms, despite you both being shifters. Genes are a law unto themselves. Are you two busy today?"

Rich nodded. "We've a hornets' nest to remove from a house in town. I'm staying close to home at the moment." He nudged Harry. "So, what did happen last night, baby bro? You seemed pally with Ted, though I could see he might not be your type. Then again, he was breathing."

"You know what Maggie told me. I've been *advised* to stay away from pure humans. Bloody shifter politics or some such nonsense I have no interest in. Anyway, Ted's got his own reasons. He says it's complicated. I think someone hurt him, and he doesn't trust men anymore, and people do like to gossip about me."

His mother patted his arm. "Well, you do have a reputation, darling. You can't deny that. And people do like to tell tales out of school. If he has to learn to trust someone again, you might not be his first choice, handsome as you are. But then I'm a biased mother." Lucy stood and gathered up the breakfast plates.

"You may have a point," Harry agreed with a sigh.

"And as I said, he's not your usual type," Rich added. "I mean he's short, sturdy, and hairy, not the glamorous sort you usually choose. And I don't think you have to sleep with him because he saved your life. I've been asking around as well. He keeps to himself, and no one seems to know why he came here. Perhaps he's an axe murderer and that's why he left Scotland in a hurry."

"Oh, I'm sure he can wield an axe," Harry said, remembering the pile of wood near the shed. "His friend, Otis, said he did most of the repairs on the cabin himself." He kept the fact that he'd spent some time with Ted to himself. "So, had we better get off, Rich? Mrs Grainger seemed keen to get rid of her unwanted neighbours."

Oona Katt rummaged in a drawer and pulled out a beige-coloured piece of knitting. "Tell her to stuff this with something and hang it up after you take down the nest. Maggie says hornets are territorial and won't nest where they think there are others."

Both men laughed. "Maggie and her superstitions."

"Still, it can't do any harm. I'll let you know what she says," Rich said.

The hornets' nest being hosted by Mrs Grainger was a fifteen-minute drive away around the lake. It had beautiful views from the rear garden, which the insects were currently keeping to themselves.

"John, my husband, wanted to deal with them," Mrs Grainger said. "But I insisted on getting proper pest control in."

"You made the right choice," Rich said. "These things can be dangerous when annoyed. There'll be about four hundred of the little buggers in there. Here." He handed over the knitting. "My grandmother says if you stuff this and put it up in the same place, it'll stop others coming. Seems daft to me, but I've learnt not to argue."

"Really?" Mrs Grainger said. "Well, Oona is a wise woman, so who am I to argue? Can't do any harm. Tea, either of you?"

Harry lifted his head up. "Yes, please, milk and one sugar each. We shouldn't be long."

An hour later and they were done. Rich's phone rang. "We can get over there now if you want. See you in about thirty minutes. Holiday let," he said. "Left them with an infestation of dog fleas. I said we'd help. We'll need to suit up. Suki won't appreciate me bringing fleas home."

"Mum wouldn't either," Harry said. "You'd think people would check, wouldn't you before bringing an animal on holiday?"

A few hours later and they had another job done. They stopped at a local pub for a sandwich and drink, then headed home again. The work phone rang once more. They often had days like this—one job after another. Harry was driving so Rich took the call. He grinned. "Rats, you say. I bet that came as a shock. But buying at auction without a visit before, you can discover all sorts when you get the keys. We can do Friday and give the place the full once-over for any other nasties. It'll take a while to get them all. It might be why the house was so cheap. Sometimes these places need to be stripped back to the brick and floorboards. Yeah, usual mates' rates for you, Bryan."

Harry chuckled. They'd worked with Bryan lots of times, as the man was a local builder and developer. He'd helped with turning the barn into the magnificent home Rich and Suki now shared. No sooner had Rich finished the call than there was another, this time on his private phone.

"Are you sure? Why didn't you say anything this morning? Have you told Mum and Gran? Okay. And Maggie? Good. We need to be certain. I know we didn't transform for a while but... Okay, okay. I'll be there soon. We're not far away."

"Suki?" Harry asked, speeding up a little.

"Yes. Says she wasn't sure she was having labour pains this morning, but she is now. She's rung her parents and help is on the way. The Cattersons can afford the *right* people to deal with any complications."

"It'll be fine," Harry said. "Our mum survived with just Gran and Maggie helping, and at least you both have some idea what to expect."

"Her mum, you remember Mitzi? She'll be over as soon as she can get here from Leeds. I wouldn't be surprised if she arrives by helicopter. At least we know our history now, with both of us being cats. There's no connection in their family to our mysterious father."

Harry nodded. "Thom said he'd been warned to stay out of the intrigue and rumour surrounding our father's death and his life, so that's what I intend to do too. No involvement with other cats for me." He put the accelerator down and drove as fast as he dared.

At the house, they found Suki with their mum, gran, and Maggie. "I'll take the head end," Rich said. "You three can deal with the business end."

"And I'll take the kitchen," Harry added. "Let me know if you need anything. I've watched every episode of *Call the Midwife,* and I make a great cup of tea. I can boil water and fetch towels. I'll try and get hold of Thom too. He'll want to know he's about to become an uncle. Good luck, brother."

Harry sat at the table in the kitchen. Photos adorned the walls. Suki's family had contacts. Her father was a member of Parliament, both human and shifter. Rich marrying into a dynasty who could trace themselves back hundreds of years gave the Katts protection. Reasons why a species could shift usually came down to some choice made thousands of years ago. No one knew why, but he had no doubt that people were trying to find out. Harry didn't waste time wondering. He worried more about the present than the past. He picked up his phone and called the eldest of the triplets, who answered straight away. Harry still found it amazing that he could ring the other side of the world and hear someone so clearly.

"Thom, it's Harry. Suki's gone into labour."

"Is she okay?"

"As far as I know. I'm staying out of it. I thought you'd like to be told. You busy?"

"Not today so I can get a lie-in. Auditions went well yesterday. You should see this place — so swish. John's taking me out to lunch tomorrow."

"Sorry, I forgot how early it is over there."

"That's all right. You okay after your fall and rescue?"

"I'm fine."

"Seen anything of your heroic rescuer?"

"I may have seen a little," Harry said.

Thom chuckled. "Only a little? That's not like you. Are you losing your touch?"

"Ted keeps himself to himself, but I haven't given up yet. He mentioned me having a pretty face and not wanting to waste any of my nine lives, so I wondered. There's something about him, but if he is one of us, he's well camouflaged, and I've never met a shifter who could totally cloak themselves. He lives in this wooden cabin in the woods which he practically built himself."

"Sounds intriguing, but if he doesn't want you to get involved, you need to back away."

"I know," Harry said. "And truth be told, he's a bit hairy to be my type. Then again, if he's interested, he knows where to find me."

Thom yawned from across the world. "I'll ring later. Love to everyone."

He ended the call before Harry could reply.

At the first sound of screaming coming from upstairs, he texted his mother to let her know he'd be back at the B&B if needed. Up in his bedroom, he played a video game for a while, but, being the cat he was, Thom's yawn had become infectious and soon Harry was curled up fast asleep on his bed, oblivious to anything else happening in the world.

"I might have guessed I'd find you here," his mother said several hours later. "Not even the helicopter landing on the lawn woke you." She sat at the bottom of the bed. "Just to let you know, you are an uncle to two beautiful girls and mother and babies are doing fine."

"And father?" Harry asked.

"I think he may be somewhat shellshocked. Those two can already yowl."

"Are they…?" Harry asked.

"I would guess so. They have the hair colouring of our side of the family. The white streak is obvious already."

"Do you ever wonder about our father?" Harry sat up and swung his legs around to sit on the edge of the bed. He hadn't talked about his dad to his mother, not wanting to bring up a difficult subject.

"I can't say I do, to be honest, not anymore. We only met a few times. He was handsome, but a lot older than me. I was going through a rebellious phase at the time. And now he's dead. Maybe it was his time—live fast and die young. You might want to consider that. From what Maggie says, the more you occupy your animal form, the shorter your human life."

"I sometimes wonder if he did get run over, or if *they*—whoever *they* may be, caught up with him and had him neutered. Maybe he's been hidden away somewhere. He was a circus performer, wasn't he?"

"Yes, and a talented one, but enough about him. He gave me you three and I'm grateful, whatever happened to him in the end."

Harry had the feeling his mother knew more but didn't press further.

She stood. "Come on, let's go and watch *Within Bow Bells*. I've a lasagne I made earlier."

When they were downstairs in the living room, Harry's phone pinged. He picked it up and showed his mother the photographs of the twins. She grinned. "I don't envy them having girls. Boys are easier."

Harry followed her to their living room. Oona was already sat in her armchair.

"Lasagne, Mum?" Lucy asked.

"Yes, please, love." The theme music played. Oona pressed pause.

"Give me five minutes to get everything," Lucy said. Harry settled on the sofa. It had been an interesting day.

Chapter Six

Ted had been busy over the last few weeks as September made way to October. They had completed the regular check of all trees in the National Park searching for Dutch Elm disease and Ash Die Back to stop any spread. The undergrowth needed to be kept in check too, removed where necessary and allowed to flourish in other places. Deer numbers also needed constant monitoring. Then there was the constant round of repairs to paths, signs, and bridges. Whatever the season, there was something to do. Ted liked being kept busy, though it didn't stop stray thoughts about a certain handsome cat shifter crossing his mind.

What Ted loved best at this time of year were the colours. Nature put on a fine show of greens to browns as autumn set in and the leaves fell providing more nourishment for the trees, and nuts and berries for the animals. This morning, he threw open his French doors and stood to smell the air, now damp after the rain had soaked the earth. He loved the smell.

"Petrichor," he whispered. The loved the sound of the word every *Doctor Who* fan knew too, and let it roll over his tongue. He wanted to strip and swim in the cold water of the river. At these times his body craved to transform, like an addict wanting their first cigarette of the morning or longing for their first taste of coffee. His phone rang.

"Mum. I wasn't expecting you. Is everything okay?"

"Your dad's had a fall and broken his ankle. You won't be surprised to learn he's feeling sorry for himself, and it's been a while since you've visited. I thought you might be able to manage a few days if you're not too busy. You know what he's like when he can't get out, and I'm needed at the big house. Even if you were here to play chess or cards with him, it would help."

Ted could imagine what a grouch his father would be, unable to get out in among the flora and fauna of the heather-covered hills. "Aye, I should be able to wangle some time. Let me check with my boss. I'll drive up to you and stay a wee while."

"That would be good, son. Is everything all right with you? We miss you." Something at the back of his mother's voice bothered him.

"I miss you too, but work keeps me busy."

"And you're taking care and staying safe?"

Ted didn't need to ask what she meant. "Yes, Mum."

"Good. I'm glad. And your dad will be so happy to see you. You know how he frets, and I'm so terrible at chess. Let me know when you're coming and I'll make your favourite dinner. I bet you can't get a decent homemade haggis down there, even if it is vegetarian. Say hi to Otis and his family for me."

"I will." But she'd rung off before he could reply. "Hm. Something's up," he said to any animal who might be listening outside. He rang his boss. Tomorrow was Wednesday and he could have until Monday. He prepared to go early the next day.

It was a long drive up to the Highlands, but the rewards came at the end — driving through Glencoe, heading down into Inverness and over the Kessock Bridge until he left the A9 to take the road to the estate on which he'd grown up. He and his parents had a cottage on the edge of the small loch. The lairds were mostly absent but the new one cared enough to get good people in to run the house and land. Being a shifter himself, unlike the previous incumbent, and high up among the most powerful in London, this huge estate was a safe space for several shifters, though Ted's foster parents had always kept him close by, worried he might transform into his beaver state without planning to. It had taken time and training from a young age to control the cravings.

While packing his bag for the trip, his thoughts had strayed back to the Katt family. It must have been a hell of a shock for Lucy Katt to find she'd given birth to three baby boys who turned into kittens with no one to explain what the hell was happening, just as it was for his parents, after so many generations of pure beavers, to discover their pup was a throwback and could become human. He'd mixed with other children on the estate but been warned to run home if his body did certain things. He'd been home schooled with a couple of others — a badger and a roe deer — both orphans taken in by families on the estate. Many human parents weren't able to cope with finding out their child was different and Ted had no doubt money exchanged hands…or even threats. And yet the Katts had kept their secret to themselves and their existence off the radar, until Thom had hit the bright lights of fame and found love.

He drove past the big house, built in the traditional Scots baronial style, over the bridge and along a track to his parents' cottage. The last of the roses still flowered around the door. It even had a picket fence. He stopped outside, opened the car door, and breathed in the fresh Scottish air. As expected, he found his mother tending the vegetable garden at the back of the house. As soon as she saw him, she struggled to her feet, brushed herself down, and stood waiting for him. He took her into his arms and held her close. It had been six months since they'd last seen each other met in real life.

After a couple of minutes, she took a step back. "You look well, laddie, though you've let your hair and beard get unruly. Come away in, you'll be famished after your trip. There's porridge from this morning or neeps and tatties some vegetable pie I made specially. Or I've bread and cheese with my homemade pickle, and you'll be wanting a drink. I'll get the kettle on."

He followed her inside to the kitchen with its huge range and old-fashioned cottage style. In the centre stood a huge wooden table.

"Tea would be lovely, Mum, and one of your cheese and pickle sandwiches would just hit the right spot. Is Dad in the front?"

"He's checking the deer. He insisted Charlie took him out. One got injured yesterday — took an antler to the shoulder — nasty. It needed culling. Venison for the house though, and the laird has a party here from London, so I can't stay long. They'll want me to help with preparing for dinner tonight and for Friday's festivities. There's going to be an autumn ball for his visitors and the estate workers. His lordship asked to see you."

That explains a few things. "Did he?"

"Now, Ted. Don't get grumpy. You know how things are."

He did. "I do. I'll listen to what he has to say. I'll get dressed up in all my finery, and I'll give all the right answers."

She patted his back. "You're a good lad, Ted. You always have been. We know it can't have been easy, especially with your kind being reintroduced to the countryside around here. We half-expected them to demand your removal, though I'm not sure how they could, and I swear, your da thought you might run off to find a partner in the wild."

"I like my human comforts too much, and I doubt any of them would want me, either. Now, come on, tell me all the gossip."

* * * *

On Friday night, he stood in front of the mirror in his childhood bedroom. He'd spent the last two days driving his father where he could, often in the rain, mostly in companionable silence. His father had never been much for words. He liked to walk and fish, and to have a wee dram, as he called it, every so often. He enjoyed a good comedy on the telly and knew how to laugh. He also adored his wife, and she him. It had been a massive disappointment when babies hadn't arrived, until they'd been given this most unusual child. The door opened behind him. His father stood on crutches.

"Let's have a look at you, Ang…" He paused. "I mean laddie. Can't have you turning up at the big house with anything out of place." Like his father, Ted was outfitted in full highland dress, from his brogues to his bow tie in the colours of his father's tartan. Donald Fraser brushed the front of Ted's Prince Charles jacket and waistcoat.

"Ay, lad. You look bonny. Your mum's waiting for us downstairs. She'll be busy tonight keeping an eye on the hired help. It should be a fine occasion, judging by the vans coming and going today. All the staff are invited as well as the neighbours. It's a big mixing of your community with ours from the estate and village."

"With one carefully making sure each know nothing about the other," Ted said.

"Aye, that's true enough. Maybe one day, but you know people fear what they don't understand. Look who they write stories about. Too many were-animals are wolves, bears, and lions and tigers, not beavers, birds, and domestic cats. Stories were created to keep people away. Throw in a few vampires and zombies and imagination runs wild. Beavers were already hunted to near extinction without it being known they could transform into humans. Your ancestors, like others, made their choice, and sacrifices have to be made."

"I know, Dad, I know."

"Come on then, no more of this maudlin talk. It's time to eat, drink, and be merry."

The house was completely lit up when they arrived, with light pouring out of every window including the towers. Space in the car park was hard to find. No doubt Jock, the head gardener, would be moaning about tyre tracks across his precious turf for the next few weeks. They were announced at the door.

"Mr and Mrs Donald and Marie Fraser, accompanied by their son."

The laird and his wife stood at the entrance to the main ballroom where the visitors gathered. There would be music, then food, then dancing. The laird was a huge man at around six-foot-six and nearly ten inches bigger than Ted, as befitted a Red Deer stag at the top of his game. He had a mighty strong grip too, as they shook hands.

"Ted. It's good to see you again. We need to make time for a brief chat later, maybe during the dancing."

Ted had guessed something was afoot. He hoped he wouldn't have to move again. He'd come to love his new home in the Lake District. He'd made a few friends and enjoyed his work. "Yes, your lordship. And might I say, the house looks beautiful this evening."

"Her ladyship and Mrs Gorton the housekeeper, with your mother's assistance, did all the work. I merely swan in and take all the credit. Shall we say my office, around nine-thirty?"

"Yes, sir. I'll be there."

For the rest of the early part of the evening, Ted found it hard to concentrate on anything other than what the laird had to say. He nibbled at the food provided, making conversation with a few locals about what he was doing now since he'd left the estate. The secret of his birth was known only to a handful of people, so at least he wouldn't face questions from the curious. He watched the hands of a grandfather clock tick by slowly until the moment came then he made his way to the laird's study on the first floor at the top of the stairs. As he climbed, he noted the portraits of those who had gone before and the various swords and claymores adorning the walls. The family had once lived in a proper castle, not this Victorian pile, which now lay in ruins next to the loch. He paused outside the door, took a deep breath, then knocked.

"Come in." The laird's voice resonated into the corridor. Ted entered to find him sat at his impressive desk in front of the window. He waved Ted to sit.

"I believe things are going well with the new job." He shuffled some papers then stared straight at Ted, clearly waiting for an answer.

"I enjoy the work, sir. I have a nice house with everything I need."

"Good. I'm pleased."

Ted longed to ask what had happened to the man who had caused all these changes in his life, but he daren't, and the laird said nothing.

"Though your parents miss you."

"And I miss them. It's been good to spend some time here." Ted couldn't help wondering where this conversation was heading. He didn't imagine for one moment the laird had requested his presence for mere chit-chat.

"As you know, Ted, our world has to take great care. If the general public knew we existed, there would be all sorts of trouble. We keep to ourselves and police ourselves. Shifter species make their own decisions within a wider network. Most operate for the good of others but there are always rogue elements. One of those rogue elements was the father of the Katt brothers. I believe you've met Richard and Henry Katt in Cumbria, as well as other members of the family."

"Yes. Harry had an accident and I rescued him. I also played a game of darts with him and his brother."

"The Katts grew up without being part of our world and without knowing their father. Thom is now settled, as is Rich, and both understand more about the world in which they find themselves, but Harry appears to have inherited a lot of his father's attributes. Let's say he puts himself about."

"I wouldn't know, sir." It wasn't a complete lie. He made up his mind to check the cabin out for bugs again.

"Good. One of our watchers in the area has at least persuaded him to avoid—how should I put this—coming into intimate contact with someone who is not a shifter. We don't want another woman finding herself pregnant with kittens. The father has many children around the world. We've traced some, but by no means all. With your unique situation, as the only one of your kind, this is a friendly request to stay away from being alone with Harry Katt. Cats are curious creatures, and we don't want him asking questions about you or your origins. Arrangements are in hand to find the right partner for him. Another relationship might compromise those plans."

"I understand, sir. Harry is good company, and it might be difficult to avoid seeing him as we both volunteer for the Mountain Rescue Service, and I don't want to give it up."

"No. Quite right. Friends is fine, in company with others. Pillow talk is another matter. We've taken great care over your existence."

"At least it's not like one of us is capable of getting pregnant."

"Fortunately not, but we don't want you to take any further risks. I'm sure you can organise your *needs* sensibly after the recent debacle. Once bitten and twice shy, and all that."

Heat rushed into Ted's cheeks and he was glad of his beard. "I've always said I will follow the will of my species. I don't transform. I keep my ability secret. There is no chance of my breeding. I keep to myself. I don't want to be exposed any more than you do, your lordship. I know we tread a fine line."

"Good. Good. I knew we could depend on you. Now, off you go and enjoy the evening and your weekend."

Ted slipped out of the room. He had a lot to think about.

Chapter Seven

"Bloody hell," Harry said, after handing over the company card to pay for the van service.

Mick smiled at him. "What can I say? It used to be easier when you didn't have a computer in the middle of everything." The bell rang behind Harry, and Mick nodded.

"Be with you in a minute, Ted," Mick said.

Harry turned. It had been a month since they'd last seen each other.

"I can wait," Ted said. He sat on one of the chairs.

"Yours giving you bother too?" Harry asked.

"Just a service. I'm leaving it here overnight, and Martina's giving me a lift home."

"About that," Mick said. "With the weather being bad, Marty's had to take the recovery vehicle out, and I'm not sure when she'll be back. You could try to get a taxi."

Harry glanced outside. It was still chucking it down. "I could give you a lift in the van."

Ted shrugged. "It's out of your way. I'll manage."

"Don't be daft. You saved my life. I owe you a rescue too."

Mick grinned. "That's true, Ted. He did. You can't argue with the lad. He does owe you. I'd take his offer or I suspect you'll be sleeping here in your car tonight. We'll have it ready for you tomorrow."

"We'd better get going, then," Harry said. "This rain shows no sign of stopping. I'll text home and let them know I'll be late."

Ten minutes later, they were sat in the Katts' van watching the wipers attempt to keep the windscreen clear. Harry turned on the headlights.

"It's been a while since I've seen you, Ted," he said. "You've been busy?" He eased the van through the gates out of the garage car park. This was not the weather to hurry.

"I went to visit my parents. They're both getting older now. Dad has injured himself and needed some distraction. Mum is rubbish at chess."

"Are you close, you and your family? They must miss you with you living up there for so long. Though saying that, I have no idea how old you are. I'm also a decent chess player if you ever fancy a game."

"My parents are both good people, though rather old-fashioned in their ways. I'm lucky, and I'll be forty next birthday. Somewhat older than you, I expect."

Harry shrugged. "Age is just a number. My father was twice my mother's age — not that I ever met him. How did they take you being gay?"

"Surprisingly well."

Harry peered through the windscreen. Ted rarely gave anything away. "You know, I think it's getting worse. I may have to leave the van at the entrance to your path."

"I can find my way home from there," Ted said. "It's not far now."

Bright headlights hit them head-on and Harry momentarily lost the road. "Shit! Fucking idiot." The van slipped on the mud, leaving Harry no choice but to go with it and hope.

"Brace yourself," he warned. Seconds later, they crashed into a tree, setting off the airbags. It took a while for them both to catch their breath and let the bags deflate.

"You all right?" Harry asked.

"I think so. You?"

"Yes, a bit shocked, that's all." He turned the engine over but the wheels spun underneath them. "Damn!"

"You *do* seem determined to use up all of your lives," Ted said.

Harry paused and stared at him. "You mentioned my lives before. You know what I am, don't you?"

Ted's face flushed red. "It's just a figure of speech," he protested.

Harry shook his head. "Not to everyone. You're a watcher, aren't you? You're like my gran's friend, Maggie."

"Maggie?"

"She's always helped look after us. She's a pagan, does healing and stuff. She's also a shifter. Not all watchers are."

Ted said nothing, but Harry noticed he didn't meet his gaze.

Harry continued. "I'm right, aren't I? You can tell what I am. Don't deny it and never play poker. You'd be useless. You know I'm a cat." Lightning flashed across the sky followed in quick succession by a clap of thunder. "Whatever, we can't stay here." Harry hated loud noises.

"No. We need to get to the cabin." Ted still hadn't answered Harry's accusation. "We're not far away. I saw the brown tourist sign a little while back."

Harry let his formidable hackles relax. "If I transform into a cat my eyesight will be better in the dark."

"You'll get wet out there," Ted said.

"I dry," Harry replied. Ted being a watcher changed everything. "We can pack my clothes into a bag for you to carry and I can change back and warm up once we're at yours. I'll get into the back of the van. Give me a few minutes."

Once outside, Harry shivered. The rain showed no signs of stopping. He opened the back and jumped in among the tools. After stripping quickly, he gathered his clothes together, then shifted. He did it so often, his body was used to the process and minutes later he was in cat form. He mewed to attract Ted's attention.

The back door opened. "Bloody hell." Ted said. "You really are a cat. Is this torch and bag for me?"

Harry nodded then jumped out.

"Good idea. I might lose you in the dark as you're not wearing a collar."

Harry hissed.

"Okay. Okay." Ted locked the van. "We follow the road for a mile or so then turn."

Harry didn't mind the wet, but he wasn't keen on the mud. By the time they reached their destination, his fur would be caked with the stuff.

They walked for a while. "Don't go too far ahead and stay off the road. My eyesight isn't brilliant in the dark. We turn here. Now we need to follow the path through the trees."

Harry skipped on ahead. Here there was no light from the road. He hoped Ted had left something on at the cabin. He scanned the area but saw nothing. He stopped. The brightness of the torch beam hit him.

"I'm right behind you," Ted said. "I always leave the garage lights on and the security system will come on when we're near enough." Ted panted as he slogged through the muddy path. "Why does it seem further away on foot?"

Harry shook himself and concentrated. He thought he saw the hint of something farther ahead of them, but he needed to be sensible and keep to the path. Ted kept the torchlight ahead of Harry. The path turned, and now, Harry could see the beam from the garage. He mewed.

"Yes, I see it too," Ted said. Wet leaves swirled around them, and Harry shivered when thunder rumbled across the sky. Without warning, arms picked him up and pressed him close. Harry snuggled into Ted's chest.

"Sorry, I didn't think. Is this all right? You were shaking," Ted said. "I thought you might like a bit of body heat."

Harry rubbed his head on Ted's chin to show him he didn't object. He wanted to tell Ted not to run. The last thing they needed was him breaking an ankle on the uneven surface. The security lights came on to show the way.

"That's better. Now, let's get both of us inside." He placed Harry on the step and opened the door. Harry hurried in, shivering from the damp. He did his best to wipe his feet on the mat in the small hallway. Ted reached down and smoothed his back.

"I'll take your bag to the bedroom."

Harry skipped after Ted through the main room to the rear of the cabin.

"The bathroom is there with towels, and you can shower if you want. I'll ring the police about the van then make us a drink. Hot chocolate sounds good, with whipped cream."

Harry mewed his agreement and watched Ted close the door before shifting back to his own body once again. Despite the heating being on, he was cold. He grabbed a towel, used the connecting door, and spent a quick five minutes warming up under an impressive shower. Once dry and dressed, he returned to the main room to find Ted sat on the sofa holding a large mug. Harry took one of the armchairs.

"Someone had already called the police about the van. You'd better call your mum. It's probably best to stay here until the rain clears. I've enough food in to feed us if you like curry—though it's vegetarian. I know cats have to eat meat."

"Cats do," Harry said. "But in human form, I don't. If I stayed human forever, I'd be fine without." He sat back and settled himself. "You didn't answer my question about being a watcher. Is that really why you came here? I suppose Maggie is getting older. Are you here to keep an eye on us?"

"Let's say I'm not here simply because of you and your family."

"No, you wouldn't be. There are others in the area." He paused. *Ted must know.* "For example, Otis and his wife, Olivia, are otters, which you must know. Rich warned me before the darts game as we'd never met before. There are some badgers in a sett near Thirlmere. There are also a few birds like Maggie. But I don't get any sense of an animal form of any sort from you. There are some dogs who live with families as well, and even a few sheep."

Ted glared at him. "I believe you're familiar with all the shifters around here in more ways than one."

Harry wouldn't let himself be embarrassed. He longed to bristle his tail. "I'm a tom cat. I'm young and single and I love to mingle. What can I say? My offer to you is still there." Ted went a slight shade of pink. Harry's anger dissipated. He did love to tease. A small smile crossed his lips. "You might want to rub the cream from your face."

Ted swept a hand over his moustache and beard. "I don't think any indulgence would be wise. Why don't you phone home and I'll warm up the curry and cook the rice."

Harry took out his phone. "I don't give up easily," he said. "We cats are known for stalking our prey."

Ted stood. "I don't doubt it for a minute. But you're not irresistible, and I think you understand the meaning of no."

This time heat rushed into Harry's cheeks. "I do. And I'm sorry. I didn't mean to overstep."

Ted leaned over and ruffled Harry's still damp hair. "You didn't. And we can still be friends, whatever the circumstances. Now, let's have something to eat. We won't be going anywhere tonight. And you need to phone your mum."

Harry took his phone into Ted's bedroom and settled on the large wooden bed covered with extra pillows. It seemed Ted was a man who liked room to snuggle. He rang home.

"Harry. Where are you? I was expecting you hours ago. The weather's awful out there. Your gran and I were beginning to worry."

"I'm all right, Mum. I'm at Ted's. I was giving him a lift home and the van slipped off the road in all the mud and hit a tree."

"But you're both okay?"

"We are. We left the van. The police know. We managed to find our way here in the dark. And in other news — Ted is a watcher."

"What? Like Maggie?"

"Yes, but he's not a shifter, or he says he isn't, and my instincts are usually good. He knows I'm a cat. He's always known."

"Harry, be careful. Watch what you say. These people can be…"

"But Gran trusts Maggie, doesn't she? And all she's ever done is help us."

"I've no doubt she also keeps people informed. You're not naïve, Harry. Just don't get involved with him. You don't have to sleep with everyone you meet."

"I know, Mum. It's a shame, though, because I like him even though he's nothing like my type, and he's at least ten years older than me. He's also rather grumpy and a vegetarian. But don't worry, I've no desire to settled into domestic bliss yet, with anyone. Anyway, I'm on the sofa tonight, which is a shame as this bed is so cosy. Maybe I'll transform and curl up on the end for the night."

"Be sensible, darling. Get a taxi back here in the morning. I'll ring the garage and get him to come out for the van — again!"

"Thanks, Mum. You're a star." He ended the call and glanced around the room. The walls were bare of photographs or paintings. Only a full-length mirror had been attached to the wall on one side. Furniture consisted of a double wardrobe, a chest of drawers, bedside tables on either side, and a shelf containing some books and plants. A TV had been fixed to the wall opposite the bed. Rugs covered some of the wooden flooring in a variety of blues, greens and browns, like the bedding and curtains. The room had a masculine feel to it, just like Ted. Harry dragged himself away from the bed to find Ted stirring a large pot.

"I've no naan bread," Ted said. "But I've mango chutney?"

"I'm fine with most things," Harry replied, taking a seat at the table. A silver fish slithered across the floor, but this wasn't the time to go bug hunting for extra protein. "I let Mum know what happened."

"Good. Though I expect she's used to you staying out late."

"I always tell her what I'm doing. We all did. Our mum and gran are amazing women, considering who and what we are and how little help Mum got. She protected us and still does." He sniffed the air. "The food smells good, and I'm hungry all of a sudden. It's been a while since I ate anything."

Ted dished the curry and rice onto two plates.

"I like a person who can cook," Harry said. He spooned curry into his mouth after blowing on it. "Mmm, tastes good and it's spicy too." His lifted his head and caught Ted's gaze then batted his eyelashes slowly — a cat's way of letting someone know the cat likes and trusts them. "So, tell me — what should I know about you to become a Ted Woodward expert?"

Chapter Eight

Ted spluttered his food. He grabbed a tea towel and cleaned up the mess.

"Something gone down the wrong way?" Harry asked with a smile on his face.

"No, I'm fine, just a hot pepper caught on my soft palette." He picked up his glass and swallowed several mouthfuls of the fizzy water.

"Have you ever tried being a vegan? I know a few people who are."

"No. I eat dairy, but I've never taken to meat. We used to have it hanging all over the house when I was young. My father was a gamekeeper, though he's mostly retired now. When the old laird died, his cousin took over and everything changed. Now, the estate is about conservation, not hunting. Dad says the laird would like to bring back wolves as predators to cull the deer as nature intended."

Harry shivered.

"Not keen on the idea?" Ted asked. "You wouldn't be alone, but the deer do a lot of damage."

"So why did you leave Scotland? Were you told to come here? You mentioned a complicated situation."

Ted wasn't sure how much to say. He could tell the same story he always did but alter the details. "I needed a change of scenery. There was a man. He was married. I didn't know, and once I did, I couldn't stay. I've not much experience with relationships."

"Oh," Harry said. "I've not had much experience either. Now sex is a different matter."

"Have you ever been in love?" Ted asked, his curiosity getting the better of him.

Harry leant back in his chair. "I thought I was supposed to be learning about you. That was a nifty turn around. And the answer is no. I thought I might be once upon a time, but she got a job offer in London and I had no desire to live in the city, unlike my brother Thom. I like what I do and I love where I live. I've no interest in finding out more about my shifter side. I know my father's name, that he was killed in a car accident, and that he has offspring all over the place, but I've no desire to find them. They can find me if they're bothered. Thom knows one of our half-sisters, but she's the only sibling I've met."

Is he talking to Ted or to the watcher he thinks I am? "Isn't your lack of curiosity unusual in a cat?"

"Maybe, but I still want to learn about you — not where you're from, but who you are. What do you love? What would you rescue from this building if it was on fire? What do you like to read or watch? What turns you on?"

Heat rushed into Ted's cheeks. Harry winked at him. "I love I can make you blush even if it is hard to see under your beard."

"I'm not playing hard to get," Ted said. "I was warned about you."

Harry shrugged. "Were you? I won't ask who by, or what they said. I hope my reputation also includes how I'm generous to my partners. Not all tomcats are out for their own pleasure. I find it interesting to discover what different shifter species bring to their beds when in human form." Harry placed the cutlery side by side on his plate.

"How many different shifter species have you slept with?" Ted tried to make the question sound as casual as possible.

Harry shook his head and smiled. "You've brought it back to me again — sneaky. Have you had special training in interrogation techniques? I don't think you're as naïve as you claim. So, is this my *Four Weddings and a Funeral* moment when I list my past lovers? Have you seen the film? My mum and gran love it. They both fancy Hugh Grant."

Ted snorted under his breath. He'd also seen the film with his foster mother. Should he admit he didn't even get anywhere near the character of Charlie's dizzying height of nine lovers? "If you want it to be. Though your private life is just that — private. In the meantime can I interest you in a pudding? I have some apple tart Olivia Haythorntwaite, Otis' wife, made for me. I've cream as well."

"Bloody hell — that's a long surname to fit on a pencil. You'd need to buy a special one from the museum."

Ted stood and picked up the plates. "I've not visited the pencil museum."

"It's more interesting than you'd think," Harry said. "And I'd love some cream. As a cat, I have to watch my milk intake, but as a human I love the stuff. I'm fine with pie."

Ted loaded the dishwasher. He warmed the desserts and put the kettle on. "Tea, after?" he asked.

"Please."

Ted watched Harry lick his lips with every mouthful. The man oozed sex appeal. "You were going to tell me…" *Do I really want to know?*

"Oh yes—my conquests. I couldn't give you a number, so I'll do species instead. Other cats, of course, though there aren't any other families locally. Several birds from a peacock—not a good idea—to pigeons and a rather cheeky robin with lots of bright red hair on his impressive chest. There have been a few cat-friendly dogs, including a magnificent mountain dog who gave the greatest cuddles, a couple of foxes, a badger, a roe deer, and a hedgehog."

"Really?" Ted asked. "Prickly?"

"Not so much. I did get stubble rash on my thighs, though."

"What was the most unusual?" *Why am I torturing myself like this?* At least Harry couldn't have slept with a beaver.

"A black panther in South America—I went there on holiday. Such a beautiful man with the most incredible cheekbones, and so lithe. So the answer is I don't know how many. I've never counted. Shall we take this tea to the sofa?"

"I'll take the armchair," Ted said.

"I wasn't suggesting we…"

"I know. As you said, you understand what taking no for an answer means." *Maybe I need to keep my distance. I feel like I want to assert my claim after all those others.*

"I do," Harry said yawning. He rose from the chair, picked up the TV remote and turned it on. "Now, let's see what Ted Woodward watches. Will it be horror, sci-fi, crime, drama, history, or even romance? I don't see you as a sports watcher — well, not football. So what is your guilty pleasure? What's your comfort watch? Let's have a look."

Harry scrolled through Ted's recent watches. "Hmm, *Masterchef* and *Hamish Macbeth*. Interesting choices."

"I like to cook. I make a mean vegetarian haggis. It's too easy to shove a ready meal in the microwave when you live by yourself. I bet your mother still cooks for you."

Harry shrugged. "Guilty as charged. And I guess you must miss Scotland."

"I do. Plockton, where *Hamish Macbeth* is set, is a stunning place, especially at sunrise and sunset."

"I've never been further north than Glasgow and Edinburgh. What's your favourite place in Scotland?"

"Hmm. That's a tough one." *Especially as I don't want to be too specific about where I'm from.* "There's still a few of the islands I need to visit. Skye is beautiful in June when the days are so long you can play golf at midnight — not that I play golf. What about you? You've obviously done some travelling."

"I've been to a few places abroad but for me nothing beats curling up on a bench by the fishpond in my mum's garden on a sunny day."

"In cat form?" Ted asked.

"Yes, the warmth on my fur is so much better than the warmth on my skin. I couldn't explain why if you asked."

"I'm surprised your mum has a fishpond."

"These are huge koi carp. She would not be pleased if any of them were damaged. They're not cheap. It's a beautiful spot with a view down the valley towards the lake."

"If you couldn't be a cat, would you miss it?"

"Part of me would like to be cat rather than human. I've always spent longer transformed than my brothers. I also liked chasing after mice and bugs more than the others when I was young and I had to promise to stay away from birds."

Ted grinned. "So you enjoy the thrill of the chase in more ways than one."

Harry stared back, meeting Ted's gaze. "Maybe I do. But I wouldn't toy with anyone's affections. I like things clear at the start so both people know what they're getting into. A few have tried to keep hold of me, but I think I'll know when I know. Sex is one thing and love is another. Anyway, what's your favourite episode of *Hamish Macbeth* then? Let's watch one."

For the next hour, Ted explained the characters and local landmarks, noting how Harry struggled to keep his eyelids from closing. No doubt if he let himself, Harry would be asleep in minutes.

He sat up on the sofa when the episode finished. "You're right. It is a beautiful place. Maybe I'll get there myself one day." He yawned and stretched his limbs.

"Looks like someone's tired. I'll get you a couple of blankets and pillows. The sofa is quite comfortable, or if you feel the need, you could transform and curl up there."

"I might just do that," Harry said.

Ted stood, picked up their mugs and put them in the dishwasher. "I'll see you in the morning then." He paused and glanced out of the French doors. "At least the weather seems to have calmed down."

Chapter Nine

Harry waited for the sound of snoring. Maybe he shouldn't, but he wanted to. In cat form, he trod softly across the living room and nudged open the door. He jumped on the bed and curled up behind Ted's knees. All he needed to do was get out before Ted discovered him there in the morning.

Harry stretched and glanced at the clock — six-thirty — he'd slept straight through.

"What the...? Harry, is that you?"

He wanted to ask who else it would be, but in his current form it would be a waste of time and effort.

Ted sat up behind him. "I need to use the bathroom. By the time I come back, I expect you to be human again. Really, Harry, you had no right to...to... sleep with me."

Wearing only pyjama bottoms, Ted stalked across the floor and almost slammed the door behind him. Harry stretched again and listened. At least the wind had dropped and the rain had stopped. He prepared himself. His body was used to changing, but he still experienced the sharp pain of every movement of bone and sinew, forgotten as soon as the process was completed. He'd transformed and was sat on the side of the bed when Ted returned.

"Oh for fuck's sake, Harry—you're naked."

Harry had no embarrassment. He glanced down. "Oh dear. So I am. It's peculiar, as a human I have hardly any body hair." Absentmindedly, he ran his hand through the white streak he and his siblings shared as cats and humans. "I wonder sometimes if we get this patch from my father. Maybe your father was hairy. *You* certainly are. Oh, now that is unusual." Harry had glanced at Ted's feet. "You have webbed toes."

Ted's face turned scarlet under his beard. "I was born with them. Some people are. Now," he said, pointing at the door, "get out there and get dressed. Some of us have work this morning. I can drop you off at your house if you like. It's on my way to the lake. I have some trees near there to assess. Someone wants to knock them down."

"A lift would be handy," Harry said, making no attempt to cover himself up. "And thank you for putting me up overnight." He stood and stretched again—*may as well show Ted what he's missing*—then padded to the bathroom. "I'll use the facilities, if that's okay."

"There's a spare toothbrush in the cupboard." Unpacified, the anger in Ted's tone was audible.

"Thank you." Harry grinned then stepped through the door. Once inside, he checked himself in the mirror. All right, he had been a bit naughty. *The webbed feet are interesting, though.* Of course, some semi-aquatic shifters had them, but humans did as well. Without warning, the door to the bathroom opened and an arm threw in his clothes. Clearly, Ted was taking no chances. He washed, dressed then checked his phone. Rich was clearly not pleased, from the several messages he'd sent that morning. The van would be out of action again, which meant they'd have to cancel a job. Maybe not much damage would have been done—if he was lucky.

In the living room, he found Ted sat at the table eating porridge with salt, from what he could sniff. Salt was a Scottish thing. His grandmother sometimes ate it the same way. To Harry, the combination tasted foul, though he'd happily lick salt from a person's fingers and be complimented for doing so.

"There's more in the saucepan if you want it, or toast. I think I have some cereal in the top cupboard."

"Tea will do," Harry said. "I'll eat the leftovers at the B&B. Mum does a great bacon butty." He poured himself a drink and sat. Composing himself, he attempted his most charming smile allied with batting his eyelashes over his bright green eyes.

"I'm sorry about the transforming. I thought I'd wake up and you'd be none the wiser."

"Forget it," Ted said. "At least the weather looks better out there. I've booked us a taxi. We'll need to walk to the road."

"Thanks. You must come to our place for dinner or something. Mum will want to thank you."

"There's no need," Ted said.

"Well, at least you could let me buy you a drink, maybe a meal, somewhere."

"You were doing me a favour bringing me home. I told you, there's no need."

"But I want to," Harry said. "It was fun getting to know you. We could be friends. We could go bowling or to the cinema. I promise you can trust me not to pounce on you."

"Maybe. Now drink up. The taxi will be here in ten minutes."

* * * *

Rich was none too pleased when Harry saw him back at the B&B. He was even less pleased to discover that Ted might be a watcher and that Harry had transformed in front of him. Rich paced the kitchen floor while they talked.

"Are you mad? Why did you stay? You could have got a taxi home."

"You know how bad the weather was," Harry protested.

"Why do you have to let your dick lead you everywhere? I hope he was worth it."

"As it happens, brother, nothing happened. We've agreed to be friends. It seems I'm not irresistible after all."

"I already know you're not irresistible, thank you very much."

"Sit down, Rich. It's making my neck ache keeping up with you."

Rich pulled out a chair and sat.

"And we both know Suki made the right choice. You're much better father material than me. How are my little nieces? Any sign of changing yet?" Harry bit into the bacon butty, glad his mother and grandmother were dealing with cleaning elsewhere in the building.

"The girls are wonderful but keeping us awake. If one wakes and screams, the other does too. Neither of us is getting enough sleep, which is making both of us cranky. How Mum coped with triplets, without the knowledge we have, I'll never know."

"I asked her about our father the other day. She didn't say much."

Rich stood and investigated the oven. "I think I'll make a sausage butty as there are leftovers and we're not going anywhere. I'll call the garage later and the insurance — see what the damage is."

"Aren't you curious about him? We don't even know his name."

"I don't need to know anything about him, and my name is Katt. As far as I'm concerned all he did was take advantage of our mother and leave her with three shapeshifting children."

Harry chewed his food, thinking. Clearly Rich retained the anger he'd always had about their sire. Maybe being a father himself had only served to increase his ire.

"I don't think Mum sees it quite that way." He kept his voice low.

"Well I do. I have two daughters and if anyone ever hurt them, I'd hunt them and deal with them, leaving no trace of their existence. Maybe someone did the same to him if he chose the wrong girl to get pregnant. You might want to think about that yourself and grow up a bit. Thom and I are settled now. You can't sow your wild oats forever."

Harry decided not to reply.

"And anyway, if this bloke Ted is a watcher, I need to speak to my father-in-law about it — he'll know…"

Harry knocked a fork from the table. It clattered on the stone floor. "No, don't do that, Rich. I'm not sure. He didn't say he was. He just knows what we are, that's all. Let's not get the Cattersons involved yet." His phone rang.

"Damn, that's the ring tone for Mountain Rescue."

Harry answered. "Hi, Malc. Problem?"

"Can you turn out, Harry? Some bloke went out with just his dog for company yesterday afternoon, texted the farmer where he's staying, but they didn't see the text until this morning. We're meeting in the car park as usual. As quick as you can."

"I'll be there. As it happens the van's out of commission so I'm available. I'll be there in fifteen." He stood immediately, leaving the plates in the sink.

"Saved by the bell," Rich said.

Harry turned. "Please don't say anything yet, Rich. Let me see how the land lies."

"Okay, but if I think it's necessary, I will. You'd better get going."

Harry grabbed his clothes and bag from the back porch and set off in the Mini to the rendezvous spot. Others were already gathered and were unpacking equipment. He glanced around but there was no sign of Ted. He wasn't sure whether to be glad or sad.

"Okay, everyone. Apparently, this guy planned a spot of wild camping up on Gibson Knott and it was certainly wild enough last night. They've sent a drone up and spotted a tent but it's flat, not pitched so he could be injured or this could turn out to be a wild goose chase."

Around him people groaned.

"Yes, I know, but we need to check. So, grab the gear and let's get going. At least the weather has calmed down, but it'll still be slippery up there so watch your footing."

"Did you hear that, Harry? Your knight in shining armour isn't with us today, so no falling off the side of a ridge this time."

Harry glared at Mick Harris, the mechanic from the garage.

"I heard," he mumbled.

It didn't take them long to find the walker due to his dog barking long and loud. It seemed he'd reached the spot where he intended to camp and discovered he'd left his tent pegs behind, then got lost in the dark when he'd decided to return. Knowing he should stay put, he'd done his best to keep under cover.

"Can you walk?" Harry asked after someone had secured the Bernese Mountain dog who'd sniffed him with interest.

"I think so. It's just my wrist. I'm not sure how damaged it is."

"Don't worry. We'll get you back. Next time, maybe check you have everything before you set out or check the weather forecast."

"I've camped in snow so I wasn't bothered about the rain and wind. Bernie always keeps me warm. He did last night."

"Still, a little more caution never hurts anyone."

Finally, three hours after they'd set off from the car park, the man was left with the ambulance and Harry returned home to his bed to curl up for a few hours and dream of a hairy man with webbed feet.

Chapter Ten

"They're doing what?" Ted stared at his phone the next day as if he couldn't believe what his friend had said.

"You heard me," Otis replied.

"But I thought they wouldn't be allowed to, not around here, not with me in the area."

"Someone has cocked up—one human department not talking to another shifter department. The pair arrive today from a park down south and they're putting them on the small rivulet which runs into the main river below your cabin. Will they know what you are? Will you be able to talk to them?"

Ted stood and walked to the French doors even though he knew he couldn't see the river from there. "They'll be so close. And as for talking to them, I've no idea. I've never met an actual real, live beaver. Can you talk to full otters?"

"Yes, but I was brought up by shifters."

"Did you have to learn how?" Ted was curious. Otis had shared little about his background.

"I spoke it around my father's family. I think I sort of always knew. I speak it with Olivia and the kids. Can Harry speak to cats?"

"I don't know. We didn't discuss it when he gave me a lift. Remember, he thinks I'm a watcher and I didn't tell him any different." He hadn't told Otis how Harry had stayed the night or seen his feet. By now, no doubt, Harry had searched the internet to discover some full humans were indeed born with webbing between their toes.

"Anyway, other than him giving me a lift in the van, I've hardly seen him since the darts match, which you took me to. I was warned by the laird not to fraternise with him — remember. He isn't considered suitable."

"They don't tell me anything much. My conversations with those in the know are one way. Maybe they want to pair you off with another beaver."

Ted's whole body stiffened. "I doubt it. All of this is because the beavers made their choice as a species not to continue in were-form. They wouldn't want any mingling of a pure beaver with a shifter. I would imagine some people are angry enough about this development. I'm not working today, so I might use the hide on the garage roof and see what's going on down there. A pair of beavers would have quite an environmental impact, but I can see why they'd choose that spot."

"Whatever you do, don't approach them. They'll stay away from you. They may not even know you're here. Anyway, I'll leave you to your day. I'm testing the water in Windemere today. There's a protest and a celebrity on the scene. Got to go. I'll call you later."

All Ted had planned to do today was catch up on cleaning, watch a few programmes, maybe even get to read, but now he made himself some sandwiches and a flask, found his warm coat, and positioned himself in the hide which looked down over the valley. He could still read and watch the hidden cameras on his phone. Around him, the birds chirped away and squirrels chased each other, beginning the gathering of nuts for the winter. The trees had changed colour and shed leaves on the forest floor leaving only the green coming from pines and firs. Soon, everything would stop growing and darkness would arrive earlier, making the days long. Ted preferred the spring. Spring was a time of rebirth and hope.

Activity lower down the valley caught his eye. The rivulet wound into the larger stream from a patch of trees farther along — an area perfect for beavers. The pair would waste no time getting started on making a lodge for themselves ready for the colder months. The National Park could have snow in October, but autumn had been mild so far. Winters had been wet rather than cold for the past few years, but too much water in the wrong place could cause its own problems for animals and humans.

A 4x4 bumped along the valley floor and headed for the trees. Ted would need to change position if he wanted to see any more. He decided to catch up with *All Creatures Great and Small* and wait for the vehicle to leave again before making a move. A couple of hours later, the vehicle reappeared. He waited for it to get to the road and wondered how the beavers would be feeling left in such new surroundings. No doubt there would be new cameras set up, so he'd need to be careful.

Dressed in his ranger's jacket, he made his way down the slope and along the Rothay. He knew the place well enough as he had mapped every tree. He had no doubt many of them would disappear with the beavers taking them down. Through the gap he saw the beginnings of an artificial den had been created. The beavers would choose whether they used it or not. A rustling noise came from ahead of him and a beaver emerged from under the woodpile. It sniffed the air. Ted crouched to stay out of the line of the camera and watched as the beaver set about taking down a small tree.

"Do you intend to hide there forever, human?"

The voice caught him unawares. He turned to see the female beaver behind him. He stared at her. She lifted her head and spoke again.

"I asked if you intended to stay there forever. And yes, you can understand what I'm saying, and I'll be able to understand you."

"How?" Ted asked. "How can I speak beaver even in human form?" It reminded him of how the TARDIS could translate all languages, like the babel fish in *Hitchhiker's Guide to the Galaxy*.

"I've no idea. I'm just a beaver. You're the one who can turn into a human. We were warned there was a creature such as you. I never thought I'd meet you, though. I must say I'm surprised we've ended up so near. They decided to relocate us here when the hippos got too close at the safari park. Maybe you and I are related, somewhere along the line."

"Did you know my parents?"

She chuckled, or the noise sounded like a chuckle. "That's human thinking. Remember, our lifespan is a lot shorter than yours, even in captivity." The other beaver appeared by her side.

"We have a neighbour, husband — a rather famous one."

Ted had no idea if he should shake hands with a beaver. "I'm Ted," he said. "Ted Woodward. I'm a ranger in the National Park. I look after the trees but do all sorts to protect the plants and animals. My cabin is at the top of the hill and to the right. I can show you the best trees to take if you like, and which I'd prefer you leave."

The male grunted. "We take as we want. Typical human, thinking you can tell us what to do. That's why we got rid of your lot. Humans have never done any good for beavers — nearly wiped us out for our fur making silly hats. We made the right choice to wipe you out of our lives instead."

Ted could understand this view. Humans did always think they were right. So many destroyed the land rather than choosing to work with it. So many denied climate change. He wouldn't blame any animal species for turning their backs on mankind.

"Now, Will. He's only doing his job. It's not his fault he was born as he was. Imagine what it must have been like growing up rejected by his kin. You and I have each other. He has to live in the human world cut off from the other side of his nature, as was decided long ago, before our time. Our species wanted nothing to do with the secrets of humans or their ways. We wanted to live our lives, build our dens, and have our families."

"I know you're right, Hetty, but it's hard to see him there — large as life. We may have chosen not to live among them, but we know what they do and what their technology and wars have cost. Now, human, you need to go back to your world and stay there. We don't want to learn anything of you. Mark certain trees to protect them if you want, but know we have work to do as your kind has chosen to place us here, and we will make the best of things."

"Would it be all right for me to see you again, even if we don't talk?" Ted asked.

"I've no idea. I'm astonished they choose to being us here. I think someone may have made a mistake. Maybe they'll transfer us again, or move you."

Ted stiffened. He didn't want to go anywhere else so soon. He'd managed to make some friends. "There are other shifters in the area," he said. "Other species."

"There may well be, but as we explained, we intend to keep ourselves to ourselves, build our dens and our dams, and raise our pups while they watch us for research and entertainment. At least we are protected here, and there are no hippos or sealions. And now we must get on. We've a lot to get done before winter sets in."

Both beavers scampered across the ground and into the water. Soon, there would be a pond and the landscape would begin to change. Ted stood, checked on the camera angles, and made his way out of the area in the opposite direction. He had a lot to consider. He hadn't thought about the politics and practicalities of this whole situation, except for how it applied to him. Secrets and lies—and someone had to see the secrets were kept and create the lies.

Back at the cabin, he made himself a mug of tea and a sandwich and settled on the sofa to watch some telly. His phone rang.

"Damn. Where did I leave it?" He used his enhanced hearing and found what he was looking for in his jacket pocket. He swiped just in time at the unknown number.

"Hello."

"Ted? I hope you don't mind me calling you Ted. We met at the hospital. My name is Lucy, Lucy Katt. It seems you make a habit of rescuing my son, Harry."

Ted grinned.

"I know you may be busy tonight with it being Halloween, but on the off-chance you're free, I wondered if you'd like to come to dinner. The family would like to thank you."

"All of them?" Ted replied, without thinking.

"Well, yes, except Thom, who is in America. Harry, Rich and his wife, and my mother, Oona. Harry tells me you're a vegetarian, but we can cater. I make a great cheese and onion pie. Please say you'll come."

"Have you spoken to Harry about this?"

"Not exactly, but I wanted to meet you."

And no doubt work out what I know, if Harry thinks I'm a watcher.

"Harry told us about your cabin, and I want to know about Scotland. My mother is from the borders. She'd love to meet you."

Ted thought for a moment. A lot of him couldn't resist. He hadn't spent time around shifters except the couple of other foster children placed on the estate for their own protection, and he was curious about the triplets' father.

"What time do you want me?" he asked.

"Seven-thirty for eight. And don't worry, there's no fancy dress to deal with. The twins are too small for Halloween yet. We'll see you later then."

Ted ended the call. *What the hell have I done?*

Chapter Eleven

Later that day, on his way to the kitchen, Harry answered the bell to the front of the hotel and opened the door. "Ted. What are you doing here?" Ted stood with a large bunch of flowers and a substantial box of chocolates.

"Umm. Your mother invited me to thank you for saving your life and giving you a bed for the night during the storm. It would have seemed churlish to turn her down. Didn't she tell you?"

"No. Clearly she wanted to surprise me." Harry leaned in. "She knows you know about us, and that you're a watcher. I had to tell her."

Ted seemed nervous. He peered over Harry's shoulder then glanced back as if he planned to make a run for it.

"Why do I try to make this place look attractive?"

Harry turned to see his mother pick up a wooden ornament from the floor — she'd given up on displaying anything breakable long ago. "Ted. You're here. Harry, for goodness' sake, show the man in. Did I not teach you manners? I'm sure Ted would like something to drink."

Harry stood back to let Ted in while his mother hurried back to the kitchen. He jumped at the sound of a loud firework, knocking into Ted.

"I'm sorry." Another loud bang sounded. He hated the noise. On Bonfire Night, he always spent the evening in his room playing music through his headphones.

Ted placed the flowers and chocolates on a chair then held Harry's arms. Harry wanted to melt into his strong chest.

"Harry, you're shaking. Is it the noise?"

Harry nodded. He put his head on Ted's shoulder. "Thom and Rich got used to fireworks, but I never did."

Ted placed a finger under his chin and lifted his head. "It's okay. You're safe here." Ted kissed his forehead and Harry's insides melted. His knees buckled. Ted held him tight.

"We'd better go through or your family will wonder where we are," Ted said. "Are you all right now?"

Harry would have been happy to stay there much longer. "Thank you. Maybe you could do the same next week when it's Bonfire Night. The noise is usually worse then."

Harry stepped away before Ted could reply, handed him the flowers and chocolates, then led Ted to the family side of the hotel. When they stepped through the door to the kitchen, Ted gasped behind him. Harry followed his line of sight to where Maggie sat at the table next to his grandmother. He glanced over his shoulder. What he could see of Ted's face had blanched.

"I told you about Maggie," he whispered.

"I wasn't expecting her to be here, that's all. I thought it would only be family."

"She's like family to us. She's always been around." Clearly her presence had shaken Ted, leaving Harry with a question—was Ted a shifter after all? Though he could see no trace of anything in the man, maybe Ted was afraid Maggie could. "Come on, let me introduce you to everyone."

Maggie stood and held out her hand. Her body shimmered with colour. "So you're the famous Ted Woodward, rescuer extraordinaire. Just as well. Harry's been getting into scrapes since he and his brothers were born."

Harry noted how the two stared at each other. What could they tell? Why had Ted kissed him? Was it just to reassure him, or was there more to it? Why had that single kiss made him feel more than any other?

"Harry, offer your friend a seat and a drink," his mother instructed.

He pulled his gaze away from Ted, who had composed himself and held out his hand for Maggie to shake. "It's good to meet you. I'm looking forward to hearing more about Harry and his brothers. Mrs Katt, these are for you. I wasn't sure which to bring so I brought both."

"Sit next to me," Harry said. The door opened behind him. Rich entered with his wife, Suki.

"Sorry, we're the last. The twins needed a feed before we left."

"My parents are there," Suki said. "Mum couldn't wait to get them to herself."

"Ted," Rich said, after taking a seat. "It's good to see you again. You must be a glutton for punishment coming to dinner with us lot. And you're a vegetarian as well."

"I've made pie for everyone," Lucy said. "Steak or cheese and onion, with mash and peas. Harry, you still haven't sorted the drinks."

Harry stood again. "Yes, Mum." He had the feeling this was going to be a long night.

Lucy served dinner and everyone tucked into their food. For a while, conversation centred on work stories and the babies. Every time a firework banged, Ted touched Harry's leg. He found it soothed and calmed him. He breathed out.

"You all right, Harry? Those bloody fireworks."

"I'm fine, Mum. I'm practicing my breathing." And Ted was stroking his thigh.

"I'd have thought you'd have been out tonight, Maggie," Ted said. "Isn't Halloween an important night for pagans?"

Is he trying to goad her? Harry checked the expression on Maggie's face, as did everyone else around the table.

"I'm not a witch, just a healer," Maggie said, shimmering as she bristled her feathers. "But then you know what else I am, as you know what some other people around this table are able to do. Harry thinks you're a watcher. Is he right? Have you been brought in to replace me?" She sipped her drink and waited while Ted continued to stroke Harry's thigh just as he would a cat. Harry found he wanted to rub his head against Ted's shoulder.

"You know I can't say anything about myself or my reasons for being here. It seems at the moment I'm here to stop Harry using up all his nine lives."

"I don't think now is the time for this conversation, Maggie," Oona said, placing her hand on her friend's arm. "And, Ted, we're grateful for what you did. Harry's always been the one who got into more bother."

Ted relaxed next to Harry, who smiled at his grandmother. "I'm sure you've lots of stories about what the triplets got up to."

"Well, there was the time he pretended he'd got stuck up a tree because he fancied one of the local firefighters," Rich said. "He was sixteen. The fire service had come to school to talk about safety, and even I could appreciate how gorgeous one of them was. Sadly his plan didn't work."

"I did get up the tree," Harry said. "But the bloke who came up to get me wasn't Mr Tall, Blond and Handsome. Not that I minded in the end. He gave great cuddles when he rescued me, and I discovered I liked men and women with a bit of body."

Oona snorted. "One day someone is going to come along and surprise you, young man. Incredible people come in all shapes and sizes. Look to what they love, what they want to protect, how much they care. That's what matters. Would they risk themselves for you?"

Harry swallowed hard and glanced at Ted. How would it feel to be in his arms? He imagined Ted would make him feel safe.

I'm twenty-six. I'm too young to want to feel safe. Shit. Do I want to settle down like Thom and Rich?

Ted leaned towards him. "Are you okay? You look like you've just had a lightbulb moment."

"Maybe I have," Harry said.

"There was another time when Harry ended up in Scotland," Rich continued.

"Frightened the living daylights out of me," Lucy said. "We searched everywhere. He was seven and it was the holidays. We'd had a new bed delivered and in cat form, he jumped in the van and settled down on our bed, which they'd taken away. In the evening we had a call to ask if we were missing a cat. They were in Glasgow. Me and a friend had to drive up and collect him. Thankfully, I didn't have to explain why he wasn't in school."

"Sounds like you're nothing but trouble, Harry."

Harry turned to meet Ted's gaze. "But so worth it." This time Harry touched Ted's muscular upper thigh, stretching his fingers higher.

"They must have been a nightmare, having three so identical, Mrs Katt."

"Please, call me Lucy. And yes, I couldn't tell them apart in either form. They avoided subjects they hated in school all the time, swapping about."

"It must have been hard teaching them not to transform when they were young, especially without help."

Harry noted Maggie's frown.

"They had *me*," she said.

"They did, but it still must have been one hell of a shock for you, Lucy."

Harry pinched Ted's thigh and he flinched.

"Sorry, I hit my toe on a table leg."

Harry could see he'd got the message.

"Is there afters, Mum?"

"Yes, I've made trifles—lemon or berry with lots of cream and custard."

"Yum. Mum's trifles are to die for. Why don't I show you around the place after?" He was desperate to get Ted away from his family, and to get him alone, maybe for more kissing. Conversation during dessert returned to safer subjects.

"I'm going to show Ted the rest of the house now, Mum."

"Fine, son."

"Thank you for a lovely meal, Mrs Katt. It was lovely to meet you all."

Harry grabbed Ted's arm and dragged Ted through the door to the entrance area. "That side of the building is the hotel. Guests have a lounge and there's a bedroom on the ground floor as well. These are the steps to our side of upstairs. The visitors have their own staircase."

"The hotel side is beautifully decorated," Ted said, taking the steps before Harry.

"Mum and Gran worked hard transforming the place after my grandfather died. I never knew him. I've no idea what he'd have made of us three."

"Your mum is incredible. Was it hard when you were young keeping you a secret?"

"Despite all the stories, we learnt quickly to control how we transformed so we didn't do it in school. I think the thought of ending up naked helped. I've often wondered if nature made a definite decision to make us more careful, though waking up without clothes has got us into bother. I have a habit of curling up to sleep in cat form. I still prefer to sleep that way. And talking of sleeping, this is my bedroom." He opened the door. "We all used to bunk here, then I moved in with Rich into the barn conversion where the business is now, and Thom had the room to himself. Once he left, I came back. I missed Mum's cooking and this room has a fantastic view of the garden." He sat on the bed while Ted ambled to the window.

Harry gazed at Ted's short and stocky frame. There was a lot of arse there to get hold of. His whole body swayed as he walked, but it suggested strength. Harry could imagine Ted welding an axe and moving logs around.

"Did you toss the caber when you lived in Scotland?" he asked.

Ted turned. "I did."

"You look like you could. I bet those arms are powerful. Are the feet a genetic thing in your family?"

Ted blushed underneath his beard. "The truth is, I don't know. I was adopted. Mum and Dad fostered me and I stayed with them. They are wonderful people. I was left on a doorstep somewhere. My birth certificate says I was born in Scotland, but I've never been sure." He sat on the window seat.

Harry longed to rush across the room and hug him. "Oh, Ted. I'm sorry. At least we had Mum and Gran, even if my father buggered off. Apparently, he's known for sowing his seed all over the place. He's dead now. Died in a hit and run on the Old Kent Road. I thought it was just a street in Monopoly, but it seems they're all real places."

Ted glanced out of the window. "I did all right. I lived in the Highlands among the mountains and lochs. Like you, I can't complain. Have you met any of your other siblings?"

Harry wasn't sure if this was a test. Ted was still a watcher and as such a possible threat. He needed to change the subject so swallowed his nerves. "You kissed me earlier and stroked my leg."

Ted stared at him. "I did. I thought you needed it. I'm sorry, did I invade your personal space? I'm not sure what came over me. You seemed…"

Harry relaxed, widened his eyes and smiled.

Ted chuckled. "Oh. Is that how you do it?"

"Do what?" Harry shifted on the bed and continued to stare. "I've no idea what you mean."

Ted strode across the room and knelt in front of him. Harry let his gaze drop. "Look at me."

Harry lifted his face and gazed.

"You changed your eyes when you looked at me. I felt like I wanted to wrap my arms around you."

"But I didn't do anything when you kissed me, at least not on purpose. I still want you to — kiss me, that is."

"Why? I'm not handsome."

Harry chuckled. "I've had handsome. I've had beautiful. I find I prefer interesting, and you intrigue me. Will you come out to dinner with me, or we could go bowling or both? You'll be able to keep a close eye on me then."

"I'm not sure I'm supposed to be *that* close."

"But you want to kiss me, don't you?"

"Perhaps," Ted said.

Harry leant forward and took Ted's face in his hands. His beard was soft. He kissed him. Ted opened his mouth and Harry responded. They stayed connected, turning slightly, tasting each other, until Harry pulled away, his stomach performing somersaults. He'd never expected to feel... He'd kissed others. He liked kissing. *It's a good job I'm sitting down. My knees are shaking.*

"Wow." It was all the conversation he could manage.

Ted stood and grinned. "I think we'd better go back downstairs before we get carried away."

Does he mean before he gets carried away? "Spoilsport," Harry said, trying to lighten the mood. "But you're right. Knowing Mum, she could be in here at any moment checking we're okay, or if we want a hot chocolate before you go out on a cold night."

Ted put his hands on Harry's arms. "Are you all right? The fireworks seem to have stopped."

"I'm better." *It's only you making me shake now.* "At least I didn't transform and hide under the bed. I used to." He turned his head at the knock on the door.

"Told you. We'll be down now, Mum."

"I'm making drinks. I wondered if you fancied a hot chocolate before you went out into the cold, Ted."

Harry glanced at Ted and they laughed out loud. "Give us a minute." He waited until he heard footsteps on the stairs.

"You don't have to stay. I can let you out the back way."

Ted nodded. "That might be best. Thank your mum. We have a busy day tomorrow checking the damage caused by the recent storm. I'll ring you about our date."

Harry perked up. "So we're having one?"

Ted nodded. "But I think we'd better keep it on the downlow. What if you come to mine on Guy Fawkes' night. It's quieter where I am, and you could pick up a Chinese on your way."

"Sounds like a plan. I won't have to explain who I'm with, and sneaking around is something I'm good at."

Five minutes later, Harry waved Ted off at the door and wandered into the family sitting room to find his gran and Maggie deep in conversation. They stopped and stared at him. He sat at one end of the sofa.

"Drinks everyone." His mother barged through the door. "Oh, has Ted gone?"

"He's got a busy day tomorrow."

"So, Maggie. D'you think he's a watcher?" Oona asked her friend.

"I'm not sure. I don't think he's a shifter. I sensed something in his manner like he was hiding something, but they've all got something to hide. I wasn't told anything about him being here. Maybe he was born human into a shifter family – it happens. He's clearly Scottish. A few important families live there. Maybe they sent him here as a punishment for some misdemeanour rather than to keep an eye on anyone in particular. He seems taken with you, Harry."

"Everyone is taken with Harry," his mother said. "I have three handsome sons."

"Thanks, Mum." He said nothing for the rest of the evening. If Ted had secrets, he could decide if and when he wanted to share them.

Chapter Twelve

Only an occasional bang penetrated the quiet of the forest as Ted tidied around the place. One thing he'd noticed about Harry's bedroom was how neat it was, along with the lack of anything loose on surfaces. Why, if cats were such fastidious creatures, did they knock everything onto the floor? During the meal, Ted had watched both Harry and his brother tap against the cutlery, nudging them closer to the edge until their mother or grandmother had met their gaze. Ted guessed they sat on their hands a lot when at the table.

He glanced over his shoulder at the tap on the door. Harry must have left the van further down the path.

"It's open," he called—no response. He strolled over to the other side of the room and pulled on the handle. Harry stood there humming to himself, wearing headphones. He took them off.

"Sorry, I put these on just in case." He stood for a moment and listened. "It's quiet here." Then he handed over the bag of food.

"Come in. Aye. Nothing much penetrates this far out. I'm glad, because they've placed a pair of beavers into the area, and loud noises might frighten them. D'you want to eat at the table?"

Harry plonked the bag on counter. "Please, it'll be easier. I wouldn't want to get sauce on your sofa."

"I'll get the plates." They sat and sorted out the food.

"Beavers," Harry said. "But they'll build dams and alter the landscape. I'm surprised you'd want them here. They might cut down some of your precious trees. Still, they seem to be popping up all over Britain now, and they are kind of cute."

"They were a native species," Ted said trying to ignore the cute comment. "Eurasian beavers have been reintroduced and they're doing well. We had some in Scotland."

"The babies are so gorgeous with their flapping tails," Harry said. "Those teeth must be incredible to take down trees like they do."

Ted ran his tongue across his mouth. Having most of his teeth removed had been painful, but now he had a perfect set and not the two huge ones at the front. He would have been called names.

"I got a variety of dishes," Harry said. "That's the good thing about Chinese, the meat and the vegetable varieties. I didn't know if you ate tofu. D'you have some water?"

"The tap stuff is good," Ted said. "It comes straight from a spring the water firms haven't yet polluted. Sorry, you don't need to hear me go on, but it makes me so angry."

"Me too. We're lucky to live in a beautiful place some people seem intent on destroying. I don't think we always appreciate what we have or do enough to protect it."

Ted dipped a spring roll into sauce and bit into it. "Umm, nice," he said. "Not too hot."

"I asked." Harry stared at him. "Don't you ever worry being out here in the middle of a forest? I don't mean lonely as such, just I'm not sure I'd like being so far away from another person."

Ted considered for a moment. "It can get claustrophobic in the forest with all the trees, but they're the reason I came here. The estate I was brought up on only had a few patches of native species — most are conifers planted to make money. Otherwise there are vast open spaces covered by scrub, heather, and gorse. It's different in the Lake District. To the north of here, there's a patch of rainforest that's protected. I met the new conservation ranger recently and it's been awarded special status."

"Rainforest?" Harry asked. "Like jungle?"

"No, this is temperate rainforest, which grows in colder places with lots of rain, but it's rare. There's all sorts of creatures as well, like this moth which only feeds on one flower called a touch-me-not for two weeks in a year."

"Why's it called a touch-me-not?" Harry asked.

"Because when anything hits the petals, the flower explodes, sending its seeds everywhere. The caterpillars have a way of feeding which doesn't set them off."

Harry grinned. "I've been told the feel of my fingers can cause explosions."

Ted spluttered his food. His face heated up. "Umm. That's good to know."

Harry picked up another spring roll, opened his mouth, placed it on his tongue, and bit into it, his eyes aglow with mischief. Ted stood.

"I'll put some music on."

"You have vinyl?" Harry asked.

"Some old stuff." He picked out a favourite record and put it on the turntable. "I hope you don't mind pop."

"Fine by me." The first song rang out.

Harry raised his eyebrows. "Wow. I wouldn't have pinned you as a fan of this particular diva of song. Have you seen her in concert? Thom took us to the O2 in London. She was fabulous."

Ted shook his head. "I've never been to a live gig."

Harry's mouth dropped open. "What, never? Now that's something we need to change." He took out his phone. "I'm going to check who we could see in the next month." He pressed buttons and scrolled. "Perfect. Tickets could be a problem, though Thom usually knows someone who knows someone. It's three weeks from now. I'll give you the exact dates so you can get the time off. Excellent, and we get a couple of nights away too. You said you'd go out with me."

"I don't know," Ted said. "People might notice we're away at the same time." *And I've been warned.*

"I don't care. I can say I'm visiting Thom and you could say you're visiting your parents or something. We can go down Friday night and return on Sunday. I'll sort everything. Please. Let's live a little."

Ted thought for a moment. *Fuck them. Harry isn't a danger to anyone. He wouldn't care what I was anyway.* "Okay. Who are we going to see?" Ted asked. He'd never been to London, or even south of Cumbria, as far as he knew. His parents had never gone on holiday.

"And how much will it cost? I have money. I don't spend much."

Harry glanced up from his phone. Ted guessed he was texting his brother. "Sorry, I didn't think about the money. I should have. The business is doing well so I can pay. Are you sure you want to go? I can be impetuous at times. As for who, that's my secret. But let's say there isn't a gay man on this planet who doesn't love her."

"Oh," Ted said. He ate the food and sipped his water and smiled to himself. *I deserve some fun and I bet a weekend with Harry would be just that — Fun with a capital F.*

Harry picked up his fork. "I still haven't learnt all about Ted. You must have so many things to do in your job," he said before spooning a combination of chicken and rice into his mouth.

"Like you wouldn't believe. The trees and animals are the least of our worries. I know we need tourists, but we waste so much time clearing up after them. Some even leave their tents behind, and you wouldn't want to know what else. We're forever patching up pathways, and as you know, some think the mountains are an easy choice for a day trip and don't plan ahead. We educate the locals in schools and clubs but we can't educate the visitors. This country is so beautiful and we work hard to keep it that way. I love lakes and mountains, especially at sunrise and sunset."

Harry grinned at him and Ted's stomach flipped. What was it about this man? Was it the risk, the danger, knowing he was supposed to stay away from him? Was it that Harry brought out his protective instincts? He didn't believe all the alpha, beta, and omega stuff he'd read in books — that was just for wolves, but maybe there was something to it after all. From the moment he'd brought Harry back to life, spluttering water and gasping for breath, he'd felt — possessive, it was the only word, though at first he'd denied it to himself. He hated lying to Harry, but Harry couldn't know the truth about him because he wasn't supposed to exist, because he might say the wrong thing to the wrong person. For some reason, the beavers didn't even want other shifters to know. Clearly, his birth had been a mistake. Ted knew the shifter world didn't like interference from humans for other purebreds, but he had no knowledge of the politics or intrigue and he didn't want to be part of that world. All he wanted was to live his life.

"Hello." Harry tinged the glass with his spoon. "I said, it's a pity we won't have much of a sunrise tomorrow. I bet the view from your veranda is spectacular. Have you seen the Northern Lights from here?"

"Sorry, mind elsewhere," Ted replied.

"On me, I hope." Harry batted his eyelashes.

"You're such a terrible flirt," Ted said.

Harry leaned over and covered Ted's hand with his own. "No, I'm a magnificent flirt. Cats are. We have the perfect redistribution system, you know. If we don't like who we live with, we find someone else, and we have to be able to persuade a person they need us. A few meows, a few purrs, a few headbutts, and leg rubs normally work. Then they wonder how they ever lived without a cat in their lives."

"I'll bear that in mind," Ted said. Harry turned Ted's hand over and stroked his palm. He shivered and stared. Tiny bolts of electricity shot up his arm.

"I think I've had enough to eat," Harry said. "Shall we adjourn to the sofa?"

"Umm, all right, if you're sure. D'you want a coffee?"

"Yes, please."

A few minutes later, Ted brought the mugs to the sofa and sat next to Harry. *Should I tell him I've only slept a few times with one man? Will he want me to top or bottom? Maybe he doesn't. How do you talk about these things? Harry's slept with women as well. He's had so much experience.* Ted sat with his knees together and his hands clasped on his thighs and said nothing.

"Are you all right?" Harry asked.

"Sort of," Ted said. "Truth is, I'm a little intimidated by you."

"Me?" Harry said. "Or what people have said about me?"

Ted turned to face him. "Both, I suppose."

"You know we don't have to do anything, don't you? We can sit here and hold hands while watching the boxset of your choice." Harry reached out and uncurled Ted's fingers then took one hand in each of his.

"See," he said.

Ted took a deep breath and gazed into Harry's green eyes. "I've only had sex with one person. It was calamitous for many reasons. I don't want to go into details. And I'm a lot older than you, and not good-looking, unlike you. To be frank, I've no idea what you see in me."

"You don't have to tell me anything, Ted. And as for the bastard who hurt you and clearly abused your trust, not everyone is like that. As for age, well, it is just a number. We'll take everything at your pace, and we've already done kissing. Maybe we should start there."

Harry let go of Ted's hands and clasped his face then edged nearer until their noses almost touched. His aroma hit Ted and dizziness threatened to overwhelm him. He wanted to bury his face into Harry's neck and breathe him in.

"Are you okay?" Harry asked without moving.

"Yes, it's your aftershave. I have a strong sense of smell."

"I'm not wearing any. This is just me and some shower gel."

"Oh." *Wow, he really smells like a pine forest.*

"Can I kiss you?" Harry met Ted's gaze. Ted nodded.

The touch of Harry's lips were soft on his own. Being nearer, Harry stroked Ted's hair. His touch was glorious. They shifted angle and Ted opened his mouth a little, tasting the familiar flavour of Chinese food. He panicked a little about his own breath, but realised they'd taste the same. Harry widened his lips and they moved in harmony, changing angles, pressing harder until Harry edged his tongue forward. After a few minutes, struggling to breathe, Ted pulled away. Harry released his face and they stared at each other, panting as if they'd run a four-minute mile.

"You can kiss," Harry said.

"I like kissing," Ted said. "But some people don't like my beard."

"I think it suits you, and the colour is gorgeous. It's soft, like fur."

"Some people don't like body hair."

"You're forgetting I've seen you naked. I have no problem with hair. Maybe it's being a cat some of the time. Humans are different. Some have hair and some don't." Harry reached out and stroked Ted's beard.

"It is so soft."

"I look after it."

Harry lifted his hand, undid one of Ted's shirt buttons, and slipped his fingers inside. Ted closed his eyes and let himself feel Harry's touch.

"This is soft too. Let's go to bed. I want to see you."

"I bought some condoms," Ted said. "I wasn't sure..."

Harry grinned. "Well, that answers one of my questions. As for who does what, I don't mind—me, you, neither." Harry stood and stretched out his hand. Ted clasped it and let himself be hauled up and escorted to the bed. He drew back the sheets. Harry jumped on the mattress.

"Come on, sex can be fun as well." He lifted his jumper over his head. He was slim but not over-muscled. Ted had a brief worry about his own body, but as Harry had said, he'd already seen it. He undid his shirt then knelt on the bed and repositioned himself so they were chest to chest. They kissed again, letting their fingers run up each other's backs. Ted kissed down Harry's neck to where it met his shoulder, then along his collar bone. Harry's groans went straight to his cock.

"I need you naked," Harry said. They both removed their rest of their clothes, flinging them off the bed.

"You are gorgeous," Ted said.

"And you're impressive." Harry lowered his gaze. "I didn't have a chance to say so the last time."

Ted shoved his feet under the bedding to hide them.

"Lie down," Harry said.

They lay facing each other, with Harry idly running his fingers over the hair on Ted's chest following the trail downwards. Ted's cock stiffened in response. He'd pulled the sheet across his lower half, embarrassed at Harry's comment.

"If I do anything you don't like, let me know."

Ted opened his mouth to reply but Harry had moved at speed to sit astride his upper body. He leaned over and kissed Ted, who responded in kind and tweaked Harry's nipple without warning. Harry groaned.

"Again. Do it again."

Ted squeezed the nipple between his finger while they kissed, changing positions and pressure.

"Fuck," Harry said pulling away. "So good." He kissed Ted's neck then again along his clavicle, returning to suck hard. Ted gasped. There would be a mark there in the morning. He wrapped his arms around Harry's back and spun him over until now he sat on Harry's chest.

"Bloody hell. Your cock is magnificent. Edge forward. I want to taste it."

Ted shuffled on his knees. Feeling bolder, he held the tip an inch from Harry's mouth. Harry stuck out his tongue and let the drip of pre-cum fall onto it.

"Give it to me, please. I want to feel it in my mouth."

Ted guided his now-hard dick inside Harry. Harry sucked as soon as he could. Ted almost lost his balance. He grabbed the metal headboard at the same time as Harry grabbed his arse and pulled him forward.

The man must have no gag reflex and flipping heck, he can suck.

Ted wanted to thrust. "Can I fuck your mouth?"

Harry nodded. Ted eased his cock in and out, not too much but enough. Oh, the feeling was glorious, and watching was better. Harry's pupils had fully dilated.

113

The man was beautiful. Ted wanted to possess him. He had to hold himself back. If he didn't, he was going to come. He pulled out.

"You have a talented mouth. Do you want me to come now?"

"Yes. The feel of you is incredible. It's like I was made for you. I want to swallow you down. You know how much cats like cream. Fuck me. I'm going to milk you dry."

Who could refuse such an offer—not Ted. Harry guided his cock back into his mouth. Ted held onto the headboard again and thrust a little deeper. Harry opened his throat. *Fucking hell! How does he do that?*

"You are amazing. You've nearly taken it all. Oh yeah. That's it." Tingles ran down Ted's spine. Every hair on his body rose.

"I'm coming," he warned. Harry's eyes shone in the lamplight. Ted gripped the headboard harder as his body emptied into Harry's mouth, spurt after spurt. Only a few drips escaped either side. Ted tried to pull out, but Harry held his arse, still sucking until he was ready to let go, then Ted sat back and stared at Harry's beautiful face. Harry licked his lips.

"Better than cream," he said smiling. "We are so doing that again."

Ted waited, unsure what to do. "You have a clever mouth," he said.

"Your cock was made to fill it. We fit together."

To his horror, Ted yawned. "Sorry, spent the day cutting down dead ash trees."

Harry pulled him down and rolled him over until they'd swapped positions. "As long as I'm not boring you."

Ted grinned as Harry stifled a yawn.

"It's catching and I've been dealing with rats all day."

"I'll keep the trees," Ted said.

Harry leaned over and kissed Ted. The connection sent shivers down his spine, but even though his cock perked a little, he yawned again.

"You could stay," Ted said. "You left the van out of sight, didn't you? We'll have the morning."

Harry rolled off next to him. "Sounds good to me." Ted wrapped himself around Harry and was asleep seconds later.

Chapter Thirteen

Harry woke with arms around him and morning wood. He glanced at the bedside clock and chuckled that Ted still had one when everyone else would check their phone.

"You're awake then."

"I am, and you're growly in a sexy way first thing. I've an hour before I need to get going, and I've been dreaming of you fucking me all night."

Ted turned to face him. "Really? We could have last ni—"

Harry put a finger to Ted's lips. "We were both tired, we've both had a sleep, and from what I can see in the dark, we're both up for some early morning joy." Harry pounced, like the cat he was, pushed Ted onto his back then sat astride him.

"I think we were somewhere like this last night." He tweaked Ted's nipple.

"Ow!"

"But you liked it. I'll kiss it better." He licked and sucked. Ted writhed under his touch. His cat's eyes let him see in the darkness.

"Where's the lube and condoms? I want you inside me."

Ted gave an audible gulp.

"Don't worry. I'll do all the work. You can just lie there."

"I'm not going to argue," Ted said. "The stuff is under the pillow."

Harry dug underneath and found what he needed. He prepped himself then positioned himself low enough to give him access to Ted's cock. Ted reached over and switched on the lamp.

"I want to see you. We don't all have great eyesight in the darkness like you."

"Fine by me. I like to be seen." Harry unwrapped the condom and rolled it over Ted's more than stunning erection.

"You don't have to," Ted said. Worry lines creased his forehead. "I know it's big. My ex wouldn't..."

"Your ex was an idiot." Harry spread more lube. He didn't say he'd taken bigger, or he'd taken two. There were some things you didn't discuss. He raised himself and guided the head of Ted's cock to his entrance, then lowered himself, breathing through the initial burn.

"You are beautiful," Ted said. "I've never..."

Harry stopped. "What? Done this before – never fucked someone?"

"No. My boyfriend wouldn't."

"Then I'm honoured to be your first." He sank until Ted filled him. Tears formed at the corner of Ted's eyes.

"Sorry, I'm being stupid. This is a little over-whelming."

Harry arched his back and leant forward to kiss Ted. He'd been intimate so many times before with all sorts of people, but for some reason he didn't understand being with Ted, kissing Ted, touching Ted — everything was different. He wanted to give Ted a memorable first time, and he wanted there to be a second and third... he could have gone on counting. He wanted to show Ted all there was to know and let him discover the joys of sex and more.

I'm getting ahead of myself.

He lifted himself up then let his body slide back down, setting a rhythm.

"I want to thrust," Ted said.

"Then do it. Fuck me, big boy. Make me walk funny. Let me feel it all day and smile remembering. Go on."

Ted fucked him. Oh, did he fuck him. Over and over again. Harry reached over to the headboard to steady himself.

"Oh God, Harry, I'm close."

Harry clasped Ted's cock. "You'll need a shower. I'm about to come all over you." Harry let go at the same time as heat rushed out deep inside him. They both shouted — names, obscenities, words that didn't make any sense. Harry wanted it to go on forever. He squeezed his arse.

"No more. I can't do any more," Ted panted. "You're amazing. I've never had an orgasm like..." He paused.

Harry lifted himself, dealt with the condom, and rolled over next to Ted. He ran his fingers across Ted's chest. "Sorry, I've made you all sticky." He placed his finger on Ted's bottom lip. Ted stuck out his tongue and licked around the tip.

Harry glanced down his body. *No, you cannot be interested in more.*

"Next time, I want to blow you," Ted said.

Harry chuckled. "So there'll be a next time?"

"Sorry, I thought…"

"Stop panicking. I know my reputation for loving and leaving, but I want more with you, Ted. I've never have had a type. I like people. I love sex. I like you. You're different and ever so slightly mysterious, and I've got to admit there's something alluring about this being a secret. You're all mine and no one knows. We have this little cabin in the wood to fuck to our hearts' content. If that's what you want."

"I shouldn't, but yes. And we must be careful."

Harry wished he could roll on top of Ted again but he needed to go and didn't have time to get distracted. He moved to sit on the edge of the bed.

Ted rolled over and lay propped on his elbow. "You'd better get off. Anything exciting on today?"

Harry shook his head. "A flea infestation in a holiday home—you?"

"More tree cutting and we've a flooded path to check, which'll be fun in this weather." Rain pattered on the windows.

"Can I call you?" Harry asked.

"I'll get us a couple of burner phones. Sometimes they check on us."

Harry didn't ask who *they* were. He stood. "Okay, I'll come round Saturday night. No one's suspicious when I go out. They've learnt not to ask questions. Is seven okay?"

"Yes, I'll get the phones by then." Ted sat up and reached out to take hold of Harry's hand.

"This was incredible, Harry."

Harry squeezed Ted then let go and gathered his clothes. "For me, too. I'm sorry, I've got to go. I wish I didn't have to. I wish I could spend all day here with you, but Rich would kill me. He hates dealing with fleas. If they're cat fleas, they bite us. And now, I'll love you and leave you." *Shit! Should I have said that? And do I?*

Outside, it was still dark and the rain was falling at a steady pace. He ran to the van, started the engine, and set off down the bumpy path. Near the exit, he turned off his lights in case a car came past. The van declared the company name, which was a disadvantage when you were trying to be secretive. Sure there was no car approaching, he set off, then switched the headlights back on again. It was a thirty-minute drive home.

Harry's mind wandered as he drove the familiar road. His thoughts turned to Ted and how much he wanted to turn back and curl up in Ted's arms.

What the hell is wrong with me? I'm usually happy to say thanks and turn away without another thought. There's just something about him. The morning traffic was increasing and he had to take more care. Still, he considered Ted.

He's solid and steady which should make him boring, but it doesn't. I know how strong he is. I bet he looks wonderful in a flannel shirt chopping wood. Memo to self, buy Ted a check shirt and get him to cut down a tree with an axe. I already know he's good in a crisis. Shit! I'm describing husband material. Is he? Is that it? Do I want to settle down? He's not allowed to be the one. But maybe he is the one. For fuck's sake, is that what I've done? Have I gone and fallen for the wrong man – the one I'm supposed to stay away from? He chuckled. *Typical me, falling for the forbidden fruit. I should end it now, but I don't want to – not yet.*

He concentrated on the road, which was steeper and narrower at this point. Their brochure advised visitors to come along the lakeside to the hotel. He turned on the bends. Across the lake, now the rain had stopped and the clouds had dispersed, the sun was rising sending out colours over the mountain. He took a left into the drive and parked the car around the back. The light was on in the hotel kitchen. His mum and gran would be cooking breakfast for their guests, a family of four and a couple visiting for a sixtieth birthday celebration.

Stepping out of the car, he sniffed the air, recognising the familiar smell of all the fireworks set off the night before. As usual, he followed his pre-prepared route. He undressed and stuffed his clothes in a bag which he hid in a bush. He flexed his body and transformed, leapt onto the wall, then to the roof of the back porch on the family side of the hotel which was under his room. He'd left the window open so once on the sill, he jumped through onto the chest of drawers then onto the bed. He wanted to curl up and sleep, but Rich would be expecting him at nine. He had just enough time for a quick shower to wash of the scent of sex. Strangely, he could smell Ted more intensely in feline form. He stretched again and was human once more.

After a shower and dressing, he sat and stared at himself in the mirror. His hair needed cutting, though he'd enjoyed how Ted had stroked him and run his fingers through the longer strands. His stomach rumbled.

I need breakfast. Good sex makes me hungry. At least he should have the family kitchen to himself.

He ambled down the stairs. He knew his mother would know he'd not slept in his room, but she wouldn't ask where he'd been or who he'd been with.

He'd texted her as usual so she wouldn't worry he'd been killed by an axe murder or something. He was about to open the kitchen door when voices said his name. He listened. Why was Maggie here so early talking to his grandmother?

"He needs to stay away from him, Oona. I don't know why. I just know what I'm told. Usually, I don't have much contact with them, but they've been insistent, so tell Lucy no more dinners. This Ted bloke for some reason is out of bounds. They don't want him upset."

Harry could hear the concern in her voice, perhaps more for herself than for him.

"It's not as if Harry has had much to do with the bloke," Oona replied. "Lucy invited him as a thank-you. Harry couldn't help that the man saved him, now, could he? And you know our Harry, he's anything for an easy life. He doesn't make waves. It won't be a problem, I'm sure. I mean, what would they do?"

Maggie didn't reply and Harry wished he could see their faces.

"Maggie? What would they do?"

"I don't know, Oona. I'm a tiny cog in a much bigger machine. There are rumours that those who step out of line disappear. Britain doesn't have large predators like other countries. There are factions within factions and levels of power. The number of humans aware of our existence is growing as shifters marry out and some aren't happy at all. The scientists—"

"You mean the St Clairs."

Harry had met Raven St Clair through his brother, but she was a writer, not a scientist.

"Say nothing, Oona. I can't say any more. I need to get off now to open the shop."

Harry waited until the back door creaked twice, opening then closing, before he strolled into the kitchen.

"Oh, Gran. I thought you'd be with Mum."

She gazed at him. "You'd better collect your clothes, young man. I won't ask whose bed you slept in last night. It looks like it's about to rain, and you don't want your things to get wet."

Harry slipped out and collected the bag. He emptied the clothes into the washer and switched it on.

"Breakfast?" His gran had moved to stand at the cooker.

"I could manage a bacon butty and a good strong mug of tea. Rich and I are off dealing with fleas this morning, and you know how much he loves that job." He sat at the table while the bacon sizzled.

"Good night?"

"You know me, Gran." He didn't go into details. She placed the sandwich and tea in front of him just as Rich stepped through the door.

"You're up then."

"I am, brother. You look rough."

"Never have twins. I have no idea how Mum coped with three of us, and we have a nanny, courtesy of Suki's parents."

"That's what you get for marrying into money." Though he was joking, his gran's frown told him not to go further with the conversation. Rich sat at the table.

"I know her people are influential," Rich said, sighing. "There's already talk of sending the twins to special schools for our kind to" — he held his hands up to make air apostrophes — "make their lives easier. I mean, I can see their point knowing how we were, but I don't want to take their money. Suki sees nothing wrong with it. I mean, we're off to this tropical island some friend of her parents owns in the Pacific and they're chartering a private plane—a bloody private jet. *We* used to go to holiday camps when we could get time away."

"It's a different world you and Thom live in now," their gran said. "You both made your choices. Love will do strange things to you. Sometimes, you have to think before you dive in too deep."

Harry had the feeling her remark was aimed at him.

"Now, get out there and earn some money, the pair of you."

Rich stood. "It's fleas, Gran. You know how I hate them."

Rich said little on the journey to the house the other side of Windermere. They picked the keys up from a local shop and parked at the back. The owner had asked them to, because who wants to see men kitted up in protective clothing and masks with spraying equipment. It didn't take long, with Harry doing upstairs and Rich the lower floor. They'd return in a couple of days.

"I'll pop to Tasker's and get us a couple of pasties," Rich said. He answered his phone as he turned the corner to the car park—thankfully it was easier to find a space to park at this time of year. Harry's thoughts wandered back to the discussion he'd overheard earlier. Maybe he should leave Ted alone, but he didn't want to. *I like him. I want to get to know him. There's something. Oh, I don't know. Thom got to marry a human. Marry!* He switched the radio on.

"And now a favourite from the seventies, *I'm Not in Love* by 10cc."

Harry put his head in his hands. It seemed even the universe was trying to tell him something.

Chapter Fourteen

Ted had this Saturday off and he had things to do. He tidied and dusted every inch of the cabin then showered and prepped himself for Harry's visit. He'd worried about his online searching, but hoped private browsing would be enough to keep out prying eyes. Yesterday, he'd bought two phones for him and Harry to use. It was like being a spy without the sharp suit and Aston Martin.

Knowing he had time until Harry arrived, Ted settled down on his sofa to read. There was a knock at the door five minutes later. Ted sprang up and hurried across the room to answer.

"Otis? Was I supposed to be expecting you?" He glanced out of the door as if he might see Harry hiding up a tree in cat form.

"No, you weren't. Olivia's taken the kits to visit her family so I was at a loose end and wondered if you fancied lunch and a pint." He stepped through the door and Harry moved back to let him.

"This place looks spick and span," Otis said.

"It's my day off. I like to keep on top of things. D'you mind if we don't go out? I've the makings of a sandwich here, and some bottles of beer? Cheese and pickle do you?" Ted opened the fridge.

"Wow, you've been stocking up."

Ted noted how Otis glanced around the room. His being here had all the makings of a low-level interrogation session without the bright light and thumb screws. *Is he here to check on me?*

"I did a big shop last night. Friday was not a good choice, but I'm flat-out next week. Why don't you sit on the sofa and I'll make us something? How are Olivia and the kits?"

"They're great. Doing well in school. They've made the swim team but are trying not to swim too well. Don't want them breaking any records. Have you seen the beavers?"

"No," Ted replied, a tad too quickly. "They'll need to be left alone to settle in. Here." He handed Otis a plate and bottle and sat in the armchair.

They both bit into their sandwich and chewed. Otis picked up Ted's book. "I've never got into fantasy or sci-fi. I'm not much of a reader. I leave such things to Olivia. She'd fill the place with books."

"I like to read when I've time to myself. I don't get much, with work and volunteering. I'm on call tomorrow, and the forecast is atrocious. There'll still be some idiots who wander off the path."

"Like Harry Katt."

It hadn't taken long for Otis to mention Harry. Perhaps he was on a fishing exercise. "Harry fell off the path," Ted said.

"How was your dinner on Halloween? All meat eaters, those Katts."

"It was fine. Mrs Katt wanted to thank me, that's all. The whole family was there and I haven't seen any of them since. Are you checking on me, Otis?"

Harry noted how his friend turned away.

"I can assure you I have no intention of getting involved with anyone." *Did that sound as if I'm protesting too much?*

"I hear you," Otis said. "I'm concerned, that's all, especially with the beavers moving in nearby. Shifters operate in the shadows. You know what it's like."

"No, really I don't, and I don't want to know. I have no interest in shifter politics. My birth was a mistake I have to live with, and I follow the rules I've been given." Anger surged through him. He needed to get a hold on himself. He stood and took the empty plates to the sink then took a couple of breaths, holding onto the counter before turning.

"Now, if you don't mind, Otis, I'd like to get on with my book."

Otis crossed the floor towards him. "I'm sorry, Ted. I don't want to pry, believe me. You could fuck Harry Katt into a mattress five times a day for all I care, but I'm under pressure here, too. All I want to do is live my life and keep my wife and children safe. You understand that, don't you?"

Ted calmed himself. "I know, Otis, but you've no reason to worry."

Did his face or voice reveal his lie? He'd always thought he had a good liar's face but he remembered what Harry had said. He hugged his friend. "Go and have a swim. Shake off some cobwebs."

Otis stepped back and opened the door. "I might just do that."

Ted stood on the doorstep and watched Otis walk down the path to the river then returned to his book to wait for Harry.

* * * *

Hours later, he was woken by the sound of a motorbike. He rushed to the door, worried about who this could be. The security floodlights lit up the front of the cabin. A man clad in black stepped off a bike and pulled off his helmet.

Fucking hell! Every bit of blood in his body flowed straight to his cock. *Who knew I had a thing for beautiful men dressed in leather?* There, large as life and twice as handsome, stood Harry Katt, beaming from ear to ear.

"D'you like it?" he asked and did a twirl. Ted covered his groin worried his hard-on could be seen from space. He gulped to wet his mouth but found he could only nod.

"I'll hide the wheels round the back."

Ted watched Harry guide the bike. This was a turn-up. He had no idea Harry was a biker. A couple of minutes later, Harry returned carrying a bag and strolled towards him.

"One of the good things about being identical triplets is we get to wear each other's clothes. The suit and bike belonged to Rich but his wife isn't keen, so he's given it to me. I thought it would be easier than parking a van with our company name on."

"Yes," Ted said, finding his voice at last. "And the suit fits you like a glove."

Harry climbed the couple of steps and kissed Ted on the lips before wriggling past him, deliberately pressing their groins together.

"If I'd known you liked leather, I'd have worn my Pride gear. Maybe next time."

Is he trying to kill me?

"I didn't know," Ted said, watching while Harry removed his boots followed by the jacket and trousers. Underneath, he wore a bright green jumper and jeans. His eyes sparkled with magic. He placed the bag on the table.

"There's a beer in the fridge if you want one."

"Yes, please. We had a busy morning."

"What's in the bag?" Ted asked.

"I thought I was supposed to be the curious one. It's a present for you. Well, for me also. And Thom's managed to get those tickets, so make sure you book the time off."

"I'm not sure," Ted said. "Otis was here earlier. He sort of warned me about you again."

Harry stepped right in front of him, invading his personal space. "Do you want to give us up?"

"No," Ted said. "But it could be dangerous."

"I've got a few lives left, thanks to you." He kissed Ted hard and wrapped his arms around him. Ted pressed back and drove his tongue into Harry's mouth, making both of them groan. He grabbed Harry's arse with and they frotted against each other. Ted kissed down Harry's neck.

"No bites," Harry said. "At least none where they can be seen. That sexy arse of yours could do with a few decorations."

"The things you make me feel, Harry Katt. I could drop to my knees here and now."

Harry's pupils darkened. "Then do it. Blow me now on your knees, please."

Ted didn't need to be asked twice. He let himself fall, opened Harry's zip, and pulled out his rock-hard cock. Without any teasing, he took as much as he could and began to suck. Harry placed his hands on Ted's head while Ted once more clasped Harry's arse to pull him closer.

"Bloody hell," Harry said. "D'you have no gag reflex either?"

Ted shook his head.

"I want to fuck your mouth. Can I?"

Ted nodded. He remained still while Harry gave a few tentative thrusts then went deeper. Ted sucked, concentrating on breathing through his nose.

"Yes," Harry said, reaching out to steady himself on the chair. "Oh yes. You are so good. Can you swallow it all? Every last drop? Shall we see? So close now. So bloody good. Nearly. Get ready. Yes!"

Ted sucked hard, swallowing every drop, milking him until Harry had nothing left and dropped to his knees. They knelt facing each other, breathing hard. Harry placed his hands on either side of Ted's face.

"I don't want to give you up, Ted Woodward."

Tears threatened to form in the corners of Ted's eyes. "I don't want to give you up either. We'll have to be careful." His stomach rumbled.

"Sorry, I'm hungry."

"Even after that load?" Harry grinned then stood and offered Ted his hand.

Ted let himself be hauled up.

"I'm starving too," Harry said, sniffing the air. "And something smells nice."

"It's curry. I put it in the slow cooker this morning. I'll add some chicken for you."

"I can eat vegetarian," Harry said.

Ted lifted the lid of the pot. "But you prefer meat."

"I won't lie. I do, but I don't want to rub your nose in it and force you to cook things you don't want to."

"Sit at the table and grab a plate."

Ted spooned out the curry alongside a couple of garlic naans. Harry talked about his day and Ted listened. It was such a change from the quiet nights he spent by himself. They made plans for their trip. Ted's pulse raced one more. *Can I do this? Go to London? No one knows me there.*

The clatter of Harry dropping his fork on his plate brought Ted back to the room. Harry patted his tummy and groaned. "That was as good as my mum's, but don't tell her I said so."

Ted stood and picked up the plates to put in the dishwasher. Harry sat on the sofa and patted the other side. "Come over here. I want to ask you something."

"Okay," Ted replied, uncertain of what would come next. He sat and turned to face Harry, whose face was now serious.

"Would you like to see me transform?" Harry asked.

"I don't know. Will it hurt you?" Ted wasn't even sure he *could* transform anymore — if it was something you simply thought about and did, or if there was some sort of metaphorical button to press.

"I'll admit, there's always some pain, but it's fleeting. I keep as flexible as I can. The real issue is the size difference. All of this has to become compact. I haven't done this with any of my shifter lovers, but I want you to know me, to see me for all I am, and a large part of me is cat."

Ted still wasn't sure, but curiosity got the better of him. "Okay, if you're sure."

Harry stood. "I've one condition." He picked up the bag and reached inside. He lifted out a package and gave it to Ted, who unwrapped the contents.

"It's a shirt."

"A blue and black check flannel shirt, to be exact. There's these as well."

"Braces?" Ted said.

"I want to see you chop wood wearing these," Harry said grinning.

"I think I can manage that." Chopping wood was literally in his blood.

"Okay, then. There may be a few bone-crunching noises, but don't worry."

Ted sat and stared, fascinated as Harry transformed. So much of what he saw was a blur. The process was quick. One moment Harry was there and seconds later in his place stood a black and white cat surrounded by discarded clothes.

"Wow."

Harry mewed then jumped onto the sofa and into Ted's lap.

Ted picked him up and wrapped his arms around this feline version of Harry, who tucked his head into Ted's neck and placed a paw on his shoulder. Warmth flooded through his body as he stroked Harry's fur along his back. *Is this serotonin or endorphins like you get from eating chocolate?*

"Do you like being cuddled."

Harry mewed.

"I'll take that as a yes."

Holding Harry like this, he had this sudden urge to tell him what a gorgeous boy he was and how he had the softest fur and a surprisingly bushy tail. This was a living creature he held in an embrace. Stroking Harry soothed his soul like meditation. He scritched Harry's ears and was rewarded with loud purrs. The noise reminded him of the most perfect engine. Did this mean Harry was happy? He had so many questions.

"Wow, this is…" *I'm talking to a cat.* "I'm not even sure what this is. I feel like I want to protect you forever when you look at me with those bright green eyes. I would fight anyone who threatened you. Is that how others feel?"

Harry rubbed his face against Ted's cheek.

"Now, I know you're marking me as yours." *Am I yours? They say cats don't have owners but have servants instead.* "I want to hold you and feed you treats. I wouldn't care if you knocked everything off the shelves if you showed me how much you missed me when I came home. Is this the power every cat has? I wish you could speak to me. Or are you laughing at me thinking there's a sucker born every minute?"

Harry made two short meows.

"You are speaking to me."

Harry blinked once.

"Do you like it when I smooth your fur?"

Another blink.

Ted rubbed a spot at the end of Harry's back just before his tail and Harry lifted his bottom. "Oh, d'you want more?" He used his fingers and rubbed harder. Harry stood and started kneading Ted's chest, his little nails breaching Ted's flesh.

"Ow."

Harry stopped and rubbed his face on Ted's nose again.

He grinned. "Does that mean you like me?"

Harry blinked, made a few turns, and curled up on Ted's chest with his eyes closed. Ted had read somewhere you didn't disturb a sleeping cat. He knew they slept for hours in a day. Having this warm weight sat on his chest changed everything. Now, he wasn't alone or lonely with this living breathing creature trusting him enough to sleep contentedly. The sounds Harry made echoed the vibrations of his body. Ted's heartbeat attempted to match the speed. The cat was Harry and Harry was the cat. They were one and the same but still different. Harry had all the urges of a feline yet was still also human.

Is it confusing for him? Is this what it would be like for me? Would I want to chop trees and make dams? Would it hurt me to transform after so long in this shape? There are so many shifters in the world of all kinds only some people know about. Were there dinosaurs? He thought about all the possible species. *I know there aren't insects, but are there mice or blue whales? Are there hummingbirds and ostriches?*

So many questions — questions he'd never dared to ask his parents, but for now all he wanted to do was to lie on his sofa with Harry curled up purring on his chest. He picked up his book, opened to his bookmark, and read.

Chapter Fifteen

Harry woke again an hour later. He opened his eyes and stared at Ted. The feeling of being held by him, touched by him, and protected by him had been almost overwhelming. For some reason he couldn't fathom, he trusted this man to take care of him, to risk his life for his. Ted stirred underneath him so Harry unfurled himself, stretched, and dug his claws into Ted's chest.

"Ow," Ted cried before moving. Harry jumped off, landing elegantly on the floor. He sat to stare up at Ted and meowed like any cat would.

"You really *are* a cat. I thought I might have had some sort of mad dream. But no, you're really a cat. It is you, isn't it, Harry? I'm not gabbling at some stray who has wandered in after food."

Harry blinked at him. He thought himself back to being human. The air around him vibrated and his cat form disappeared to be replaced by a naked man.

"Oh," Ted said. "I'd forgotten."

Harry loved the way Ted blushed.

"You've seen me like this before," he said, and twirled like a doll in a music box. He loved to show off.

"Yes, but the context is different. Then you weren't standing starkers in my living room with me fully dressed."

"You could strip as well and we could make out on the sofa if you want. Or maybe I could put on your dressing gown and you could make us a big mug of tea and some biscuits. I thought I saw some Hobnobs in the cupboard, and I'm starving again. Transforming takes a lot of energy."

He turned and sashayed across the room, shaking his arse and feeling Ted's gaze on him. "Don't forget the tea," he said, before grabbing the robe and heading for the bathroom.

Once inside, he used the loo then sat on the lid. *Did I do the right thing? I don't think Ted is really a watcher, but there's something special about him. More than something.* He gazed at himself in the mirror. "You like him, don't you? Maybe more than like him."

Harry had never been in love. He hadn't transformed in front of anyone other than his family before, or let another human hold him in their arms as a cat, but he'd wanted Ted to see.

"Let's face it. You were testing him," he whispered. In cat form, all Harry had seen in Ted's eyes was love. He knew how people were with pets. His brother Thom had told him all about how he moved in with his now husband in cat form. People were protective of their pets, or the good ones were, and Harry was certain Ted was a good one. He'd witnessed the need to protect in Ted's expression, and in Ted's arms he knew he'd be safe as cat or human. He chuckled to himself.

"Face it. You have feelings for this man."

"You all right in there?" Ted called from the living room. "You don't want your tea to go cold, and I can eat whole packets of Hobnobs."

Harry wrapped the robe around himself and tied the belt. "You'd better have left me some," he said, opening the door.

"I have cakes as well, with real cream," Ted said. His smile lit up the room like a sun rising over the horizon, spreading its warmth over the land.

"You have me all figured out," Harry said, plonking himself on the sofa.

"Not yet," Ted replied. "And I do have about a million questions."

Harry dunked a biscuit into his tea for the perfect amount of time then let it melt on his tongue before answering, "I may not have all the answers."

"I've never lived with a proper pet. Dad had working dogs but they didn't live in the house. Do you know the power you have? I swear I would have fought all-comers to protect you. Is that normal?"

"I've never had a pet either. I remember Thom wanted a gerbil but can you imagine? My mum said a very definite no. I wish I could say all humans are the same, but I'd be lying. Cat lovers are a distinct group. Cats get away with being aloof and their owners just give them more, though we can be loving too. Dogs are different because they're pack animals."

"Even the cats were working animals on the estate."

Harry paused for a moment. *How much should I tell him? In for a penny, et cetera.*

"There are some things I haven't told you. I wasn't sure what you knew. All my instincts tell me you're not a danger. I've been told to stay away from you because of my family. My father is a mystery we were told not to attempt to solve it. Apparently he earned his nickname, The Wanderer, and he has many offspring who are called the Wanderlings. All Thom discovered is that he was abandoned by his family so took revenge by sleeping with humans and creating more of his line. Mum was young and she says going through a rebellious stage when she met him. My father was twice her age and charming. She had no idea what he was until we were born."

Harry ate more biscuits waiting for Ted to reply.

"Remember, I've no idea who my parents were at all." Ted stared ahead. His whole body leeched sadness, making Harry wish he was a cat again and could spring into Ted's arms.

"So we both have mysterious ancestors." He paused and Harry worried what was coming next. Ted turned to face him again, moving so their thighs touched.

"Do you like being a cat?"

"I do," Harry replied. "As a teenager it gave me an excuse for needing more sleep. My gran said at least if I was sleeping, I was out of trouble. As the youngest by a few hours, I was spoilt. Thom and Rich were supposed to be the sensible ones, until Thom went off to London."

"And now he's about to become a movie star."

"Hopefully, though he'll have to be careful. You'd be surprised which other stars have a similar secret."

"As a human, can you do cat-like things?"

Harry chuckled. "I think we've discovered that's not so. I don't always land on my feet. I can shape my body differently and jump higher. Shifters all have some abilities which match their animal form, like extra strength, or being able to hold their breath longer."

Ted's body lurched as if someone had stuck him with an electric prod. *Curious.*

"I bet your friend, Otis, could swim for some time."

"Yes, I imagine so." Ted had tensed. Harry took his hand.

"Are you really a watcher? It's just—"

Ted snatched his hand away. "There are things I can't say, Harry. All I can tell you is that I know of shifters."

"Thom met some other shifters in London—the St Clair family, the parents of Raven St Clair, the writer. He told me a little about them. They're doctors investigating genetics. All very hush-hush, apparently." *Should I have said that? Too late now.*

Ted wrapped his arms around himself. "I think we should stop talking about this subject."

Harry knew fear when he saw it. "Okay. Sorry, curiosity comes with being a cat."

Ted stared at him. "And we know what curiosity can lead to. Please, Harry, don't talk to anyone else about the St Clair family—I care too much for you."

Shit! He's serious.

"I care for you too, and I've no ambition to dig into mysteries. All that bothers me is not seeing you. I don't want to stop. Do you?"

"I should, but no. We just have to be careful and keep things on the down low."

Harry stood. "Come to bed with me. I'll make you forget the rest of the world."

Ted held out his hand and let Harry lift him from the sofa. They stood face-to-face.

"That's quite a boast."

Harry led Ted to the bed. Once there, Harry undid the belt on the robe and dropped it around him.

Ted needed to take a breath. Despite Harry's claim, he had his own ideas for what should happen next.

"Lie down on the bed on your front," he whispered, not quite believing what he was saying.

Harry raised an eyebrow. "As you wish."

Ted chuckled, recognising the quote, which dissipated the tension in his muscles.

"Hmm, you'd suit being a pirate. You look good in black — the dread pirate Harry. Maybe we could find a ship and sail away together from all of this. Just the two of us travelling around the world." For a moment, Ted stared at him, imagining such a possibility then he stripped and knelt next to Harry on the bed.

"Would you like that?"

"Would I get to wear a sexy white blouse, leather pants, fancy boots, and an eye patch?"

"I think that could be arranged."

He reached out a hand and ran his finger down Harry's back from neck to arse. Harry shivered under the touch. He did it again, this time using all four fingers. Harry's skin was soft and smooth. He guessed the man looked after himself, but then he was a cat and cats spent a lot of time washing themselves and were fastidious about cleanliness. Harry had no marks, no moles, though sometimes Ted would swear his skin changed colour, forming patterns of black and white that matched his fur.

"You like to be touched?"

"Yes," Harry said. "But it has to be the right person. Cats are picky. We need to find the right person and when we do that person usually gets no choice."

Ted reached over to his top drawer and took out the massage oil then he positioned himself over Harry. He opened the jar and the smell hit the air.

Harry sniffed. "Lavender, I love the smell."

Ted dug his fingers into the pot. "This'll be cold but it'll warm up." He'd checked online what to do, never having massaged anyone before. He started at Harry's neck and shoulders not pressing too hard. This was about touch. Harry groaned.

"God, you're good. Oh, yeah, just there."

Ted worked his way down Harry's back. The scent of sweet flowers filled the room. Before he used his hands, he kissed each cheek, resisting the urge to bite and leave his mark.

"You have a peach of an arse."

"Why thank you, kind sir. Your palms are massaging them perfectly. You could do this for a living."

Ted ran one digit down the gap between each cheek, stopping at Harry's hole. His oiled finger slipped in with ease. Harry lifted himself to meet Ted. He slipped in another and fucked Harry slowly. His own cock was now hard as iron.

"Fuck me," Harry whispered. "I need you inside me, but I need to turn over. I want to see your face."

"Yes," Ted croaked as all moisture left his mouth.

While Harry turned, Ted took a condom from the drawer, covered himself, and used a little more lube. Harry had placed a pillow under his bottom. Ted moved between his legs then eased into Harry until his balls hit flesh. He fucked him tentatively at first then increased the pace, his gaze locked on Harry's green eyes.

Harry shifted a little and placed his legs on Ted's shoulders. He eased deeper, hitting that little bundle of nerves.

"Yes," Harry cried. He grabbed his cock and started to pump, which sent Ted over the edge. His orgasm slammed into him out of nowhere. He loved this. He loved having Harry underneath him, making Harry his and his alone.

"Don't stop," Harry said. "Please just a little bit longer. So good. So…" Harry threw his head back and pumped his cock. Ted watched his face. He was beautiful.

No one is going to take you from me, Harry Katt. I don't care what they say. From now on, if you want to be, you are mine and I'm yours, and that's all there is to it.

Chapter Sixteen

Harry stretched then opened his eyes and squinted into the half-light emanating from the living area. There was no sign of Ted. He listened, expecting to hear the sound of falling water from the shower but instead he recognised the sound of chopping coming from outside. He glanced at his watch. It was already gone nine and the sun was attempting to shine. After using the bathroom and putting on his clothes, he hurried to the door.

"Fuck me."

Ted stood dressed in the shirt and braces Harry had bought accompanied by a kilt, complete with sporran, held up by a thick belt. In his hands he held an axe which he swung at a log, splitting it in two with one strike.

The air was cold and still. Frost lay on the ground and the early morning mist had begun to burn off as the winter sun attempted to give a little warmth to the day. Ted was glorious — every inch the lumberjack of Harry's fantasies.

"I hope you've got pants on under there," he called out. "Or you'll have blue balls in this weather."

Ted grinned. "Och, laddie. You know a true Scotsman doesnae wear anything under his kilt." Ted picked up another log and with one blow spilt this one in half, then into quarters, ready to use in his wood-burning fire.

Harry grabbed the mat from the floor. Before Ted knew what he was doing, Harry placed it at his feet, lifted the kilt and took Ted's cock into his hand and mouth. He needed to take Ted and make him come like this. True to his word, Ted had nothing on. Did the man feel the cold at all?

Harry sucked hard. He intended this to be quick and dirty. Ted clasped his head and shoulder, holding his hair and tugging at it.

"Is this okay?" Ted asked.

Harry made a noise he hoped Ted interpreted as a yes. By now, Ted's erect cock filled his mouth but he didn't gag, instead he used one hand to stroke and sucked at the head.

"Yes," Ted said, squeezing Harry's shoulder. "Don't stop."

Harry had no intention of stopping until he'd swallowed every drop of what Ted had to give.

"Oh my God, Harry." With those words, Ted emptied into Harry's mouth — warm cum on a cold day.

"No more," Ted said. "You've had it all. I need to sit down before I fall down. Come out from under there."

Harry lifted the kilt over his head and gazed up at Ted. He licked his lips and smiled, then shivered.

"Come on, you beautiful idiot, let's get you inside in the warm. You bring the mat and I'll bring the logs."

Back inside, Ted lit the fire, creating a wonderful glow.

"I'll make tea," Harry said. "Do you like pancakes?"

"I do," Ted said.

"I'll make us some for breakfast."

"I usually have porridge." Ted came up behind Harry as he stood in front of the kettle and encased Harry in his arms. Harry leaned into the embrace. *This could be something I could have every morning if I get this right.*

"Well, today we're having pancakes. Do you have any maple syrup?"

"Top cupboard."

Harry reached up and took out a bottle. "Wow, this is the good stuff, imported from Canada. Does it taste different?"

"It tastes better, made from proper Canadian maple trees. The trees need to be over thirty years old to get the best flavour. They boil the sap to make the syrup in huge vats. I'd love to go to Canada to see it done one day."

"We could go on our ship when we sail across the ocean," Harry said. Behind him, Ted sighed.

"I can dream, can't I?"

The kettle boiled and Harry made the tea. "Sit at the table. I need to make up the batter."

It didn't take long and soon Harry was turning out perfectly made pancakes just like his mother had taught him. "Mum used to make them every Shrove Tuesday for us. We ate so many. I like savoury ones too." He stacked up a stack for each of them, keeping them warm on the plate, then brought them to the table.

"I suppose we couldn't add ice cream," Harry said sheepishly.

Ted frowned at him while he covered his pile in the wonderfully smelling syrup. "For breakfast? Really?"

Harry chuckled. "Who knew you were such a pancake purist? All right." He covered his own in the sugary delicacy and used his fork to cut off a chunk.

"Oh, wow," he said, when the taste hit his tongue. "That is so good." He wolfed down the lot, hardly breathing between mouthfuls. "I must tell Mum about this stuff."

"I get it from a deli in Bowness," Ted said. "You can order online. They have all sorts of tasty stuff."

Harry sat back, wiped his lips, patted his stomach, then swigged back a mouthful of tea. "What a perfect way to start the day — giving a gorgeous kilt-wearing lumberjack a blowjob and sticky, sugary, pancakes washed down with builder's tea — magnificent."

"Can you stay?" Ted asked.

"I texted Mum last night I wouldn't be home — she worries. I can stay, but I'll need to go this afternoon. Rich and I are up early dealing with a rat infestation in Gretna."

"Sounds fun," Ted said.

"Rich loves rats."

"What, literally?" Ted stared at him. Harry wasn't sure how to reply.

"Well, he is a cat. We both are. It's in our nature. You said the estate you grew up on had working cats to deal with vermin."

"Have you ever eaten them?"

"I used to, but not now I'm older. Rich has been known to throw a few on the barbecue. Does it shock you?"

"I don't know. I suppose you can't help what you are — you're a carnivore and you have to eat meat."

"I do. Come on, we've got all day, and I can think of better things to do than talk about rats. You could show me your forest. I wouldn't mind seeing if we can spot the beavers."

"It's cold," Ted said. "And we don't want to risk being seen."

"Shame. I saw a programme about them once. Beavers are amazing engineers. They cut down trees just using their teeth. Imagine if you had to rather than using an axe. And the dams they build are so clever. They completely transform the landscape."

Ted picked up their plates. "They don't come out from their holts during the day so we wouldn't see anything, and the area is fenced off with warnings to stay away. There are cameras all over the place."

There was an edge to Ted's voice. Harry decided not to push the idea. "So we stay in and cuddle on the sofa then. We can binge watch something."

"I'd like that," Ted said.

"How about something funny? Have you seen *Ghosts*?"

"No," Ted replied. Harry explained the premise.

"Okay, sounds good to me." Ted picked up the remote and searched for the programme. A few minutes into the first episode and they were both already laughing.

The day passed quickly. Harry fell asleep at various times, as he often did when sat in front of a fire with a warm body next to him. After waking up the third time, Ted suggested Scrabble. As usual, Harry attempted to make as many rude words as he could.

"In our version you get extra points for them," he said.

"Well not in mine."

"Spoilsport, and anyway, your set doesn't have enough of the letter K. I mean there's fuck, dick, prick, cock—you can't write them all. We made extra of that letter for when we played. Rich used to learn new rude words to get more points."

Ted placed a seven-letter word on the board using all his tiles. "And that's fifty extra points to me."

Harry pouted. "I can't win now. I concede. I need to get going before it gets icy out there. Mum's already fretting about me having the bike." He leaned over and kissed Ted. "It's been lovely being here."

"It's been lovely having you here. I'm not sure what I'm doing this week."

Harry sighed. "We're busy. I might not be able to do next weekend either, but we'll have the concert soon after."

"You still haven't told me where we're going," Ted said.

Harry smiled. "I told you, it's a surprise. I've booked the tickets and Thom said we can stay at Tyler's flat. I've everything worked out so stop worrying. I know you're still not sure."

"I'm not, but I want to go."

"Then it's decided." Harry jumped up. He took his leathers and slipped into them, followed by his boots and helmet, then did a twirl. "Sex on a stick, no?"

Ted's grin told him all he needed to know as he walked towards him. "Undoubtedly."

"I'll use the burner to ring you. Maybe I'll talk dirty to you."

"Stop it," Ted said. He opened the outer door.

Harry skipped down the steps, collected his bike, and started the engine. He waved at Ted in the doorway and set off. The drive home didn't take long, though the weather conditions meant he had to concentrate on the road. His mother greeted him at the door.

"You didn't call me today. You've been out a while."

He edged past her. "You're letting all the cold air in, Mum. And you can dig all you like, I'm not telling you anything."

"You are being careful, though, aren't you?"

"Of course," Harry said.

"Rich phoned to remind you about the early start tomorrow."

"I remembered." He put the helmet in the hall cupboard. "Any chance of a hot chocolate, please?"

"Seeing as you ask so nicely." She patted his cheek. "I worry about you, that's all. The other two are married now, but you're still here. Promise me you won't do anything silly."

"Mum, stop fussing. By the time you were my age you had us three running around and you were developing this place."

"That doesn't matter. We're not talking about me. You're my babies. I love you."

Harry kissed her cheek. "And I love you too." He stepped through the door to the kitchen. "Is there any cake left?" he asked.

His mother followed him. "You know better than to ask. In this house, there's always cake."

Chapter Seventeen

November had gone from cold and frosty to cool and damp—very damp. It hadn't stopped raining for the last two days—two days Ted had spent outdoors clearing overgrown paths and checking on the safety of as many access points as possible. He got home on Wednesday night with plans to shower, eat, and sleep. He didn't even bother to dress, but wrapped himself in his robe, cooked a lasagne, and plonked himself on the sofa.

He woke up later to a half-eaten dinner and the noise of a motorbike. He checked his phone but there was nothing from Harry. Ted listened and realised there was more than one engine. He got to the window to see the taillights of two vehicles racing away into the forest.

"Damn." *Probably some idiots, but they're heading towards the beavers.* He picked up his usual phone and rang the police then the wildlife officer on call—there was an emergency number for this kind of event. He dressed at speed, intending to go out and check for himself, when he heard a quiet knock at the door. He opened it. At first, he thought there was no one there.

"Human, let me in. No one must see me."

Ted looked down to see the male beaver. He stood to one side and it scurried past him. Ted checked outside then locked up and turned around.

"What are you doing here?" he asked the beaver, still unsure how they both understood each other.

"Men on loud vehicles. They're breaking up our dam, throwing things around. I was taking down a tree and got away from them but my mate is in the lodge. She'll be scared. All our work. We're supposed to be safe here. We were better off with the hippos."

Ted grabbed his coat. "I've already reported them. The rangers should be here soon. I'll come out with you now. You stay under cover. I know where I'm going." He took his most powerful torch from the shelf. "I'm sure she'll be safe. They'll most likely make a mess and not want to go into the water."

He opened the door and watched the beaver disappear into the darkness before stepping out into the drizzle. The simplest route was down into the valley and along the river. No doubt the beaver would have gone the same way, taking the connecting water route back to its lodge. Ted hoped it would be sensible and stay away from the intruders.

The grass underfoot was slippery and he nearly ended up on his arse a few times. The revving of the bikes pierced the silence of the woods before he saw their owners making more noise with their shouting and whooping. Why did humans enjoy destroying things in this way—disturbing creatures who did no harm to anyone? He'd never understand.

Back on the road, a police siren sounded and he saw flashing blue lights. He waved his torch hoping they'd see, then turned it down and made his way along the small tributary that flowed down the hillside into the Rothay at the bottom of the valley. The sound of engines grew louder. He had no idea what he'd do — two more-than-likely-young men versus him weren't good odds but he knew every tree in this area and where to hide if necessary.

He got to the beavers' home in a matter of minutes. The space and the pond were much bigger — fewer trees standing and more damming the area to create a different habitat. The intruders were racing in circles, cutting up the muddy ground. They'd strewn branches all over the area. One wrong step and both of them could end up in trouble.

"Stop them," a voice whispered behind him.

"There's someone here." One of the bikers attempted to stop but the mud had other ideas and the bike slipped into the pond, taking the driver with it and trapping him on the edge. His cry pierced the quiet of the night. Ted turned up his torch.

The other youth, seeing him, turned and fled. leaving his partner-in-crime behind. Ted hoped he'd end up with the police.

"So much for friends," he murmured, then headed to where the other lad was screaming under the weight of his bike.

"My leg. Get this thing off me."

Ted flashed his torch at the scene in front of him and winced. The sharp point of a bone had punctured both skin and denim.

"Don't move," he said. He tried lifting the bike but the front wheel was embedded in the mud. He took out his phone and called for an ambulance. Unable to do anything else, he removed his coat and pressed it to the wound.

"What the hell did you think you were doing?" he asked, failing to keep the anger out of his tone.

"It was just a bit of fun. My dad said the beavers ate the fish in the river and he loves to fish. We thought they'd go somewhere else if we broke up the dam."

"Then tell your dad he's an idiot. Beavers don't eat anything but stuff from trees when they chew them and cut them down. They're protected, and they were released here for a purpose. You and your mate are in a lot of trouble."

Tears flowed down the biker's face. Ted guessed he was still a teenager. From out of the trees, he heard voices and saw lights flashing.

"Over here," he called. "Quick as you can."

Police appeared along with a couple of rangers he recognised.

"We caught the other one back there. So what's happened here then?"

Ted didn't know this constable. He lifted his coat and the PC took a sharp intake of breath.

"Hmm, nasty. Have you called for the paramedics?"

"Yes. He claims he was trying to protect the fish from being eaten by the beavers."

The rangers were inspecting the damage done to the lodge. One turned to address the injured youth, "Hopefully, for your sake, they're safe inside."

The sound of a siren came from across the valley.

"I'll inform them of the situation," the other PC said, and hurried off back through the trees. The boy screamed again.

"Can't you give me something?"

"We can get this bike off of you."

It took three of them, but they managed and dragged him carefully from the water. Ted held up his leg.

"This uniform will need a proper clean," the constable grumbled. The boy whimpered.

"I'm sorry. It was Ryan's idea."

"I'd sure it was, laddie. I'm sure it was."

The paramedics arrived ten minutes later, checked the boy over, then lifted him, screaming once more, onto a stretcher.

"The painkiller will kick in soon."

Ted sat on one of the felled trees. His cold, damp clothes stuck to his skin. He shivered. One of the rangers made his way over and sat next to him.

"We've checked everything here. All we can do is return when it's light and keep an eye on the cameras tonight. Are you all right? It's not the weather to be wandering about in the dark."

"Yeah. I'm fine. I work outdoors in all sorts. I can find my own way back to my cabin. I brought my biggest torch."

"You're the tree bloke, aren't you — Ted Woodward. Appropriate name."

"You're not the first to say that and yes, trees are my remit, but I muck in with all the park ranger tasks. You get off now." He held his hand out and the ranger shook it. "At least the rain has stopped."

"We've had flooding in places from the river. It's one of the reasons we brought the beavers here and they'd made a good start. With any luck, we won't have any more bother."

"The lad thought the beaver eat fish. Maybe the locals need some education."

"We had hoped to get them in under the radar, but the news is out now so we could hold a meeting." The ranger stood. "I'm Craig, by the way, Craig Braithwaite. Thanks for contacting us. Having you on the spot is useful."

You don't know how much I could help if the beavers will let me. Ted remained seated. He wanted to stay to see if the beavers emerged from the lodge with no one else around.

"Craig, we'll take the route along the valley," the taller ranger said. "You take care, Ted, and thanks for your help."

Ted waved them off then sat and waited despite the cold. He deliberately kept out of the sight of the camera. After ten minutes, with a rustle and a splash of water, the beavers emerged at the side of the pond. They surveyed the scene.

"Humans!"

"We're not all bad," Ted said.

"No. Thank you for what you did."

Ted nodded. "As long as you're all right. The rangers are coming back tomorrow to help tidy up the area. They were idiot lads who thought you ate fish. Craig, one of the rangers, is planning to do a talk for the locals."

"Humph, human and ignorant." The female picked up a branch and dragged it to the edge of the dam.

"If you need me, you know where I am. Despite what you think of me, I want to help."

He couldn't hear what the female said as she muttered to herself, collecting broken branches.

"We will, and thank you again."

Ted stood, checked on his route, then made his way back home through the trees, marking each one with an equal sign to help him find his way the next time. The torch cast shadows and every so often he detected a movement among the fallen leaves when some small creature carried on with its nocturnal activities. Above him an owl hooted and another called in reply. Was that a flap of wings above reminding him birds were predators too? Across the valley a fox screeched, no doubt also out hunting. There were more creatures than him wandering through the woods in the dark. He was grateful to see the light from his home.

Back in the cabin, he stripped off his damp clothes and threw them in the washer then, in the bathroom, he turned on the shower and let the warm water run down his body. Somehow mud had permeated everywhere and soil flowed down the plug hole for some time. After washing his hair and towelling it dry — which didn't take long, as water rolled off his hair-covered skin — he grabbed his robe for the second time that evening, ambled to the kitchen to make some hot chocolate, then sat once again on the sofa. He glanced at the clock. It wasn't midnight, but he knew Harry had planned early night. He and Rich were off to the Midlands in the morning to deal with an infestation of bedbugs at a university. He'd probably be there until Sunday.

He sighed. He missed Harry. The noise of his mobile made him jump. Otis. Word had travelled fast.

"Hi, Otis."

"Are you okay? I got a report there'd been an incident with the beavers."

Ted explained, leaving out the information about the beaver coming to him. He'd grown more wary of sharing things of late.

"Do you think they'll let them stay?"

Ted wasn't sure how to answer. "That's up to the wildlife people."

"As long as you're all right."

"Better than the laddie with the broken leg. I know my way around even in the dark. I'll be fine after a night's sleep." He yawned, hoping Otis would take the hint.

"I'll let you get off. Let's have a proper catch-up soon."

"Yeah, that'd be good. Night." He pressed red and plugged the mobile in to charge.

He turned on the TV and listened to the news while drinking his chocolate. Nothing on there made him feel any better. Once he'd finished and tidied, he dragged his tired body into bed, managed to read two pages of his book, then fell asleep to be woken by his alarm several hours later.

Chapter Eighteen

It had been a long weekend and Harry was looking forward to a few hours of sleep in his own bed and the possibility of some time with Ted. Treating room after room in university accommodation for bedbugs, during term time, had been exhausting. At least the spray they used allowed the students to return the same day and they wouldn't have to come back. The stats on how quickly bedbugs could spread were mind-boggling.

"Suki called this morning," Rich said when they reached the M6. "Her parents are coming for dinner tonight and they specifically asked for you to join us."

"What?" Harry said, not sure if he should be worried. The Cattersons moved in elite circles and Harry had no interest in facing their questioning over anything. "Why me?"

"I don't know, but can you please do me a favour and come. At least I'll have someone from my side there. They're arriving this afternoon to see the twins.

Dinner is seven-for-seven-thirty. Please, Harry. I don't ask many favours. Just turn on your legendary charm."

"Flattery? Really?" But Rich was right. He didn't ask much, and they were a good team. Maybe he could fit in a visit to Ted early in the week before they went on their weekend away.

"All right. Do I have to wear a suit, or is it smart casual?"

"Smart I think—not jeans. The Cattersons consider them to be work clothes. Without a tie should be okay. It's at our place, not some posh restaurant."

Harry was glad, but eating out did also mean less 'difficult' conversations. "Then I shall come but leave before ten because it's been a long few days and us cats need our sleep."

Sunday driving up the motorway proved to be less busy going north and Harry managed a few catnaps along the way. Rich preferred to drive, which Harry had no problem with. When he opened his eyes three hours later they were at Windemere and a few minutes from home.

Rich dropped him at the house. Harry popped into the lounge and said hello to his mother and gran then took the stairs two at a time to his bedroom to call Ted.

"Be careful," Ted advised when Harry explained about the dinner. "I don't know much about the Cattersons, but Leo Catterson is something big in the government—human and shifter. He's a wealthy man."

"I know. Rich says he uses private jets to travel. Can you imagine?"

"No, but our laird is the same—another rich man, but maybe different in attitude."

Harry wondered what Ted meant but didn't ask. They kept their calls brief. "I'd better go. I'll try and get over midweek and let you know the plans for the weekend, or some of them." He wanted to casually end the conversation with the words I love you, as he had sort of done before, but they weren't there yet.

"Take care on your bike," Ted said. "I hope you're not planning to make me ride pillion down to the big city."

"I'd like to see you in leathers sometime." Harry chuckled at the thought. "Have a good week."

"You, too, and call me tonight if you need to."

Harry put the phone back in its hiding place, set a timer on his watch, and curled up on the bed.

His alarm woke him a few hours later and his stomach rumbled. He'd be glad of a decent dinner, at least. He showered and dressed in a simple black shirt and trousers combination—black suited him—and placed a small diamond stud in each ear. His white streak stood out more prominently when he wore one colour. He examined himself. Should he leave the stubble that had grown over the last few days? Perhaps he should even grow a beard. He ran his fingers over his chin and decided to leave it. Sometimes he missed having whiskers.

Rather than his usual trainers or steel-toe-capped boots, he sat on his bed and slipped his feet into his black brogues polished to within an inch of their lives then grabbed the jacket that went with the trousers and did a twirl in front of the mirror.

"Yep. I'll do."

Downstairs, he found his mum and gran in the living room catching up with their weekly fix of *Within Bow Bells*.

"You look handsome," his gran said. "Off somewhere nice?"

"Only to Rich's. The Cattersons have invited themselves to dinner and he wants me there for moral support."

A worried look crossed his mother's face. "Be careful what you say in front of them. Leo Catterson is a man with power and influence. I wish Rich hadn't married into the family, but Suki is so down-to-earth, unlike the rest of them. Rich will need your support. He's the steady one out of the three of you, but you and Thom — you got the charm."

From our mysterious father, no doubt.

He kissed both of them on the tops of their heads. "I can't help being this handsome, and I'll be discretion itself and try not to speak too much."

At the back door, he stuck his hand out to find a few drops of rain. He grabbed an umbrella, unfurled it, and ran down the path they'd laid to the converted barn. A Bentley stood in one of the parking spaces with a bored-looking driver in the front seat. Of course, the Cattersons wouldn't drive themselves.

Harry stood under the shelter and pressed the doorbell. A harassed Rich appeared quickly.

"Thank goodness you're here. The twins are asleep at last, I've run out of small talk, and I've no interest in politics — human or shifter. Suzie's gone to help Suki in the kitchen and I'm left with him. The man is huge."

Leo Catterson was a Maine Coon in his cat form. In human form, he stood around six-foot-five and had a mass of ginger hair and a deep booming voice Harry imagined would carry across any room.

"Before we go in, I need to tell you they've brought someone with them. Her name is Tasha. She's some sort of relation to Suzie Catterson, and I suspect they're trying to pair the two of you off. It has nothing to do with me, and I don't think she knew anything either. She's in the kitchen with Suki and her mum at the moment."

"Humph," Harry said. "Bloody typical to send the women off to cook."

Rich blushed. "I know. The daft thing is, I made the dessert and the sauce for the steak, and I'm a better cook than Suki, but she insisted, with her parents being here. We'd better go in. Try not to say anything controversial, if only to make my life easier."

Harry frowned. "Okay, as it's you." He fixed a smile on his face and followed Rich into the lounge, hoping Tasha would turn out to be as annoyed as him at this obvious attempt at a set-up.

"Mr Catterson," Harry said holding out his hand. "It's good to meet you again." He winced at the grip crushing his fingers.

"Harry, it's good to meet you again. I've just been talking to Rich about expanding your business — taking on more workers or even setting up other branches."

Bloody hell, he wastes no time with pleasantries, does he?

"We have pests down in the Home Counties too, even in Parliament and Number Ten."

I bet you do.

"Perhaps you can convince him. I'd like him to be able to keep my daughter in the style to which she has always been accustomed."

Rich shook his head behind his father-in-law.

"I'm not sure," Harry said, taking the glass of champagne Rich passed him. The bubbles went up his nose. "We like being hands-on rather than delegating tasks, and we're prepared to travel. We've just carried out a big job in Birmingham which will bring in a tidy profit. The business is doing well. We rarely get a day off. We could expand here with a couple of trainees, but expansion and getting the right staff brings its own problems."

"Just remember, it's better if we keep the jobs in the family, so to speak."

Harry and Rich nodded, knowing exactly what Leo Catterson meant.

"If we can find them, we will."

Suki appeared at the door. "Dinner will be served in five minutes so if you could go to the dining room."

Rich breathed an audible sigh of relief. "Thanks, darling. Leo, Harry. Shall we?"

The dining room was big enough for a large table and had French doors that opened to a beautiful garden. Multi-coloured lights could be seen twinkling in the dark. They took their seats with Harry placed next to Suzie Catterson. She was striking in a different way to her husband. Her almost white hair, tinged brown at the ends, shone in the light from the ceiling, and like all Birmans, she had astonishingly blue eyes. Opposite him sat Tasha, who shared Suzie's Birman colouring.

Rich took the seat at the head of the table with his father-in-law choosing to sit at the other end.

Harry glanced at Rich and nodded towards Tasha, not wanting to embarrass his brother by making his own introduction.

"Yes," Rich said. "Suzie, you know my brother Harry from the wedding, and Harry this is Natasha Felixstone, Suki's…"

"Cousin," Tasha replied. "On her mother's side of the family. It's good to meet you. Suki's told me a lot about you and your brother Thom."

"All good, I hope," Harry said flashing his best smile.

"No one's all good. Being so would make life boring."

Several sets of eyebrows raised, including Harry's. This woman clearly had a mind of her own that Leo Catterson did not approve of. Harry suspected they hoped to marry her off to keep her out of trouble, and if he was a candidate, others had been rejected before him.

Rich passed around the wine while Suki presented them with plates of scallops and bacon then sat next to Tasha.

"What is it you do?" Harry asked—if Tasha did anything. Suki had battled her parents to train as a physiotherapist and owned a practice now run by her partner while she was on maternity leave.

"I'm an animal keeper at a safari park in the Midlands. I specialise in the welfare of big cats."

Harry spluttered the mouthful of wine he'd sipped. He grabbed his napkin and wiped his face. "Sorry, I wasn't expecting that answer."

Tasha grinned at him and her stunning blue eyes twinkled. "No one expects that answer. I've been told it's not a proper job for a girl."

"Really?" Harry replied. "Isn't any job a proper job for a woman—or a man, for that matter?" He glanced around at the people at the table. "Haven't we got over this gender bias in everything now? I mean, we can be both human and animal—have dual personalities."

"This starter is delicious, darling," Suzie Catterson said.

Harry glanced across the table to see Tasha wink at him. He couldn't help but like her already, and if he'd been single, he would have been interested.

"Yes, the scallops are perfect, Suki, and isn't this shallot sauce your recipe, Rich? My brother is a great cook, Tasha, but many men are brilliant chefs, aren't they? Why should women be stuck in the kitchen. Rich is even brave enough to change a nappy, but we've both got strong stomachs with our job."

"You're in pest control, I believe," Tasha said. "And, Rich, Harry is right. This sauce is perfect."

Harry knew Rich didn't know whether to smile or frown. "My brother has many skills—both my brothers. You know my oldest sibling is an actor, soon to be a superhero."

"Wow. I love Marvel and DC films. I saw Thom on the stage when he played the cat in panto. He was so good. I believe your father was a performer as well. H—" Tasha stopped abruptly and rubbed her leg.

"If everyone's finished." Suki stood and cleared the plates. "Tasha, could you help me with the main course, please."

Diplomatic as always, Suki removed the source of her father's frown from the room.

"I see there was an incident with the beavers while we were away," Rich said.

Shit. Harry could have done without this change in conversation. Had Ted's name been mentioned?

"Beavers. Interesting lot. Didn't know you had some here." Leo Catterson appeared to just be making conversation.

"I read they were taken out of a safari park," Rich continued. "That Mountain Rescue bloke who saved your arse called the alarm on the idiots who tried to trash the place."

Harry had no chance to get Rich to stop talking. He couldn't even reach to kick him under the table At least his tendency to forget names came in handy and he hadn't named Ted.

"Interesting species, the beaver. Do you know there are no were-beavers now. They decided to breed the human out of themselves and wanted nothing to do with the human world, though there were rumours of a throwback."

The hairs on Harry's neck rose. He needed to end this conversation now.

"Of course, the geneticists got interested about whether you could resurrect a species from extinction. Bloody daft, as far as I'm concerned. Can you imagine dinosaur shifters?"

"Tasha seems like a nice person," Harry said.

Leo took the bite. "She is, but she has too many opinions. She needs to settle down and have a family. Give herself something else to think about."

Bloody hell, we've slipped back to the 1950s.

"Right. I need a visit to the gentlemen's room — prostate is a bugger."

Harry waited until Leo had left them then turned to Rich and glared.

"What?" Rich asked.

"Don't mention Ted."

"Okay." Rich didn't question, preferring an easy life.

"He doesn't like people knowing about him. He told me at the dinner we had when I showed him around. I don't think he's much for people — prefers trees."

"That genetics thing is worrying," Rich said. "Can you imagine a shifter T-Rex? Ye Gods."

"And we all know what happened when they messed about with DNA in *Jurassic Park*, don't we?"

Rich shuddered. "I'm happy living my life. I don't want to be wealthy. I want to be comfortable. I have no interest in power. Suki agrees with me. She..."

Voices came from the hallway.

"So, d'you reckon United have any chance at a trophy this season?" He nodded at the door just before it opened. Leo entered followed by Suzie.

"Dinner is coming. The steaks are cooked to perfection."

Harry grinned. For all of them it meant the beef was blue and therefore, hardly touched by heat.

Suki and Tasha entered the room carrying plates and dishes loaded with food.

"Steak for everyone. There are three times cooked chips, mushrooms, tomatoes, peas, and Rich's peppercorn sauce. Help yourselves."

This time talk of the twins dominated most of conversation. Harry and Rich told stories of their childhoods and got Leo to talk about his family and how he and Suzie met, along with their villas in the Bahamas and Rhodes and their apartment in New York. This was definitely how the other half lived.

Dessert was a cheesecake covered in whipped cream. Everyone praised the cook. Leo patted his stomach.

"That was a beautiful meal. And now, I fear we must go. I've got to be in London in the morning, so the jet is waiting for us to leave."

"I'd like to stay for a while," Tasha said, flashing what Harry guessed was her sweetest smile at Leo and at him.

Leo chortled deep in his throat. "Of course, my dear. Max will take us first then come back for you."

The perks of the rich – private jets and chauffeured cars.

"Thank you."

While Rich and Suki said goodbye to his in-laws, Tasha pulled Harry to one side.

"I wanted a word with you. I need to make something clear."

"Okay," Harry said.

"I know your reputation. Suki told me. I have no interest in being another notch on your bedpost or entry in your little black book."

Harry laughed. "I don't have a book or any notches on my bedpost, just a few scratches. And you're safe from any advances, I can assure you. I had no knowledge of this set-up."

"Me neither. I wouldn't have come if I'd thought they were matchmaking again."

Harry nodded. "I get that. I've no idea why they should be so interested in us."

Tasha opened her mouth as if to answer then decided not to. "Anyway, I'm glad that's sorted because I think you're kind of fun. And the thing—is I'm not interested in a relationship, men or women. I don't want children, and I'm happy by myself. Friends I like, but I have no use for lovers."

"Well, we're clear then." Harry didn't plan on mentioning he was already taken—because he was—very taken.

"Good. I like to be on the same page. And now I need a proper drink, not this fizzy stuff. And as Max is driving, I can have a couple, though I need a clear head for work in the morning." She poured herself a brandy. Harry declined.

"Your job sounds fascinating," he said.

"It is. Our tigers have just had cubs. It's such a privilege to watch them grow. Have you ever met a big cat shifter?"

Rich came back into the room before Harry could answer.

"What are you two still doing here? Let's sit somewhere more comfortable, shall we? Suki is checking on the girls." They strolled through the double doors to the lounge and sat on the sofas.

"They sleep well then," Harry said.

"Like kittens. When they're awake they're terrors, but asleep they're angels."

Harry finally relaxed and yawned. It had been a long day. Something about what Leo Catterson had said bothered him, and clearly Tasha had some worries. What if someone *was* trying to recreate shifters from extinct animals? He yawned again.

"Looks like someone else should be in his bed," Suki said.

"I do. I'll get off now. Thank you for the lovely meal, Suki. It's also been great to meet you, Tasha."

Rich followed him to the door. "I'll see you tomorrow. Thanks for doing that tonight."

"You are welcome." He yawned. "God, I'm knackered. I need some shut-eye." And just like the twins, Harry hoped his brain would put his worries to one side and allow him to sleep like a kitten.

Chapter Nineteen

On Friday night Ted waited, pacing the floor, with his bag packed for the trip to London. At least Harry had told him their destination if not who they were going to see. He yawned, tired having spent the week cutting down diseased elms. It was a job he hated. He and a couple of other rangers had also removed weeds and shrubs to give more room for growth of other species. It was a cold, dirty task, especially in the rain and occasional fluttering of snowflakes, but a necessary one and better than checking and emptying parking meters, though there were fewer of them with card payments and phone apps.

He turned at the security light coming on and a tap on the door. "It's open."

Harry stepped in from the porch with a huge smile of his face and wellies on his feet.

"I've parked just off the road," he said. "I've hired a car and told Mum and Gran I'm catching up with an old acquaintance. I didn't give any details. The less I say, the less I have to remember."

"I've said nothing," Ted replied. "Otis is away visiting his in-laws, and no one else would visit. If necessary, I'll say I went home for a brief visit."

"It's muddy out there. Do you have wellies?"

Ted grinned. "I do, though not as fancy as yours. Mine are black and without multi-coloured polka-dots."

Ted threw on his heavy coat, stepped into the boots, and picked up his bag. Harry had been right. A few flakes of snow made a half-hearted effort to settle with no effect.

"The forecast is for cold but no precipitation," Harry said. "Though I rented a 4x4 just in case."

With his bag stowed next to Harry's in the boot, Ted climbed into the passenger seat, glad of the warmth from the heater. Harry leaned over and kissed him. Ted found he liked the casualness of their contact and returned the kiss.

"It's good to see you too. So, do I get to know anymore yet?"

"Some," Harry said. "We're not driving all the way to London, but I couldn't risk anyone seeing us at the local station. "I'm driving to Preston. We can leave the car there in the long-stay car park and pick it up when we return. It might be a waste of money, but it seemed more sensible than taking a car to nearer London. We'll take the train to Euston from Preston. I have the keys for Tyler's flat."

"Sounds good," Ted said. "I've stowed my car in the garage so it looks as if I'm not here. We'd better get going. It's getting dark already. It's a good job you've allowed more time for the M6."

In the end, the journey went smoothly as most of the traffic seemed to be heading in the other direction and the rain held off. They arrived in ample time for the train, parked, found their way to the right platform and waited along with other passengers.

"I haven't been on a train before," Ted said.

"Not even one of those steam trains in the Highlands?"

"Nope. Never. And I haven't been to London, either. I'm sort of equally excited and terrified. I'm glad we're staying at your brother's flat. I wouldn't have liked all the people in a hotel. I'm not sure how I'll be on the streets."

"We can get taxis. I've downloaded an app. Here's the train now and it's on time."

Once inside, Ted glanced around. "It's narrower than I expected."

"I think the word is streamlined."

"Like you," Ted replied.

"I'll take that as a compliment for now, as long as you realise it's genetics, not exercise, and don't start getting self-conscious about anything."

"The tables are useful." They sat opposite each other next to the window. "And the seats are comfortable."

The train eased out of the station, heading into the dark. "It's a pity we can't see out. I'd have liked to have seen some of the countryside. When do we get there?"

"Just after eight. We can get a taxi to Tyler's flat and order takeaway. There's a good place on the same street. I'll get us a coffee now we're on our way. I don't know about you, but it's been a long week."

Left to his own devices, Ted took out his phone and was surprised to find the train had Wi-Fi. He opened up his Free Cell app. He preferred the old-fashioned card games to anything else. By the time Harry returned, he'd completed three games.

"Right then, do I get any more clues about who we're going to see tomorrow?"

"Nope," Harry said. "But I did wonder what you fancied doing during the day. There are so many things to see. We'd be able to fit in a matinee as well, if we can get tickets and don't choose anything too long."

"I don't know," Ted said. "I'd like to go to the British Museum, and maybe the Science Museum. There's the National Portrait Gallery as well, and the Tate or the V&A—so many places—and there's a lot to see just walking around. We could go to Covent Garden on Sunday morning for breakfast and to the market. Have you been often?"

"A few times visiting Thom and Tyler, but I haven't been to any of the usual tourist places. It'll be such fun doing all this with you."

Three hours passed in a flash.

"The towns are closer together here," Ted said. "You'd imagine the whole country was covered with houses from what we see in the news about overcrowding, but we know there are so many empty spaces."

"We live in one of the most beautiful places in the country," Harry said. "And you were brought up in the Highlands, with huge open areas in both."

"I know but I imagined that the south of England would be covered in buildings without anything else, especially the south-east."

Harry gave him what Ted thought was an indulgent smile. "London has lots of parks."

"I know, but remember I'm now the furthest south I've been. I don't even own a passport—never needed one."

"Well, you won't need one where we're going, though London can take some getting used to. I couldn't live there all the time. Last time Rich and I were down there, we went on a tour of the sewers."

"Why on earth would they have a tour of the sewers, let alone find that people want to visit them?"

"It was fascinating. They are huge in places and have some beautiful designs and stonework. You'd be amazed."

"I think I'll pass. I'd rather go through the parks and look at the plants and trees. I bet they're beautiful in spring and summer. Most of the trees will have lost their leaves by now."

"We can come back next year."

Ted stared out of the window. They weren't far away from their destination now. He didn't like to think that far ahead. For whatever reason, they were dicing with uncertainty. Part of Ted's reason for taking this risk was the fact that there might come a time when he couldn't do anything. Living for what they had in the here and now was all they had.

"Ted?"

"Sorry, I got distracted by the lights."

Harry reached out a hand and touched his. Automatically, Ted checked to see if anyone was watching, but no one lifted their gaze from their phones or laptops.

"Let's have this weekend, shall we? One day at a time. No talk of anything else."

Ted nodded. "Living for the moment."

"Exactly."

The train slowed and people started to gather their belongings ready to disembark. When he stepped onto the platform, Ted could swear there were more people there than he'd seen in his life. Boards flashed with adverts, and the noise assaulted his ears. Harry clasped his arm.

"I know. Hold on to me. The taxi rank is this way. We'll probably have to wait."

They did, but finally their black cab stopped in front of a large house. Harry opened the gate and Ted followed him up the path.

Harry dug in his coat pocket and pulled out a set of keys. "The flat is on the first floor. Let's hurry or the colonel will be out to investigate and find us a job to do."

They hurried up the stairs. Once inside, Harry wrapped his arms around Ted and kissed him."

"What was that for?" Ted asked.

"Because we can, and because I like kissing you, even with the beard."

Ted ran his hand across his face. "I'm not shaving it."

"I wouldn't ask you to. It's part of you, and it's so soft. Right, I'll show you around."

Ted glanced up at the ceiling. "It's got all its original features, as *Homes Under the Hammer* would mention. I bet it's worth a fortune."

"Tyler's father owns the whole house and those either side. He's a big-time lawyer. His sister is also a lawyer. They used to share this place. I'll tell you the story of how Thom and Tyler met over a pizza later. We're in this bedroom."

Harry opened the door to a lovely room with a king-size bed and a large window with a view of the street. Ted put his bag on the bed and unpacked his clothes to hang them up. Harry took his hand.

"Come on. The bathroom is opposite and through here is the living room and the kitchen. The kitchen overlooks the fire escape and the lane at the back. The flat runs the full length of front to back. It's a big place for round here. Sit and I'll make us tea. The takeaway menu is in the drawer under the coffee table."

Ted sat on the sofa and stretched his legs. Glancing around, he thought his cabin was about half the size of the flat—if that. Harry returned with tea and they ordered. They spent a lot of the rest of the evening eating, with Harry telling the tale of how Thom, in cat form, had wheedled his way into the house. Ted laughed at the problems of getting around when naked.

"Have you ever been caught out?" he asked.

"More than once," Harry replied. "I'll tell you some more stories another time. Have you worked out a plan for tomorrow?"

"Yes," Ted said. "A big breakfast at the greasy spoon down the road, then the Tube to the British Museum. Depending on how long it takes, maybe the Science Museum or V&A, lunch, the theatre, a quick bite to eat then the concert."

"Great." Harry yawned. "But now I think it's time for bed."

Chapter Twenty

Harry waited for Ted to finish in the bathroom. He yawned again. It turned out travelling by train was as tiring as driving yourself. He glanced around the room. All the personal stuff had gone now, which pleased Harry—he had no desire to have sex and catch a glimpse of his brother's face smiling next to his hot boyfriend while in the throes of passion. Thom and Tyler had bought a house with a garden big enough to keep beehives out of the city, and they and their friends and family only used the flat as a stopover. He leaned over, checked the top drawer, and chuckled. Had Tyler deliberately left some important items there?

Ted ambled through the door wearing a T-shirt, sleep shorts and more notably slippers. "I can't remember the last time I showered in a bath." He stopped and stared in Harry's direction.

Harry gazed at his body then felt his face. "What is it? Have I got a bogey or something?"

"No, it's just...well... I can't believe you're here with me, being as gorgeous as you are with me being—"

Harry sat up. "Stop it and come here." He pulled back the duvet. He'd thought of lying there naked but figured Ted might find such behaviour intimidating. Ted joined him on the bed and Harry reached up to stroke his hair.

"Wow, it's dry already."

"Water sort of runs off me." Ted turned towards him so they faced each other and dragged the cover over them both. Harry kissed him—a brief kiss on the lips to reassure him.

"This weekend is our weekend," he said. "There's no one I would rather be here with than you. Maybe its karma, maybe it's fate, or maybe you have an intoxicating musk I can't resist. Whatever it was that drew me to you, doesn't want you to ever go away. This is the real deal for me." He didn't quite get to the love word, though he had little doubt there was love in his thoughts as he lay there gazing into Ted's soft brown eyes.

"It's real for me too," Ted whispered. "I have to keep pinching myself so I know I'm not dreaming."

Harry slipped his hand under Ted's T-shirt and caressed Ted's skin with his fingers until he reached a nipple and gave it a quick squeeze. Ted moaned.

"Is that real enough for you?"

"It's a start," Ted replied, grinning. "What else have you got?"

"Slip out of those shorts and turn over and I'll show you."

Ted moved faster than a whirling dervish while Harry reached under his pillow for the lube and slicked up his cock.

"Lift your leg."

Ted did so without questioning and Harry shifted forward to tuck his erection between Ted's sturdy thighs. He reached around and wrapped his lubed-up palm around Ted's shaft, which hardened on contact.

"Oh," Ted said. "Is this okay? You don't want to…?"

"This works for both of us, though you might want to stick the T-shirt under you or you'll be the one sleeping in a damp patch. You can help me with your ample interest. You're a lot for one hand." Ted's calloused fingers touched his own and Harry began to thrust, letting the feeling build for both of them. He tried kissing Ted's back but he couldn't concentrate on everything. Men might be hopeless at multi-tasking, but cats were worse.

"Feels good," Ted moaned, his baritone voice low and as sexy as anything. For a moment, Harry wondered if Ted sang. He'd have to find out.

"I like being wrapped around you," Harry replied. "And you have such muscley thighs that are squeezing me just right."

Ted flexed.

"Yeah, there…" Tingles ran down Harry's spine. His balls, now heavy and full, felt ready to explode. He gripped Ted tighter when Ted sped up his movements.

"Coming," Ted said as hot liquid covered Harry's hand. With a couple of thrusts, he came too, leaving them both panting, desperate for air. Harry kissed the back of Ted's neck and nuzzled closer. Ted cleaned up his thighs.

"Are we staying like this?" he asked.

Harry didn't have the energy to change position and was already three-quarters asleep. "Yes please. So tired now. I'll be big spoon. Turn off the light."

The room plunged into darkness and Harry was asleep in seconds.

* * * *

Harry awoke to the feeling of someone stroking his back and he arched his body to get closer to Ted's touch then realised something was different.

Fuck! I've transformed in my sleep. He opened his eyes to find Ted staring at him. He hopped off the bed to the floor, stretched and transformed. Ted didn't lean over so he had privacy. Once back in human form, he slipped back under the duvet to face Ted.

"Does that happen often?" Ted asked. "Not that I mind."

"No, just when I'm tired and feel safe. And I feel safe with you. I'm sorry for my lack of control."

Ted reached out and stroked his hair. "Don't apologise. It was a surprise, but I'm honoured you feel secure enough to be yourself in whatever form."

Both their stomachs rumbled.

"We need a good breakfast," Harry said. He glanced at the window. "And It looks like the sun is trying to shine."

"Are we taking the Tube?" Ted asked. "I want to see what it's like though I know there could be lots of people."

"The café is at the end of the block then we can choose bus or Tube." Harry's phone beeped. "I'll check this text," he said pressing the screen. "It's from my brother. It seems we've got special seats in a VIP area tonight, as we're using John Ballantyne's season tickets. Thom says I should use his disguise kit while we're out, because otherwise people might think I'm him and want Thom Katt's autograph." Harry lifted his head and caught Ted's concerned expression.

"I now. I'm sorry I didn't think I might attract attention. He says the kit is in the second drawer next to his bed. Thom uses it all the time. He also suggests wearing a big coat to make me look larger."

Ted had paled under his beard.

"Are you all right?" Harry asked.

"I worried about anyone seeing me with you. What if someone takes our photo? I forgot that you're identical to a TV star from a show set in this very city."

Harry stood and kissed Ted. "Come on. It'll be fine. We'd better check out this disguise. I'll feel like some sort of secret agent."

In the bedroom, Harry opened the drawer.

"Oh my God — a huge bushy beard and there's some sort of special glue they use in the show." He picked it up. "I don't think I'll need this as I already have more facial hair than Thom. There's dye to cover my white streak, and the hat will cover my hair."

He painted his hair. "It's strange how different I look just doing that. There are coloured contact lenses as well and a little mole for my cheek as well."

Having made all the changes to his appearance, he checked himself in the mirror. "I don't think I'd recognise myself. No one will want my picture, especially if I'm wearing sunglasses as well."

Ted passed him the hat and Harry — with some reluctance — placed it on his head. "There. What d'you think?

"You look different, especially having brown eyes."

"But still sexy?" Harry asked.

Ted smiled. "Always sexy. Shall we go?"

"Yes, we've a full day ahead."

* * * *

After a hearty breakfast, they decided to take a taxi to the British Museum rather than face the crowds and escalators.

"It's so big," Ted said as they approached.

"And full of things found in other cultures," Harry replied, and instantly regretted what he'd said.

"I suppose so," Ted agreed. "And some of them should be returned, but not everyone could afford to go to see such things in their home countries, and there are British antiquities too, like the finds at Sutton Hoo. I booked us into a tour which starts in half an hour and covers a lot of ground with a guide. We can go back to anything we want to see."

"Good idea," Harry said, as they stepped into the entrance area where people in a variety of groupings wandered about, staring at their phones and no doubt attempting to work out where to go.

They found a seat and glanced through the guidebook. Harry paused at the Egyptian entry. "These people had the right idea. They worshipped cats."

"And the cats have never forgotten," Ted replied. "Some of us still get down on our knees."

"That's true," Harry replied, grinning. "And I think that's the first time I've heard you using innuendo."

"It's your bad influence rubbing off on me."

Harry turned to face Ted. "Are you flirting with me?"

"I thought I'd give it a go."

Harry nudged Ted. "I like it. I'd like to kiss you, but I'd better not here. Look. there's a group gathering over there." He glanced at his watch. "Let's go and check it out."

For the next ninety minutes, their group were guided around several galleries — Roman, British, African and Egyptian, and given a load of information about everything from Anglo-Saxon masks to mummies. Harry found it difficult to take it all in and found he had itchy palms that wanted to knock all these artefacts to the floor. Ted, on the other hand, stood transfixed while the guide explained how the mummies were created and the ceremonies surrounding funerals and burials. Harry only perked up when cats were mentioned. They hurried on again to the final gallery where people argued over the rights and wrongs of the Elgin Marbles, which one visitor had expected to be actual marbles, and had wondered why there was such a fuss. Of course, they finished in the shop. While Ted ambled around checking everything, Harry made his excuses, found a bench to sit on, and watched the world go by, glad of his disguise. Ted appeared fifteen minutes later carrying a bag. He took out a box and handed it to Harry.

"I got you a little something."

Harry grinned and opened the present. In it was a tiny statue of the black cat they'd seen in the Egyptian section.

"I don't think it will break if you knock it on to the floor. I know your mother doesn't have china or glass ornaments."

Harry nodded. "It was a good job all those things were in cases. I could have gone mad in there. Don't know what makes us do it — it's a compulsion even if someone is watching — to be defiant. Mum used it as an excuse to make us clear the table after meals, but we had to pick everything up not knock it over."

Ted turned to face him. "Do you always feel like a cat?"

Harry stared out into the crowd. *Do I?*

"That's hard to answer. When I am a cat, I know I'm human as well, but the feline instincts are stronger. When I'm human, I still have those patterns of behaviour — I have the need to sleep, but also to play and hunt. We played a lot of video games as kids. Lessons were hard because we found it hard to concentrate. Thom threw himself into dance and drama, while Rich got into science. We had a teacher who was into entomology — the study of insects. Rich found them fascinating. He thinks people should eat more."

"Yuck." Ted pulled a face. "What about you?"

Harry shrugged. He'd kept it to himself that he enjoyed history and art, and even with Ted he kept to his usual answer because it didn't fit into his usual happy-go-lucky persona. "Me? I've never been interested in anything in particular. I just followed my brother for a simple life. Maybe one day I'll find my niche." He glanced at his watch again.

"We'd better get moving. The play starts at two. After, we can get a taxi home to change and one back to the arena."

"Let's walk," Ted said. "We can do it in twenty minutes if we go along Shaftsbury Avenue to Leicester Square then via Charing Cross to Trafalgar Square. I checked the route online. I'd like to see these places I've only heard of on a Monopoly board. I wonder why some got included and others didn't."

Along the route, they passed numerous theatres and other well-known buildings. Harry wished they could take photos, but he knew the rules about evidence —

better safe than sorry — even when using their burner phones.

At Trafalgar Square, Harry had to resist chasing the pigeons, unlike the small child who got to do it without anyone commenting. "Let's go in the Portrait Gallery. We've an hour to see what we can then grab a sandwich."

Ted wandered around, glancing at people who were important enough to have their portrait painted, while Harry sat and stared at those in the Tudor collection.

"There are so many symbols in these paintings," Harry said when Ted joined him. "Can you see the eyes and ears on the dress in this one? It's to warn people she had spies everywhere. They made copies and sent them around the country so people could get an image of their queen, and they were all painted to a standard pattern. Our teacher loved showing us the secret stuff in art and how it was used for propaganda."

"Our tutor told us all about the paintings in the big house. There were a few of us kids on the estate. I always preferred the outdoors. My father gave me my love of nature. We tramped all over the moors, mountains and hills."

"Sounds idyllic," Harry said.

"In a way it was, but we knew little of the outside world. We didn't have a television and I was only allowed supervised access to a computer. Moving to Cumbria has given me much more freedom, and I've watched so many boxsets." Ted stood. "We'd better get a move on. Maybe we'll return one day and see more."

Back outside again, they bought food from a stall and sat on a bench under Nelson's column. The sun attempted to warm them but a bitter wind swept across the open space and Harry shivered despite the padded coat and knitted hat.

"I hoped this beard might keep me warmer," he said.

"It sort of suits you," Ted replied.

"Thom? Is that you under your disguise?"

Harry raised his chin to see a woman staring. "Raven."

She gazed at him as if she knew something wasn't quite right. "Which one are you, because you're not Thom? Your accent is stronger and your voice a little deeper, though you are wearing his disguise kit. He wears the mole on the right." She sat next to him on the end of the bench. Ted tensed on the other side of him.

"I'm Harry, here for a weekend visit. It's..." He searched for a name. "Ewan's first time in London. Ewan, this is Raven St Clair, a friend of Tyler and Thom."

Ted said nothing.

"He's a bit awestruck. He has some of your books."

"Really? Which one is your favourite?"

Ted muttered a title.

"I'll send Harry a signed copy of the next one for you."

Harry needed to rescue the situation. "It's such a coincidence seeing you here with over eight million people in this city."

"It is, isn't it?"

Raven glanced over to one of the lions at the sound of her name being called. "Sorry, got to go. That's my partner, and we're off to a book signing. We've both new books out." She took out her phone and noted something. "There. Now I'll remember and I'll send you a copy."

"That would be great." Harry kept Raven in view as she hurried through the crowds to her partner then set off without looking back at them.

"Don't worry. She won't say anything," he said. "She and her family don't agree on many things, and she lives in Glasgow now. It'll be fine." He wanted to reassure himself as well. What were the chances of meeting Raven in London, miles away from where they both lived? "Come on, let's walk to the theatre. It'll be fun to see if we can solve who the murderer is in *Mousetrap.*"

"I haven't read the book," Ted said. "You read Christie though. I saw some on your bookshelves."

Harry elbowed him. "I have read it, but I've read so many, I can't exactly remember. No sneaking a look online either. And tonight we have the concert to look forward to, so try not to fret." Despite his words of reassurance, Harry guessed fretting was exactly what Ted would do.

Chapter Twenty-One

"I can't believe you worked out who did it," Harry said when they were back at the flat. "I think I've just read too many to remember."

Ted grinned in triumph. "Just a lucky guess."

Harry enveloped him and hugged him tight and Ted allowed himself to melt into his arms. "Nah, you're just clever, that's all." He tapped Ted's temple. "It's the power of your little grey cells but now, we'd better get ready. You've more surprises tonight."

"Really?" He extricated himself form Harry's embrace. "I'm nervous enough as it is. I don't think I could manage a whole meal. You weren't planning on us eating somewhere posh, were you?"

Harry buttoned up his shirt. "No, they have hospitality. I've booked us a taxi, and the ticket details for the concert are in my phone. We have to go to a certain entrance because we're not sitting in the crowd."

Ted's stomach rumbled with hunger and more than a little fear. He'd found the huge numbers of people on the streets of London intimidating enough. "What if I can't cope with the noise and all the fans?"

"You'll be fine," Harry said. "I'm excited myself."

The cab dropped them at the designated door. Ted waited while Harry flashed his phone at the man.

"Thank you, sir. Mr Ballantyne has confirmed you will be using his suite tickets tonight. Sally will show you up to the correct place." He eased open the door. Ted half-expected they'd enter into the land of Oz, not a concrete corridor that led to a lift.

"If you follow me, please, Mr Katt, I'll show you where you can leave your coats then along to the bar. Food is laid out there, should you be hungry."

Ted followed Harry and the thought struck him that maybe this time Harry was playing his brother for real, despite the beard.

"And here we are. I'll be around if you need any help, or ask anyone else with a badge. I'm sure you'll have a lovely evening."

Harry nudged him. "I'm sure we will."

Ted glanced around. A few people sat on chairs at the bar. "Is that thingamy from the news?" he asked Harry.

"Sit. I'll get us a couple of drinks and explain."

Ted took a seat furthest away from anyone else. More people arrived. Surely, that was a politician he recognised, with a woman and a couple of teenagers.

Harry strolled over from the bar. Someone said hello to him and he nodded rather than engaging in conversation.

"Do they think you're Thom or are they just being polite? Maybe he's known among VIPs even wearing a beard," Ted whispered, leaning in. "Won't they think it's odd you're not here with Tyler?"

"They may do, but he couldn't afford these prices on his soap salary—not yet. If anyone asks we can say you're a relative of John Ballantyne's from Scotland. The tickets belong to him, but he can't be here all the time and he's loaned them to Thom and Tyler before. There are only thirty-or-so people allowed in this section and no photographers. The seats are just outside this box."

Ted glanced through the glass at the arena. "I bet this costs a fortune."

"I would expect it does, but it also gives people privacy, which I know is important to you, so relax and enjoy yourself watching everyone's favourite Australian pop princess."

"Really?"

"Yes, really. And I want to see you make some moves."

"I don't dance," Ted said. "I mean, I've done Scottish dancing but not disco. I've never even been to a club." He'd never dared even at university.

"Oh, I wish I could take you to one later. Maybe another time. They're setting out the buffet. Let's get something to eat. I can hear your tummy rumbling from here despite your earlier protests."

Ted found it funny that even the wealthy and often famous still queued for food. He followed Harry and piled the extensive vegetarian selection onto a real china plate and collected real cutlery, not plastic.

How the posh people live. I sound resentful. Am I?

More people with faces he recognised arrived. Ted attempted to make himself smaller and picked at his food, which was delicious.

"You're quiet," Harry said.

"Truth? I'm feeling a little overwhelmed being here with all these celebrities when I'm no one. At least none of them appear to be shifters in this VIP area."

"No, thankfully."

"That could have been awkward for you," he added.

Harry nodded. "Thom said no one has ever approached him, so I figured we'd be safe, but maybe people are discreet." He swallowed one of the canapes in a single mouthful. "The food is good."

Ted glanced out through the glass. "It's looks like the arena is beginning to fill now. I don't know how they do these performances night after night to all these people. They put their reputations on the line every time. I get nervous enough giving kids and other groups talks about safety outdoors and how to treat the forest and wildlife."

"I know I couldn't do what Thom does," Harry said. "But he loves it. Each to their own. I suppose. The support act is on soon. Let's go to our seats."

Their positions gave them a full view of the stage and one-way screens gave their section protection from prying eyes. The staging for the show was massive, with a runway through the middle of the floor. When the music started, there was little point in talking. With the arena almost full, the first act bounced onto the stage and began.

All Ted could say was the group were loud and clearly aimed at teenage girls, judging by the audience. Next to him, Harry sang along to every tune and danced in his seat.

"They're good, aren't they?"

"Sorry," Ted said. "It's hard to hear you." He searched around the arena. Every so often he caught the tell-tale trace of a shifter. A nervous knot grew in his stomach. In the box, everyone else seemed occupied with the performance, though he noticed a few people stood at the back who were, Ted judged from their stern demeanours, there as bodyguards or a police escort.

The first act did an hour. Back in the bar, Ted thought about asking to go back to the flat.

"Are you excited yet?" Harry asked. He seemed so hyped, Ted didn't have the heart to let him down.

"I'm looking forward to the main attraction, but this sort of thing isn't for me—too loud and too many people."

Harry nudged him and winked. "There'll just be the two of us later, so don't wear yourself out bopping."

"That's more likely to be you."

The lights flashed in the bar, telling them to return to their seats. Everything went dark in the arena except for one spotlight aimed high up and into their vision came the star of the show sitting on a trapeze. The music started, her voice rang out and bright flashes of colour filled the stage as she was lowered. Ted held his breath, hoping she'd make it in one piece. He wasn't keen on heights. Harry leaned closer to him.

"She's amazing, isn't she? My dad did a trapeze act. He travelled with various circuses all over the world. Hence his nickname and my unknown collection of half-siblings."

Ted stared ahead. *Maybe I had brothers and sisters. I'll never know. Like my parents, all will be long gone now.* A wave of sadness washed over him, sprinkled with a little jealousy that Harry, at least, had his family when Ted had been rejected by his because of what he was.

All around him people sang and danced. He wanted to join in. Harry kept asking if he was all right.

"I'm fine," he replied, more times than he could remember. "I told you, it's loud and peoplely."

The next two hours seemed to last forever. Ted tried to join in singing along to her most famous hits so Harry was able to enjoy himself. Two people didn't have to enjoy the same thing to be together, did they?

But he's younger than me. He's a cat. He doesn't know what I am. I have to live my life in secret. Maybe it's better we part now before we're in too deep, even if I'm already in too deep.

His brain argued back and fro as if there were two entities, one on each shoulder, not good and bad, just with different views on what he should do — what was right and if what was right aligned with what he longed for in his heart of hearts.

Do I love him?

That question was the simplest of all his brain posed.

Yes, with all my heart and soul. Now he chuckled. *How melodramatic can I get? I sound like the heroine in a Mills and Boon or something.* He'd never read a Mills and Boon so had no real idea.

"Come on, party-pooper. At least stand up and dance for the encore."

Ted let Harry pull him up and attempted to lift his feet and shake his hips until at last the night was over. Most of the other VIP guests had cars waiting for them. Their taxi came and Ted listened to Harry talk about the night, making the appropriate answers until they arrived back at the flat.

"I need tea," he said. Harry had collapsed and spread himself over the sofa. "D'you want one?"

"Tea? Yes, please, and Tyler always has biscuits somewhere."

Harry was humming a familiar tune when Ted returned with the mugs and a packet of chocolate Hobnobs. He patted the sofa.

"Sit next to me and tell me what's been going though that handsome head of yours all night."

Ted took a deep breath. He had no idea where to begin or even what to say.

"I'm not sure I can say things here — in the light." He swallowed some tea.

"Okay then." Ted noticed Harry's throat ripple as he took in a deep breath. "Let's go next door." He stood and stretched out a hand. Ted took it. Harry pulled him up — Harry's strength caught him unawares — and he let himself be led to the bedroom. They shed most of their clothes at speed and slipped beneath the duvet. Harry opened his arms.

"Come here."

Ted reached for the light switch so only the glow of the streetlamps lit the room through a small gap in the curtains. He lay on his side and placed his head on Harry's shoulder. Warm fingertips traced lines over his skin.

"Okay. I'm listening."

What do I say? There's so much I can't say even now.

"We're different in so many ways, you and I?" He waited for Harry to answer, but no reply came.

"I'm much older than you and I'm much less experienced in all sorts of things. You wanted me to have fun tonight and I didn't. It was too loud and there were so many people. We don't have the same interests."

Still nothing.

"I'm happy at home, or in the forest, or in the hills and mountains. I'm a vegetarian."

Harry snorted.

Well, at least it was some sort of reaction. Frustrated, he continued, "Are you ever going to say something?"

Harry shifted then kissed Ted. Little sparks of electricity danced over any part of his skin Harry touched. Ted thought he might turn into a mushy puddle as he returned the kiss, opened his mouth, and let Harry slip in his tongue until it met his own. Harry pressed their bodies together. Ted's cock rose to attention against Harry's hardening erection.

He wasn't sure how long this lasted—time either stopped or stretched into infinity, it was hard to tell the difference. He wanted Harry inside him now, but sex wasn't the answer, even wonderful sex that took his breath away and made all his senses come alive. It took all his strength to edge away and create some distance between them.

"Tell me you don't love me?" Harry said.

Ted had to admit it was a bold move. *Do I tell the truth or lie? I don't want to lie, but let's face it, my whole life is a lie, but I can't tell him that. If I'm in danger for whatever reason, I will not put him in danger too.*

"I can't."

"I don't care how old you are. I don't care if you like quiet. I grew up in the countryside. I love it. Being here has shown me it's all right to visit, but I'm not like Thom. I like people but one at a time, not in huge crowds. I don't care what you eat as long as you don't judge me for something I can't help. I know you have a deep dark secret of some kind—I'm not stupid. I'm a cat—we sense these things in people. I also know there's a reason why you haven't told me and I accept that. I know I've slept with lots of others and you might find it intimidating, and truth be told, you're not my usual type, but there's something. When I hear your voice or see you in the flesh, something calls to me. I can't explain it. You make my senses sing like no one else has. Being with you feels right. I don't think I've ever been in love with anyone because how I feel about you is so different. I can't put it into words, and I've said enough of them now. But know this. I do not want to lose you. If there's music to face, I want to face it with you and be by your side."

Tears slipped over Ted's cheeks and he wiped them away. "There are things I can't tell you. I do have feelings for you—so strong that sometimes they scare me. All I want for now is to feel you inside me with nothing between us. Can we?"

"I get tested all the time, I'm on PrEP, and I've always used condoms. Are you sure?"

"I'm sure. I've been tested too. There's been no one else until you." Ted slipped off his boxer briefs and lay on his back. He slipped a pillow beneath his hips and bent his knees, exposing his arse. His cock lay dormant on his stomach but he knew a few touches would send tingles throughout his body.

Harry turned on the lamp. "I want to see you," he said.

Ted nodded. "Show me what you're going to put inside me."

Harry sat up and positioned himself on Ted's chest. He took hold of his cock and nudged Ted's lips. Ted opened his mouth and licked at the tip, tasting the bitter drops of liquid. He took in the tip and sucked, swirling his tongue around, feeling the veins running along the surface like ridges of bark on a tree.

Harry's cat's eyes shone in the lamplight. His face showed an ecstasy Ted hadn't ever seen in another. He couldn't wait. He enclosed Harry's cock in his palm.

"I want you to take this and fuck me. I want to know I've been fucked. I want to feel your warmth inside me and know it's there. Do it, Harry. Do me now."

Harry's cock jerked in his hand.

"I didn't think I could get any harder." Harry reached over to the bedside table and gave Ted the lude.

"Slick me up and I'll do you."

Ted loved the feel of Harry in his hands and couldn't wait to feel him in his arse, hitting that spot over and over until he could take no more. He wanted to remember this night forever.

"Now," he said.

In seconds, Ted found his legs being lifted over Harry's shoulders. He'd never felt so exposed in his life but he didn't care. Harry finger-fucked him, opening him up, then positioned himself.

"You're sure about the condoms?" he asked.

"Are you?"

"Oh yes. I want to be inside you and fill you up. I can't wait."

"Then fuck me. I'm yours."

Harry didn't wait. He didn't take his time either. He thrust inside Ted in one fluid motion.

"Yes," Ted cried. "More. How does it feel?"

"Amazing," Harry said. "I didn't think it would be so different but it is." He nudged Ted's prostate, making him arch his back, wanting more.

"There. Just there." Harry loomed over him. He leant backwards and began. Thrust after thrust, hitting the same spot again and again, sent Ted somewhere else. He knew his mouth uttered words but he had no idea what they were. He closed his eyes, wanting only to feel. His cock throbbed, desperate for attention but he resisted. He wanted this to go on forever. Harry pounded him — that was the only description his brain could manage.

"I'm close," Harry said. "Touch yourself."

Ted wrapped his fingers around his erection, sending shivers down his spine. His balls, now heavy, were ready to let go of their load. Harry opened his mouth and threw back his head. Heat rushed inside him and his orgasm barrelled through him, sending out streams of white liquid, which hit Harry above him and covered his body up to his chin.

"Oh, God. So fucking good," Harry said. "You're all full of me. I love knowing that."

Ted let go of himself and Harry shifted Ted's legs and the pillow and fell on top of him. They lay there breathing. Ted enclosed Harry in his arms. He knew the truth now. Nothing could ever stop him loving this man. Harry was his.

After a few minutes, Harry rolled off him. They lay facing each other.

"We're all sticky," Harry said as he ran his finger through the mess. "But I can't be bothered to go to the bathroom now. Can you stand my breath?"

"If you can stand mine."

Ted lifted his arm and Harry tucked himself in. He made a noise almost like a purr rather than snoring. Ted closed his eyes and drifted away, all troubles forgotten for a little while.

* * * *

"Ugh," Harry said next to him. "I need to shower. How come you're all clean?" He kissed him. "And have minty fresh breath?"

"I'm an early riser," Ted said.

Harry lifted his eyebrows.

"Stop it. Go and get clean, and I'll make us a tea before we go out and hunt breakfast and look for anything interesting in Covent Garden. Will you be wearing the disguise again?" Ted asked.

"I thought I might, though not the lenses as they made my eyes itchy. Judging by the frost I saw through the window, wearing a woolly hat and big coat might be sensible."

This time they did take the Tube. It took Ted a couple of steps to jump on the escalator—he wasn't keen but wasn't about to admit it to Harry.

At Covent Garden, they found a rather more up-market café for breakfast, allowing Ted to treat himself to avocado on toast and mixed berry pancakes while Harry tucked into a full English—minus tomato—and even more tea.

Ted bought a few trinkets for the cabin while Harry wandered off. Knowing to stay put from mountain rescue training, he found the nearest bench warmed by the weak sun and settled onto it to people watch. He reckoned he must have counted every nationality and so many languages as people milled around in the space.

"Found you," a voice said over his shoulder. Harry sat next to him carrying a parcel. "We'll need to get back to the flat ready to catch the train," Harry said. "I'm sorry it's been so quick."

Ted leaned his head on Harry's shoulder. "Been treating yourself?"

"You'll see, but not now."

Two hours later, they were on a train heading back north to who knew what. Ted longed to see his cabin and forest again, but he had a growing sense of concern, and although he and Harry had agreed to continue, he couldn't help but worry.

The journey went surprisingly smoothly, with Ted driving the final part from Preston to home. Back at the cabin, everything seemed to be as he left it. He sniffed the air, checking for any different smells.

"I'd better get going though I don't want to," Harry said. He wrapped his arms around Ted and pulled him close. "It's been amazing having this time with you." He stepped back and picked up the parcel.

"This is for you?"

"Do I open it now?"

"If you want."

Ted recognised the shape was a painting. He pulled off the paper and stared.

"Do you like it?" Harry asked. "I thought with you having them as neighbours, it would be appropriate here."

The painting showed a beaver family with a dammed creek and trees in various stages of removal. Harry couldn't have any idea what this might mean to Ted.

"It's beautiful," he said, trying to get control of the swirl of thoughts in his mind. "And similar to the creek with our beavers." *Since when did they become our beavers – be careful?* "I'll find a space for it."

"I'm glad you like it. I wasn't sure. It's an original, not a print. You never know, it might be worth something if the artist becomes famous." Harry kissed him. "I'll call you to arrange something."

"Yes. Please," Ted said, not knowing what else to say.

Minutes later, the sound of a car engine turning over further down the path filled Ted's heart with gloom. Solitude had been something he enjoyed, but now Harry had left, a sense of loneliness hit him. He glanced outside. The sun was already gone and the sky had clouded over. The anticipated rain had arrived, so there would be no tree hugging to calm himself. Instead, he decided to clean the house to take his mind off everything.

Hours later, as he lay with his feet up on the sofa watching the news, there was a tap at the door. Wary, he opened it to find the male beaver stood there. The beaver glanced from side to side. "Let me in." Ted stepped back and the beaver scampered to the middle of the room.

"What's the matter?" he asked. "Are those idiots back?"

"No, this is about you. We've discovered...don't ask how...that someone is looking for you. You need to be wary of strangers. You may be in danger. We don't know who or why, this is nothing to do with us beavers. We may wish you didn't exist, but we mean you no harm. That is not our way, but it is the way of others. Don't trust anyone." He glanced around again. "I need to get back. Don't come near us again."

Harry opened the door and the beaver disappeared into the darkness without turning around.

After locking up, setting the outside alarms, and checking every window, Ted sank onto the sofa. *Who wants me and why?* He thought about Harry. Could this all be an elaborate plan to trap him? No. He trusted Harry, but was he right to do so? Maybe someone else was pulling Harry's strings and watching, despite how careful they'd been. He needed to think, and he needed an escape plan, but how much of this should he share with Harry, if anything at all?

Chapter Twenty-Two

Harry paid the taxi and stepped out of the car at the front of the B&B, where a few cars were parked to the side. They had guests even at this time of year. He hoped to get up to his bedroom without meeting anyone, but those hopes were dashed when his mother appeared at the door.

"I wasn't sure if that was you or another guest. There's a conference in a big hotel in Windemere but some people have chosen to stay here because we're cheaper and more...accommodating."

In cat form, Harry's hackles would have risen. Instead he shivered.

"Come into the kitchen and get warm. Tell me how Thom is doing."

Harry had no option but to follow his mother. "Where's Gran?"

"She was feeling a little under the weather, so she's gone to her bedroom. I'll pop in on her later. Don't worry, it's just a cold, and this weather affects her arthritis. Maggie will probably turn up with one of her potions in the morning, if I know anything."

He followed his mother through the door and sat at the table while she let the kettle boil and took the biscuit tin out of the cupboard.

"Are you eating with us tonight? I've some lasagne for the guests who asked, and you know I always have spare."

"I'll take it up to my room, if that's all right. It's been a long couple of days and train travel is surprisingly tiring."

"Right you are, love. I'll warm some for you now while you tell me what you've been up to."

Guilt swept over him. He hated lying to his mother, but it wouldn't be the first time. "Thom's fine." *Though not actually in London.* "We went to a few museums and a concert — you know, hung out. It made a nice change. He's all excited about getting the superhero role — if he gets it. It'll make him a star. Me and Rich will have to change our hair colour or something or people will mistake us for him all the time."

"I suppose they will. The tricks you and your brothers used to play on everyone. Oh, talking of brothers, Rich says to remind you you've got the follow-up visit to check on the rat situation at Mere Farm."

"They'll never get rid of them no matter how hard they try. They bought a farm as a vanity project and rats come with the territory. We told them, but clearly they've more money than sense, and who are we to turn away money?" He yawned.

The oven pinged. "Here," his mother said, handing him a tray with a bowl of food and a pot of grated Parmesan. "I'll come up later with a hot chocolate when I visit your gran."

Harry threw his bag over his shoulder and took the back staircase to the family side of the house and his bedroom. Halfway up, his secret phone pinged. He smiled, knowing it would be a message from Ted. *You have got it so bad.*

In his bedroom, the put the tray on the bed and dug out the phone.

Keep an eye out for strangers. Someone is looking for me. Be wary of anyone asking strange questions. Thank you for the weekend. Don't call or text. I'll contact when I can.

Harry stared at the words. His mother had a hotel full of strangers. Could one of the guests be a worry? He decided to check them out in the morning. His stomach rumbled. He'd had nothing but a bag of crisps since breakfast. He sat back on the bed and ate the lasagne then scrolled through YouTube, hoping to distract himself. His mother woke him from a nap at nine with a mug of hot chocolate topped with a large swirl of cream. He bolted the door behind her. Tonight, he'd sleep in cat form with one eye open, just in case.

* * * *

The following morning, Harry volunteered to take breakfasts into the dining room for his mother while waiting for Rich to appear with the van. Ten people occupied the space on the other side of the house. To his surprise, only five were shifters, so this was a mixed conference. Most sat in pairs except for a well-dressed woman with a London accent—a fox shifter—with glorious red hair. The other singleton was a man, who in other circumstances would have taken his breath away and woken up his cock. The man was a jaguar, a

204

predator like himself, but massive and intimidating. He couldn't imagine how the other guests, two badgers and a pair of dogs — German Shepherds — would feel in his presence. The man oozed power.

Each set of guests treated *him* differently too, according to their species, and Harry regretted offering to help. He delivered plates to those awaiting a cooked breakfast and hurried out of the door. Once in the entrance, he turned to look through a glass panel and his gaze met the man staring back at him like he was a tasty snack he'd be more than happy to devour. *I need to talk to Ted.*

Rich awaited him in the kitchen. Harry longed to tell him he couldn't work and shoot off to the cabin, but whatever was happening, Ted had told him not to, and anyway, he'd be at work. *But what if he's gone — just done a moonlight flit?*

"Ready?" Rich said. "It's likely to take us over an hour to get there. I feel guilty asking them for money but we have a business to run. I get the feeling they think rats are urban creatures who only live in sewers. They asked us to get rid of the spiders too."

"They'll learn," Harry said. "Or they'll go bankrupt attempting to live the good life. I'll grab my coat."

On the journey, Harry's thoughts whirled with so many what ifs. After thirty minutes on the road, Rich broke the silence.

"What's up with you? I thought you'd have been full of your weekend with Thom. How is he?"

"I didn't see him in the end, but the weekend was fine."

"Hmm. Suki reckons you've got a secret lover tucked away or you'd have shown more interest in Tasha."

"Does she now? Strange how your in-laws should be interested in my love life. I don't know if I can trust you anymore."

Harry lurched forward as Rich braked hard, swerved into a lay-by, then stopped.

"What the fuck, Rich?"

"What the fuck, indeed. What was that comment about? What's going on in your tiny mind? Your head's been somewhere else for weeks."

Harry turned to face Rich. "Can I trust you?"

"Of course you can trust me. I'm your brother."

Harry checked in all directions. He even considered whether the van might be bugged. "There's a seat over there. Let's sit outside."

"It's cold."

"I know, but I've got to talk to someone."

"Okay. I can see you're worried."

They sat on the bench. Anyone passing would think the van had broken down.

"Tell me," Rich said. "I swear this will go no further."

"I'm depending on you. I need to talk and I can't involve Mum or Gran. I was in London with someone over the weekend—someone I have strong feelings for."

"I'm listening."

"He lives a few miles from us and works locally."

"He," Rich said.

"Yes. *He*. We've been seeing each other for a while."

"Do I know him?"

Harry nodded.

"So what's the drama?"

Harry stuffed his hands into his pockets. "I'm not sure. He has a secret and I'm sort of okay with that, so we've kept everything on the downlow. And no, he's not married."

"Is he one of us?"

"I don't think so, but he knows about our existence."

"Hang on," Rich said, grabbing Harry's arm. "This is Ted you're talking about, isn't it?"

Harry nodded.

"But he's older than you, and nothing like your usual type. He's not what you'd call handsome, is he? Still, I suppose beauty is in the eye of the beholder, as they say. And he has some big secret? Is he in danger? Is he putting you — or all of us — in danger too?"

"I think *he* might be. He left Scotland because of a bad break-up. Maybe it's something to do with that. Maybe this bloke wouldn't take no for an answer and has come looking for him. He texted me last night telling me not to ring or text him even on the burner phones we have. And this morning, there's this bloke staying at the hotel. He's a shifter — a jaguar."

"A big cat? Here? I wonder if my father-in-law knows. Non-native species are supposed to report their entry into the country."

"He's here for a conference, Mum says. I didn't tell her what he was. You know she doesn't want to know unless we think she needs to. There are others staying at our place, and not all are shifters. But what if he's searching for Ted? I need to warn him. I'm worried I'll get to his cabin in the woods and he'll have gone." Harry stared at the floor, squeezing his eyes. He didn't want to cry in front of Rich.

"Shit, bro. You've got it bad, haven't you?"

"Yes. I've never felt like this about anyone before. I've no idea why, but something draws me to him. He makes me feel protected, but now he could be in danger, and I need to warn him about this bloke."

"I bet you've forgotten we've a match tonight with Jack and Alfie, so come out and play darts with us first then go to his place when we've finished. You could do with some ordinary conversation, and there'll be fewer people about later on." He glanced at his watch. "We'd better get going. Come on, I'm sure it won't be as bad as you think."

Rich was an optimist. Harry had said so when he set his cap at Suki Catterson, daughter of a millionaire, especially as she'd rebuffed Harry's advances. But Rich had been right, so perhaps he was right about the situation with Ted too.

* * * *

As he wasn't going home after the darts, Harry dressed in his leathers and took his bike to their local, The Miner's Arms. The other three were already there when he arrived and were talking to the other team from the Drover's Inn on the other side of the lake. They all knew each other from school and other local events.

"Everyone all right for a drink?" he asked.

Rich lifted a pint. "I got one for you. We're both on the non-alcoholic stuff."

"Probably wise. It's raining cats and dogs out there. I wouldn't be surprised if there's some local flooding." He took off his jacket, pulled over a stool and sipped his pint. "So what's the gossip?"

"We were just talking about the state of Windemere. All this rain will mean more sewage ending up there. It's not good for business. Who wants to go paddle boarding or kayaking among all that?" Everyone nodded. It was a topic of much local complaint.

"How's business for you two?" Jack asked.

"Can't complain. There are always pests, though some of them are people. Today, we had to convince a couple we couldn't keep all rats and mice away from their farm. They've moved here from the city. I think they've watched too many of those TV shows which do the same. They're going to face a steep learning curve."

"Ay, lots of farmers whose families have been here for years are facing money problems and diversifying as much as they can."

"I've got some good news," Andy of the Drover's team said with a big grin on his face.

"I'm glad someone has, boy." Jack slapped his back. "Spill then."

"I'm going to be a dad."

"Well, that's great news," Rich said. "But try not to have twins. My two already work as a team. I dread to think what they'll be like as teenagers. Even them getting to the terrible twos is scaring the life out of me."

"It's the great thing about being an uncle," Harry said. "I can waltz in, have all the fun, and waltz out again — perfect."

"Someone will pin you down one day, laddie," Jack said. "Even Alfie here has found himself a girl who can stand him, and you've got a bigger pool to cast your net over."

"Nah," Harry said. "I'm happy to go fishing and return my catch to the sea. Anyway, isn't it time we beat you and got our revenge for last time?"

The match was a close one but ended as Harry had hoped, going down to the last game and final dart as he hit double eight to win. He went to the bar to log their victory with the innkeeper and to buy a last round for them all. Stood waiting, his hackles rose, feeling a body behind him and hot breath on his neck.

"How fortunate to find you here. I have to say those leather trousers suit you and this T-shirt shows off your other assets. The view certainly improved when you returned to the bar."

"I'm not interested," Harry said. "I'm here with my brother and some mates, not to be chatted up." He didn't even turn around.

"That's rather ungracious comment to a visitor, and your family has been so welcoming."

"They don't know what you are," Harry said. "I do."

"Oh, I know you do. And I know what you are too. Us cats, we are all the same." His accent became more pronounced.

"I don't think so."

"Not what I've been told." A hand caressed the small of his back. He had no room to get away, pressed as he was against the bar-top.

"Your reputation precedes you. And nights on the road can get lonely. I thought we could keep each other warm in this chilly place. I don't know how you stand such cold."

Stan put more pints on the tray. Harry grimaced when the man cupped his arse.

"You all right, Harry? Need a hand with those?"

"Yeah, please."

"I'll help," the man said. "And I haven't introduced myself. My name is Alonzo Vicario Ferrara de Souza."

"Is it?"

De Souza picked up a tray. "I'll have a dirty martini, innkeeper, if you could bring it over."

Harry was stuck. De Souza followed him back to the table and pulled a chair over. "Evening, gentlemen. I hope you don't mind me joining you. I'm here for a conference and staying at the Katt family hotel."

Mike from the Drover's team nodded. "Are you a salesman like me?"

"No, I'm a recruitment specialist. I head-hunt specific people for certain important roles — people who will be paid a significant amount of money. I'm giving several talks and seminars, then tomorrow, I'm off to Edinburgh."

"Are you looking for anyone in particular?" Alfie asked.

"Not exactly. You must get lots of people coming and going around here, though I can understand anyone choosing to stay with such beautiful scenery."

"Aye, laddie, a few of us are incomers. My wife caught me on holiday, and I ended up here."

"I thought I detected a Scottish accent. I love Scotland. I was friendly with a man from the Highlands once, but we had a falling out. I did hear he relocated to this area."

Harry nudged Rich. "We get a lot of visitors. Most don't stay, though they might buy second homes and price all the locals out of the market."

"Tell me about it," Alfie said. "It'll take us ages to save enough."

The discussion turned to house prices and the cost of living. Harry breathed a sigh of relief while de Souza frowned.

"Well, I don't know about you lot, but we've a job over in Yorkshire tomorrow so an early start. Harry, you ready to go?"

"Time we were off too, Alfie," Jack agreed. "Your mum will be staring at the clock."

"More like looking at the TV hoping she can get her programme done before I get back."

The four of them stood leaving the Drover's team sat with de Souza. All Harry could do was hope they didn't know Ted. None of them worked in the same field, so there was no reason they should.

Outside, Rich rolled out the ramp they used to wheel heavy stuff into the van. With some effort, Harry got his bike inside, with help from Alfie, then joined Rich in the front seat. He hoped they hadn't been seen in the dark of the car park and no one had come out while they were there.

"I'll drop you off somewhere along the way," Rich said. "And give Mum a heads-up about this bloke in case he asks her and Gran any questions. Be sensible, won't you?"

"I need to warn him. It was pretty clear that bloke was digging for information. The bastard grabbed my arse at the bar. I couldn't get out of his way. I wanted to punch him, but didn't want to cause a scene."

Rich pulled into a lay-by on a smaller road. They manoeuvred the bike out of the back. He took hold of Harry's arms then hugged him. "Please be careful, little bro. None of us could bear it if anything happened to you."

"I love him," Harry replied. It was the first time he'd said those words out loud.

Rich patted his back. "Then that's all that matters. Go. If you can, call me."

Harry stepped away, mounted his bike, and sped off into the night.

Chapter Twenty-Three

Ted had spent the day working, trying to act as normally as possible. He figured if he was in the middle of nowhere, it would be less easy for somebody to find him. Now, he paced the floor of his cabin. He wanted to call Harry. He needed Harry's arms around him, or even Harry in cat form to cuddle and soothe his frazzled nerves.

I should phone home and tell them, or tell Otis. But I don't want to leave – not again. Maybe this was another journalist who had discovered his story. Had that bastard left a trail of information? Surely other shifters had faced such scrutiny. *Or is this something different – more sinister. Why should anyone be interested in me? Okay, I know I'm different, that I'm not supposed to exist. Is that it? Does someone want to know how or why I was born? Am I unique?* He paused.

"I shouldn't exist," he said out loud.

"Ted, let me in." The voice startled him. He hurried to the door.

"Harry, is that you?"

"Yes, let me in."

Ted unbolted the door and turned the key in the lock. Caught up in his own thoughts, he hadn't noticed the security light come on, but he hadn't heard Harry's bike either. He opened the door and Harry dived in past him. He locked up again in the hope of calming the hoard of butterflies now occupying his empty stomach.

"Harry, what are...?" Before he could finish his question, Harry had enclosed him in his arms and held him tight. He kissed him.

"Thank goodness, you're all right." Talk and kisses. Talk and kisses. Ted couldn't keep up with either.

"Harry, slow down. What is it? Did you say something about an ex-boyfriend of mine being here? And you're sure no one followed you? Sit on the sofa with me."

Once sat, Harry took Ted's hand. "I need to tell you something before anything else."

"Okay. I'm listening." *I should be telling him to go. Whoever that person is, definitely isn't the journalist who tried to fool me.*

Harry turned to face him and held both his hands. "Ted. I love you. I'm in love with you. I don't want to lose you, and whatever is going on, I will do everything in my power to help and protect you. You mean the world to me. I thought love was for fools, but it seems I'm a fool too, just like Thom and Rich."

The butterflies in his stomach stopped fluttering. *Harry loves me. Beautiful, funny, sexy, Harry Katt loves me.* In any other circumstances those words would have made him the happiest man on the planet. He'd have shouted from the mountain tops that he loved Harry too. But now how did he answer? Harry was staring at him — waiting — his eyes full of emotion. Silence hung in the air like an early morning mist over the valley.

"You don't have to say you feel the same way, Ted. I needed you to know all the facts if you have to decide about anything."

Come on. Say something. You can't leave him hanging like this. It's time to tell him the truth and give him all the facts. He took a deep breath and slowly let it out.

"Harry, you know I have feelings for you, but there's something I need to tell you first."

"No, you don't. It doesn't matter — whatever *it* is."

He clasped Harry's hands tighter. "It does. You need to know everything. It's time I told you who — or what — I am."

Harry squeezed his hand.

"I suppose I begin at the beginning."

"As the song says, that's a very good place to start." Harry managed a smile, which just about got to his eyes.

Ted snorted. "Yeah, Maria von Trapp and I have so much in common. Okay, to begin with my name isn't Ted Woodward, or at least it wasn't until I came here with a new identity. Even the name I had before is the one my foster parents chose, and it's so Scottish. My true parents didn't name me. I was found one morning outside a house and as far as I know, not in this country. The people who lived at the house were shifters and took me in."

Harry opened his mouth then clearly changed his mind about asking the question.

"You were right to wonder about me. I'm not human. I, like you, am a shifter, but I'm not supposed to exist. I am unique. I know that's quite a claim. My species decided some time ago they wanted nothing to do with humans and for several generations none were born and they believed the plan had worked. Then, out of nowhere, I appeared — a throwback."

"Is it possible for a shifter species to become extinct?"

"The beavers tried to make them so. After all, humans had come close to making them extinct."

"So that's what you are. You're a beaver, but I can't tell. Maggie couldn't tell either."

"It's what I am, but as I said, I shouldn't exist. Some people are fascinated I do, but the group I was delivered to—I don't know all the ins and outs of the politics—they agreed with the beavers' decision and their right to choose. I couldn't exist so I had to be hidden and I could never transform. I've been human since I was young enough to control my abilities. I haven't transformed for nearly forty years, which is why no one can tell."

"Wow, there are so many shifter species whose numbers have fallen or who've become extinct. I suppose this explains your webbed feet."

Ted nodded as heat rushed into his cheeks. "I hide them, though there are people born with webbed hands and feet who aren't shifters. Anyway, I lived for years in Scotland. It wasn't a bad life, though I was envious of those who could be who they were meant to be."

"I can't imagine what it must be like for you to not be able to do what comes naturally to a beaver. As well as your feet, it explains a few other things—you being a vegetarian." He lifted his hand and stroked Ted's hair. Ted leaned into his touch. "The gorgeous colour and softness of your hair, and..." He paused and smiled. "The way you piled the chips on your plate one on top of the other like they were branches forming a dam. Nature will out, like us knocking things off tables and shelves and following any flying insect around a room. We all keep certain features in human form."

"Did I really do that with chips?"

Harry nodded. "You did."

"Bloody hell. I didn't realise. Even such daft behaviour could have exposed me. I had it drilled into me as a child how some groups had advocated for my death to avoid me breeding or being used in experiments, but eventually curiosity or the simple need for physical contact led me to a relationship with a man who turned out to be a journalist investigating if shifters existed. I thought he cared for me, but I was a means to an end. I don't know what happened to him, but I was brought here and met you. That's everything. I bet you've lots of questions. I'll do my best to answer."

Harry cupped his cheek. "No, I don't. That you are a beaver doesn't matter to me. I get why you didn't tell me the truth. We've all lied about what we are to protect ourselves. What worries me is what happens now."

"It worries me too. I might have to leave here, and…" He didn't want to say the words. *Leave you.*

"Is there anyone you need to tell, or should tell?"

"There's Otis, and I suppose I need to tell the laird."

"Are your foster parents shifters?"

"No, but they're aware. Dad was a friend of the previous laird. They've taken in many waifs and strays like me over the years. I'll call in the morning and let them know about this bloke. Can you stay?"

"I hid my bike behind your woodpile and I want to be with you."

This could be our last night if they insist I leave here. I could end up anywhere and I can't ask him to up sticks and leave his family for someone he's only known a few months.

"Let's go to bed. I need to hold you. When you were a cat, holding you made me feel calm and warm inside."

"That's one of our superpowers," Harry said. "In either form, though not all cats like to cuddle. It depends on if you were taught as a kitten like we were. For me, being held is a joy."

Harry stood and stretched out his arm to haul Ted from the sofa and lead him to the bed. He pulled back the cover then lifted Ted's jumper over his head, followed by his T-shirt. Despite all they'd done, Ted's body hair still made him self-conscious, as did the lack of defined muscles compared to Harry's sinuous form.

"Stop it," Harry said touching Ted's chest. "I can read your mind." He pulled his own T-shirt over his head and removed his leathers and briefs in one.

"Anyway, if we're comparing, in one place you've inches on me in length and girth." His smirk sent more heat into Ted's face.

"You're incorrigible, Harry Katt." He couldn't help but smile while Harry slipped off his socks.

"Oh no. I'm easily incorriged." He dropped to his knees, then undid Ted's belt and zip then lowered Ted's trousers and boxers. "I mean, look at this beautiful thing nestled among such a gorgeous background. Though I see you've been tidying a bit."

Will my face ever cool? He sat as his knees wobbled when Harry ran a nail along the underside of his now more-than-interested cock. Harry touched the head with the tip of his tongue, glanced up and Ted nodded. He took a strong grip of the base then enclosed Ted's erection in his warm mouth and sucked. Ted leant back with his arms supporting him on either side and let himself feel. His orgasm caught him by surprise, so he didn't have time to warn Harry, who still managed to swallow every drop.

"Put your hands through my hair," Harry said, his breath increasing. Ted realised what he was doing and threaded his fingers through the strands, tugging slightly. Harry lifted his face so their eyes met and Ted's heart missed a beat or two—those eyes blazed with light in the darkened room. *I love him, but I need him safe. If they send me somewhere. If I tell him anything. He'll follow.*

"You are so beautiful," Ted said as Harry came under his own touch. "Please come to bed. I need to hold you."

Harry slipped in next to him then into Ted's arms. Once again, he turned his gaze on Ted. "Promise me you won't disappear."

Ted sighed. "I can't promise anything, my angel. Nothing in my life has been my decision."

Harry tensed in his embrace. "We could leave—just the two of us, and tell no one where we are. We could jump on my bike and go anywhere."

"It's not so simple." He stroked Harry's face. "We'd both have to become someone else and we'd need documents. Let's just be together now, not think about the past or the future—live in the moment. I love you."

"And I love you too." Harry made tiny snoring noises within minutes like the cat he was, while Ted stared into the darkness.

Chapter Twenty-Four

"I don't want to go," Harry said the next morning. It was pitch-black outside.

Ted clasped his hand. "I told you, I'll call Otis, and I need you to find out if this man is still at your mum's place. If we know where he is, Otis may know what to do, though to be truthful, I've no idea what his exact role is in all this."

Harry put his other hand over Ted's. "You will tell me what's going on, won't you? You won't just leave saying nothing? I couldn't bear it." Tears welled in the corner of his eyes. "I'm in love with you, and I want to be with you. I don't care what you are, and anyway, I think beavers are cute."

"I'll do my best, but my life has never been in my own hands—or paws—and, as I've been told so often, I'm not supposed to exist."

"But you do. You're here in front of me. I've held you in my arms. We've made love, Ted. That must mean something."

"Of course it does. You mean the world to me, Harry. I didn't expect to feel this way ever, but you sashayed into my heart like the cat you are. If that bloke is still around it could be dangerous for both of us and your family, and I don't want you to do anything stupid. If he's there, text me." He stood.

"You'd better go if you're going to sneak back into your bedroom."

Harry stood then enveloped Ted in his arms and kissed him until Ted pulled away.

"I love you, Harry Katt."

"And I love you, Ted Woodward. Please be careful."

Ted nodded. "You, too." He unlocked the door and opened it for Harry to go.

"Nothing seems disturbed," he said, glancing from side to side. Harry stepped across the threshold and took hold of Ted's hand, only letting go when he'd walked too far. His knees wobbled and his body shook.

I don't want to go. But he knew he had no choice. Ted needed him to check on de Souza. He collected his bike and put on his helmet. He waved before pushing it to the road. He didn't look back, not daring to in case he found himself running back. He had to trust Ted's words and go and do his bit to help, whatever the consequences.

* * * *

Back home, Harry climbed up to his window in cat form, transformed, and got ready to face the day. He found his mum and gran in the kitchen cooking breakfasts for the guests. He made himself a mug of tea and sat at the table.

"Is de Souza still here?" He tried to keep his tone casual. "He turned up at the pub last night when we were playing darts and tried to chat me up. I thought I might stay out of his way."

"No, he left earlier. Said he'd been called away by his firm."

His gran handed Harry two pieces of toast. "He's a handsome bloke," she said.

"Too pushy for me."

The back door opened and Rich stepped through. He glanced at Harry. "You've forgotten, haven't you? A customer over near Keswick has found a huge wasp nest clearing out an overgrown garden and wants us to get rid of it."

"Sorry."

"Late night?" Rich asked. Both his mum and gran smirked.

Rich squeezed Harry's shoulder. "We'd better get going then, before you fall asleep. I'll drive."

Once outside, Rich hurried Harry towards the van. "You can tell me on the way."

Harry got in the passenger seat and took out his phone. "I need to text Ted to let him know that bloke de Souza has checked out. Who knows where he is. He could be at Ted's already. Ted is a shifter, Rich, a special one, and he's in danger." He texted the message.

Rich didn't wait to ask questions, but Harry was too preoccupied to ask why. He started the engine and set off. Harry's phone beeped minutes later.

Don't worry. I'm with Otis and not at home. Going to a safe place. Will call when I can.

"Is he okay?" Rich asked.

"Yes, he's with Otis and de Souza is in the wind."

Rich halted the van at the crossroads, waiting to turn right. A large car turned left into the road they were leaving.

"That's Leo Catterson's car, isn't it?" Harry said. "Rich, what have you done? You said you wouldn't say anything about Ted."

"I said something vague to Suki about de Souza, but she knew his name. I didn't want to worry you. Her family know all about Ted, Harry. I told you my father-in-law has influence. He's friends with the laird of the estate where Ted grew up. They're all part of some sort of alliance. I didn't ask the details. And…well… Otis works for him. He's come here to see de Souza, but it seems he's fled. That means Ted should be safe."

"Turn around. I need to know where Ted is. Rich, I love him."

Despite, Harry's pleading, Rich turned the van into the main road. "You need to stay away, Harry. Let them do what they need to do. This is above us. I don't know why Ted is important and I don't want to know. I guess as we can't tell his species that he's something special, but I'm happy with my life, my wife, and my kids. I don't know what you're mixed up in, but I want you safe as well. Leo is no danger to him. Suki wouldn't lie to me. Just sit tight. We'll get this job done and tonight find out later what's going on."

Harry nodded. He had every intention of jumping back in the van and driving off as soon as they got to the customer's house. His phone beeped again.

I'm at a safe house. Don't do anything silly. Stay away from the cabin.

He stared at the words. All he could do was trust what Ted told him. He wiped his brow and put the mobile back in his pocket. They did the job. His phone stayed quiet. He had to believe Ted was fine, that de Souza hadn't found him and was being dealt with, but the man was a big cat. Britain didn't have shifters big or strong enough to deal with an animal that size unless there were some no one knew about who worked for the council — bodyguards or secret agents. Humans with a gun could take down such a threat. Someone like Max maybe, who drove for the Cattersons.

When they got back to the B&B, Leo Catterson's car was still there. Max stood at the front door. Harry wanted to rush straight in.

"I need to speak to him," he protested when Rich grabbed his arm.

"No. Let me. I promise if there's anything you need to know, I'll tell you."

"Don't lie to me, Rich."

"I won't. Go on. Get yourself a stiff drink or something. Chances are this will have all blown over and Ted will be back in his cabin by morning." He took hold of Harry's arms. "You've got to be positive, little bro. You know you matter to him."

"Yeah, but he might not get to decide what happens, Rich. He's not been allowed to choose for himself up to now, so why should this be different? You know they wanted me to stay away. They even tried to set me up with Tasha." He paused. "D'you think she could have anything to do with de Souza? She works with big cats, doesn't she?"

"I doubt it, or Leo wouldn't have let her near here. Stop creating more problems than there are already. I thought Thom was the one with the imagination among us, not you. Now, go and wait. Things will get sorted. If I find out anything, I promise I'll tell you."

"Please, Rich. I need to know I can depend on you — we're family — brothers in arms — one for all and all for one."

"I told you, I'll do my best."

Rich had a simple view that people were essentially good. Until now, Harry hadn't thought too deeply about anything — just lived his life and had fun, but now, as Rich said, all he could do was wait.

* * * *

Harry spent the next two hours wearing a groove into his bedroom carpet, holding on to his phone in case Ted or Rich rang to let him know what was going on. Lights flashed on in the yard outside and he rushed to the window to see Leo Catterson's car leaving. A few seconds later, Rich appeared, hot-footing it to the house.

He stood frozen, not knowing what to do until Rich burst through his bedroom door.

"They're taking Ted out of the country by plane. There's a small airstrip over on Watney Island. Leo is on his way there now. What do you want to do?"

"I've got to see him," Harry said. "Maybe they'll let me go with him."

"But what about here? What about Mum and Gran? You might not be allowed to see or speak to us again, Harry, and you've no idea where he's going."

"I do care about everyone else, but I can't explain how I feel about him. You knew Suki was the one for you from the moment you saw her, didn't you? And Ted saved my life — literally. I know it's been a ridiculously short time, but when you know, you know."

"And you're prepared to give up everything for him?"

"I'm prepared to try."

"Do you have a spare helmet?"

Harry nodded.

They hurried down the stairs. Harry paused, seeing his mum and gran sitting in the lounge watching the TV.

"You off out again, laddie?"

He kissed the top of his gran's head. "Yes, Gran — galivanting again."

"Keep an eye on him, Rich."

"Yes, Mum."

Harry stood behind his mother's chair and hugged her. "I love you, Mum."

"Ah, yer soft idiot."

"Love you too, Gran."

Before they could question him further, he glanced at Rich and they rushed to collect the bike.

"It'll be quicker on this," Harry said. "I have to get there in time."

Rich sat behind him and they set off. Harry kept up a steady speed, hoping they wouldn't get caught by a police patrol — not that there were many off the main roads, and he knew this area like the back of his hand.

He had no idea what he would do if he got there and the plane hadn't left. What might Ted be thinking now? He had to concentrate on the road and though he wasn't bothered about the speed cameras, he slowed when they drove through the series of towns on the main road.

Just under an hour later, they arrived at the aerodrome and pulled in behind an outbuilding to the side of the main car park. Harry took off his helmet and moved to where he could see the runway. A plane stood waiting, with Leo Catterson's car parked beside it, and Max stood at the foot of a staircase. He'd never get past him.

"Damn."

"What is it?" Rich asked from behind him.

"Max is guarding the plane."

Rich placed a hand on his shoulder. "Well at least Ted's still here. Try ringing him."

Harry fished out his phone from inside his jacket and pressed the numbers to reach Ted. He tried both phones but got answers from neither.

"Nothing. I don't know what to do. I could run over and shout. Maybe Ted would hear me. At least I might get to say goodbye."

"Or get yourself killed."

Harry frowned at Rich.

"What? You don't really know what's going on, Harry. Look, I've an idea. It might work or it might not."

Harry took hold of Rich's arm. "I'm prepared to do anything, Rich."

"Okay. As a cat, you're smaller. Maybe you might be able to sneak behind the car and jump onto the stairway. Max is positioned to search this way, and you're not the type of cat he's checking for. You might be able to get into the plane and hide under a seat or something."

Harry could have wept. "That's fucking brilliant." He hugged Rich. "I fucking love you, bro."

"And I love you too."

"If I manage to do this, can you explain to everyone?"

"You know I will."

"Look, the pilots are crossing the runway from the main building. If I go now, Max may be distracted. You can put on my clothes so there's no trace I was here. Say I forced the information out of you or something, or I was listening through the window." He hoped Rich wouldn't get into trouble, and they would understand he meant no harm to Ted.

He stretched then transformed and ran from hiding place to shadow until he reached the car. Just as he did, Leo Catterson appeared at the top of the steps and the engine started. He needed to go, now. Max strode to the other side of the car and opened the door. Harry took his chance and jumped, reaching the top step with ease before tucking himself into a small space just inside the doorway. One of the pilots stepped out of the cockpit and sealed the plane.

I'm in. I did it.

"Please fasten your seatbelt, Mr Woodward. We are about to take off." A female voice spoke from the main part of the aircraft. "I'll be in the cockpit until we're airborne."

"Yes, I understand."

Harry wanted to emerge from his hiding place stop the sadness in Ted's voice. He imagined him staring out of the window into the dark. He wanted to let him know he wasn't alone, but until the plane was off the ground, he hunkered down, hoping the take-off wasn't too bumpy. He needed to wait until there was no chance to land in Britain, not that he knew which direction they were flying in.

The plane's engine roared and Harry attempted to squeeze into the smallest space. He thanked the pilot silently for a smooth lift-off then did what cats did when they had nothing else to do—he slept.

Chapter Twenty-Five

Alone in the main body of the plane, Ted stared out of the window into the night. Somewhere down there in the darkness, Harry was probably pacing, not knowing what to do. They'd taken Ted's phones, and although he realised they were trying to protect him from something, once again he was being whisked away to somewhere else, a place he wouldn't know anyone, and a place without Harry. He covered his face with his hands even though there was no one there to see him and wept.

It had been a mad few hours getting to this point. Otis had appeared and whisked him away to what he called a safe house.

"This is ridiculous. A safe house? It's like something out of an American crime show. Why is this jaguar after me? And I can't believe I'm saying that either."

Otis had shrugged. "Truthfully, I don't know. It's above my pay grade. I'm sure Mr Catterson will explain when you meet him."

But no one had explained. He'd been bundled into a posh car by a burly man called Max to find it occupied by another large man who, like Harry, was a cat but on a much bigger scale.

"What the hell is going on?" Ted had asked.

"We're keeping you safe, as was agreed many years ago."

"I don't understand."

"You don't need to understand. You know what you are and that you are unique. There are some shifter types who would like to investigate you and they have no worries about whether you are alive or dead when they do. And then you got mixed up with Harry Katt. Together you created the perfect storm. Harry is one of the Wanderlings."

"Meaning?"

"His father broke all conventions and slept with human women. We don't. We don't breed cross species and we don't breed with humans who haven't consented and know what might happen. Thackery chose to ignore the rules for his own reasons. We still haven't located all of his offspring."

Ted had slumped in his seat. He noted they didn't mention locating this Thackery, which must be the name of Harry's father. "Will I be able to see Harry again?"

"No. We have our own plans for that young man. It's for the best. We're putting you on a plane tonight. It'll be you and the crew in my jet. You'll find out your destination when you get there, and you'll be safe."

He'd remained silent from then onwards, even as he trudged up the steps into the private jet.

"Mr Woodward?"

Ted wiped his eyes and glanced up.

"I'm Livy, the co-pilot. I'm sorry you've been left for a couple of hours. We keep staff to a minimum on these flights. If you get hungry, there's food in the galley at the back of the plane, as well as drinks. The facilities are back there too, and a bedroom if you want to sleep. This journey will take a while, so you might find getting some rest is beneficial."

"I don't suppose there's any point in me asking where we're going?"

She smiled. "No. We don't know your final destination. We're only given the next place to fly to or over. We don't know much more than you do. It's safer that way."

"Do you often work for Mr Catterson?"

"He's a regular customer. This is his plane. Usually the captain flies his own, but for important customers, he'll fly their personal jets."

Ted picked up the television remote control. *Maybe I can get some news.*

"You have access to many films and boxsets," Livy informed him. "But there's no live feed. If you need anything, press the buzzer."

He watched her return to the cockpit and yawned. His body clock was telling him he needed sleep and so, with nothing else to do, he stood and made his way to the rear of the plane, used the facilities in the sumptuous bathroom, then lay down on the large bed and stared at the ceiling. He'd almost dropped off when the bed dipped next to him then something landed on his chest. He opened his eyes to see a cat sat staring at him. For a moment, he thought he must be dreaming. He closed his eyes and opened them again. The cat mewed then headbutted his nose.

"Harry?" He couldn't believe he was saying that name. The cat blinked.

He shifted so he was sitting up and took the cat into his arms. It wriggled in closer and placed a paw around Ted's arm. The cat had a narrow white stripe like the one on Harry's head. He wanted to believe.

Without warning, it sprang out of Ted's arms onto the bed and stretched. The air appeared to shimmer and instead of a cat a man sat in front of him—a naked man—a naked Harry Katt with the hugest grin.

"What the fuck? Harry? How? Where did—?"

"Did you think I'd let them take you away from me?"

Despite his naked state, Harry crawled up the bed and sat astride Ted then smothered him with kisses. Ted held him close, feeling warm flesh under his fingers.

"I should pinch you to check I'm not dreaming," he said between kisses.

"Even better," Harry replied, rubbing a finger over Ted's nipple. "I'll pinch you."

"Ow. That hurt."

Harry sat back on his heels then undid the zip on Ted's trousers and pulled out his cock. "Nice to know you're happy to see me. Cocks don't lie."

He spread himself over Ted, positioning his body so their groins met.

"Someone might come in," Ted said between groans.

"Nah, these people would knock, and they're busy piloting the plane. Private jets are something else, aren't they? How the other half live, eh?"

"Ay. God, Harry. The things you make me feel."

Harry spat on his hand and reached between them. "That's better. A little lubrication from both of us helps. Lift your hips so I can pull these trews, as you call them, down a little. We wouldn't want anything precious getting caught by a zip, now, would we?"

Ted laughed. No one had ever made him laugh like Harry, even in the throes of passion. And even though he had a thousand questions, he let Harry have his way. Happiness flooded every part of him."

"What are you grinning at?" Harry asked.

"You. You being here. Us doing this. Oh, us doing this. Oh, yeah, just there."

Harry kissed him again and they came together, moaning into each other, until their orgasms slowed and they needed to breathe. Ted held Harry tight.

"No one is taking you away from me. Wherever I'm going, I want you to be there with me — if you want to."

Harry rolled over next to him. "I wouldn't be here if I didn't want to be with you. Only Rich knows I am. He overheard Leo Catterson making arrangements for you. We rode my bike to the airfield, I transformed then sneaked onto the plane — sometimes being small and black helps."

"I can't believe you're here." *I can't believe you've given everything up to be with me.* "I need to clean up and change. We'll have to find something for you to wear."

"Or I could just lie around naked and transform if I need to hide."

Ted shifted to the edge of the bed and stood. He stripped then grabbed a towel, followed by a bathrobe.

"Here, put this on for now."

Harry stroked the robe. "Oh, it's so fluffy. Only the best, but I think both of us could fit in here — Leo

Catterson is a big man. Is there anything to eat? I'm starving and I need the loo."

"The ensuite is through there. I'll go make us a sandwich. There's a galley at the back "

Ted dressed in another T-shirt and found a pair of shorts then padded over the shagpile carpet to the door. He hummed to himself as he prepared the food and made hot chocolate—they'd have to share a mug in case anyone came in and Harry had to hide quickly. Harry would lick off the swirly cream, anyway.

"Mr Woodward?"

Ted dropped the knife. "Sorry, I didn't hear you."

Livy smiled at him. "We're trained to be quiet. Just to let you know, we'll be in the air for another six hours then we'll land to refuel and take on another pilot to rotate and allow us to sleep. We'll have to wake you up when we land, but you can use one of the seats in the bedroom and strap in there."

"Thank you. I don't suppose I get to know where we're landing?"

"Not officially. We're not taking the straight route to the final destination is all I know, but we're used to that with particular clients."

"I bet you are."

"I'll leave you to it, then."

She turned and left him alone once more. Realising he'd taken ham to make the sandwich for Harry, he put it back and made him another cheese toastie. He found Harry sat up in bed flicking through options on the huge TV.

"I haven't found any porn yet," he said. "Oh good, a toastie. That cheese smells great."

"Eat up and we'll get some sleep. I'll lock the door. We'll be landing somewhere in a few hours." He explained what Livy had said.

"I can curl up small and hide under the bed."

Ted nodded. "But we need to work out a plan, Harry. I've no idea where we're going, and they could put you back on the plane when we land. We're not out of the woods yet."

* * * *

A knock woke Ted in the early hours of the morning. Harry, in cat from, jumped from the bed and hid out of sight.

"Mr Woodward, we'll be landing in a few minutes. It shouldn't take too long. I'll let you know when we're taking off again. So if you could strap yourself in one of the seats, please."

Ted rubbed his eyes. "I'm moving now, thanks."

He waited a few minutes. "I think you're safe now." Harry emerged, transformed, from the ensuite wearing the robe.

"You'd better get strapped in too."

Harry glanced out of the window. "It's light outside. I think we've travelled eastwards. This airport is huge. I'd guess we're in Dubai." He took the seat next to Ted.

"I think you should stay hidden until we get to wherever it is we're going. I doubt we'll land at a big airport or go through the usual customs. Rich men have power."

"I've been thinking. Maybe you could hide me in your bag. Then when we get wherever they're taking us to, we'll have to plead and hope. I could argue I know too much."

Ted took Harry's hand. "We need to wait and see where we end up. Some countries don't allow gay couples. They could stick me somewhere with no freedom at all. We don't know. I want to be myself as well, Harry. Even if it hurts to transform after so long. I want to know what it's like to swim and build as a beaver."

"I get that," Harry said. "I can't imagine not being a cat. I wonder where we'll head to next."

"Could be anywhere, if they aren't flying direct. This is a big plane but it'll still need to refuel. What did you tell your mum?"

"Nothing. She'll be pissed with me. Rich will tell her I've gone, but I left everything behind. I am the epitome of travelling light. I didn't want to be without you, and I didn't want you to be all alone again in a place where you knew no one. Surely, they'll see having someone they can trust living with you is a good thing." Harry laid his head on Ted's shoulder. Ted didn't tell him about his conversation with Leo Catterson.

"We're moving."

The internal phone rang and Ted picked it up.

"The plane will be taking off again soon, Mr Woodward." This time the voice was male.

"I'm prepared for take-off," Ted said.

"Good. Please feel free to move around once the lights go green over the door."

Ted held the arms of the seat. He'd discovered he wasn't keen on this bit. Harry laid a hand over his.

"At least I'm not trying to squeeze in a small space with my paws wrapped around something this time," he said. Minutes later, they were back in the air again.

They stopped a few more times over the next Ted didn't know how many hours. He attempted to act normally, sitting on the luxurious leather seating reading—at least he had his glasses—or watching television while Harry stayed hidden in the bedroom. He still had no idea where they were heading or in some cases, where they'd landed, but he was glad he wasn't doing this in an economy seat surrounded by others and, knowing his luck, a screaming child or a drunken stag party.

They'd taken his watch so he had no idea how long they'd been in the air, and he'd given up trying to work out the direction from the sun. It was now dark again when Simon, according to his badge, one of the new co-pilots, stepped into the lounge.

"We'll be landing at our final destination soon, sir. If you could pack your belongings and be ready in thirty minutes?"

"I don't suppose you can tell me where we are?" Ted stared up at the handsome older man.

"No, sir. That would lose me my job."

"Fair enough." Ted stood.

In the bedroom, he found Harry sleeping under the duvet and woke him up. Harry stretched, jumped into Ted's arms, then headbutted his nose. Warmth swelled in Ted's chest as he stroked Harry's back.

"We're landing at our final destination soon. I've been told to pack. Are you sure you'll be all right in my bag?"

Harry blinked once.

"I'll make sure to keep hold of you so you're not thrown in a boot or something, like we discussed. If we can get where we're going without them seeing you and being able to whisk you away, then we might stand a chance. I don't know, but I want to try."

Harry blinked once again.

"Right, I'd better get sorted."

The landing proved somewhat less smooth than before and Ted guessed they might have arrived at a rather more informal setting. At the bottom of the steps, he tried to see anything that might help, but all was dark except for one building where the crew were talking to someone. He glanced up at the noise of a helicopter and saw lights approaching. He leaned over.

"Can you hear that?" he whispered. "It seems we're going somewhere else. I can't see anything here. We're definitely not at an airport. Don't worry. I'll keep you with me."

The helicopter landed nearby. Simon directed Ted towards it. "You'll be travelling in this to your final destination," he said. "Good luck."

A huge red-headed man, who appeared strangely familiar, stepped out of the cockpit. *Is that the right word?* He held out his hand. His grip was firm, and Ted thought he'd crick his neck meeting his gaze.

"It's good to meet you, Ted. I'll be taking you to your new home. My name is Ralph McStagg. You know my cousin."

The laird, of course – the man's deer form was hardly visible, suggesting it had been some time since he'd transformed. "Yes, I do."

"Get in, and I'll tell you as much as I can."

Ted climbed into the chopper and sat with his bag on his lap. They rose steadily then set off into the dark and into Ted's new life.

Chapter Twenty-Six

All Harry could hear was the whirring of helicopter blades. He wished he could stick his head out of the opening Ted had made so he could get more air. He'd managed to sleep on the plane, but there was no chance of that now. The conversation between Ted and the pilot was muffled so he had no idea if Ted knew where they were yet.

Harry couldn't tell how long they were in the air, only that the chopper seemed to rise and fall, suggesting they were flying over mountains and into valleys. It was warm but not hot. Finally, they maintained a downward trajectory and landed.

"I think we're here," Ted whispered, before he pulled the zip, leaving only a small gap.

More muffled speech and movement. Ted carried him then, at last, placed the bag on solid ground. He unzipped and light flooded inside, making Harry blink.

"Quick. Jump out and hide somewhere. I've lots to tell you but I need to get rid of Ralph first."

Harry leapt from the bag and hid under the large bed.

"Love you," Ted said, and closed the door, leaving Harry alone and frustrated once more. Being a cat, he couldn't not jump back on the bed to examine his surroundings.

The bedroom was large, with a door on the other side of the room ajar enough to reveal a bathroom. The walls and floors suggested a cabin much like the one Ted had lived in before, made of wood, though Harry was happy to see a radiator on one wall. Other than that, the walls were bare and the furniture sparse. Harry padded over to the bathroom.

Wow, this place is huge. The shower and bath are big enough for two. He grinned at the thought. *Don't get ahead of yourself. They could throw you out straight away. Better have a quick wee.*

He strolled back under the bed, curled up, and promptly fell asleep like cats do. He had no idea how much time had passed when Ted woke him.

"Harry, you can come out now. He's gone. I thought the helicopter leaving might have disturbed you."

Harry made his way from under the bed then jumped up into Ted's arms. Ted placed him back on the bed.

"You transform, and I'll get you some clothes. We'll have to make do for now. Ralph said to let his factor know what I need to get the place sorted, but that the fridge and freezer are well-stocked."

Harry turned back into a human and stretched out all the kinks of being small for a longer time then waited for Ted to return.

He grinned when Ted's eyes widened, taking in the sight in front of him. Harry didn't care and leant back, showing off. "I love how it still surprises you I'm naked even though you know I will be. Now, sit here and tell me everything."

Ted explained who Ralph was. "He owns this huge estate we're on."

"So we're in New Zealand?"

"Yes. They want me to work in the forests of the estate. The rest is given over to sheep farming and I know nothing about that, but I do know trees and rivers. There's a small area of forest nearby with a stream. He says I'll be able to be myself because the only shifters in the country are here for a reason and entry is strictly controlled. I can swim, take down trees, and build a dam. I can be a beaver."

Harry pushed away his worries and wrapped his arms around Ted and hugged him. "It won't be easy — the first time."

Ted shook slightly. "I know. I'm prepared. And I don't intend to rush into anything. But we're here, and we're together, and perhaps you should put on some clothes, then I'll show you the rest of the place. Ralph said there's no other house within five miles of here, so no one can see. We have the place to ourselves."

"It's got everything we need," Harry said. The tour hadn't taken long as there was only one other large room which served as a living, dining and kitchen space. "Let's go outside."

The smile on Ted's face told Harry all he needed to know. He reached for the handle and swung open the door.

"Oh my God. It's beautiful, like being back home but on a larger scale." Ahead of them stretched grassland. To the side, a wooded area covered a huge space, but the backdrop was the most spectacular, as mountains, some still capped with snow, reached up to the bright blue sky. The cabin had a garden filled with flowers and buzzing insects making Harry want to run around and chase things.

Ted placed an arm around his shoulder. "It's magnificent, isn't it? It reminds me of home. There's a vegetable garden round the back and a small wind turbine, so the house is self-sufficient."

"It's like the scenery in *Lord of the Rings*. We're living in the Shire and the mountain over there could be Mount Doom."

"I hope not," Ted said. "Let's have something to eat. There's a barbecue at the back and enough steaks in the freezer—they didn't think about me being a vegetarian, but I can make a veggie pizza as there's also an oven."

"All the mod cons. Come on, then. I can man the barbie and you the oven."

For a while, they sat on the decking at the back of the house and watched the sun go down.

"It'll be the longest day on this side of the world next month," Ted said. "And Christmas."

"It'll seem weird having Christmas in the warm, though it's not quite like having a barbecue on the beach like the Aussies. Let's go for a walk in the woods and see if we can find this stream they mentioned. I bet the stars are amazing in this sky with no lights from nearby towns or cities to spoil the view."

Harry took Ted's hand and they strolled through the trees. The leaf canopy obscured most of the remaining light, but Harry found his way while Ted named the variety of each tree.

"This place is old," he said. "I thought it might be all varieties of pine, but there are some deciduous trees here, and I've no idea what most of them are. I've a lot to learn about the native varieties and which are protected. I can hear water from over there."

I may have the eyesight, but Ted has the best hearing and sense of smell. Harry set off in the direction Ted pointed to until the trees opened into an empty space with a small stream running through it. Harry lifted his gaze to the sky.

"Wow, look at the stars." He spun around as a silver glow from above created a circle of light around them. He pulled Ted to the floor and they both stared.

"It's like a fairy glade," Ted said. "Any minute now I expect an elf to appear."

"It's beautiful, and all yours to turn into a beaver paradise."

"Maybe, but for now all I want to do is lie here with you."

All around them, the sounds of the forest tinkled and twittered. Harry had no idea what creatures existed in the dark, and for now he didn't care. He rolled over on top of Ted and kissed him.

"I want you to fuck me here under these starry skies in the forest among the trees you love."

Ted sat up and lifted his arms. Harry pulled off Ted's T-shirt then his own. He kissed Ted's chest with its covering of auburn hair, following the line lower and lower.

"Take them off," he whispered, when he reached the edge of Ted's jeans.

"I've an idea," Ted said. He stood, offered his hand to Harry and hauled him up then picked up their discarded T-shirts and led him to a large tree. He lay the shirts on the forest floor then took off his jeans and boxers and sat with his back against the bark.

"Ride me."

Harry grinned then reached into his pocket before throwing off his oversized shorts. He waved the small packet of lube in the air.

"I found some in the bathroom on the plane and thought it might come in handy."

Harry knelt astride Ted's thighs, bent forward and prepped himself while Ted took his cock in hand and stroked.

"Have you some for me?" Ted asked.

Harry squeezed the last of the lube on the tip of Ted's erection and lifted himself, ready to let Ted slide inside him. "Are you sure?" he asked.

"Yes. God, your eyes are so bright in the dark. I can hardly see a thing, but the smells and the sounds are incredible. I can hear the insects and the fluttering of wings through the trees."

Harry positioned himself then let his body drop inch by inch until he was full. He wriggled, getting into position, and they wrapped their arms around each other, meeting chest to chest and mouth to mouth so as much of one as possible was touching the other.

"You are so beautiful," Ted said in between kisses. "I want to be with you for the rest of my life, like this, holding you, feeling the heat of you around me, listening to you breathe."

Harry gasped. "Oh yeah, there. That's perfect. I bet I'm leaking all over you." He groaned, not caring how loudly. "Yes. Fuck me, Ted. I love the way you feel. This place is magical. I've tingles down my spine."

Ted held him tighter and thrust upwards.

"Please. So good the way you fill me up. Yes, that's it." He didn't even need to use his hands, just the closeness of their bodies and the friction they provided was enough as his orgasm burst free. Ted kept moving inside him as his muscles contracted.

"I love you," Ted yelled, and heat bloomed inside Harry, filling him. "This is so glorious with nothing between us knowing my cum will still be there."

Harry kissed Ted's neck, not caring it would leave a mark. Ted was his and he wanted Ted's body to say so. "Next time we can use a plug, though you'd have to order one, then you can fuck me again using it as lube."

"Bloody hell, I think my cock just twitched at the thought of you walking around like that."

As Ted spoke, the moon appeared through the gap in the canopy and lit up Ted's face.

"I love you," Harry said. "I think I loved you from the time you came to see me in hospital, and from when you stroked my leg under the table with everyone there."

Ted wiped a tear from his eye. "I suppose we'd better go back to the cabin. Who knows what might be out here?"

Harry lifted himself off, feeling the immediate sense of emptiness. *Maybe a butt plug would be a good idea.* They dressed speedily then strolled hand in hand back to the cabin, and to bed.

* * * *

Harry woke the next day to sunshine streaming through the curtains. It took him a minute or two to remember where he was. Ted groaned next to him and opened his eyes.

"Morning, sweetheart. D'you know, I've no idea what day it is. It'll still be yesterday back home."

Guilt smacked Harry in the chest. Would his mum be worried? Rich would tell her a little, but not too much for her own safety. Ted jumped out of bed.

"I'll hit the shower then find us something for breakfast."

Harry found something else to wear — too big again. They'd need to do something about clothes. He hummed as he dressed, thinking of the night before. The knock on the front door woke him from his musings. He hid in the large wardrobe and waited, listening to the murmuring of conversation followed by the creak of the bedroom door opening.

"You can come out now, Mr Katt. I think we have some things to discuss, don't you?"

Chapter Twenty-Seven

"They had cameras," Ted said.

"Everywhere?" Harry asked.

Ralph McStagg stepped forward. The room seemed much smaller with all three of them in the space. "No, not everywhere, but they do cover the front and back of the house. You wouldn't expect us to not take your security seriously considering your circumstances, now, would you?"

Ted placed himself in front of Harry. "I want him to stay. I'll go out of my mind here on my own. We love each other." His heart swelled with joy uttering those words.

"We're aware of your relationship, and we'd had word Harry here had disappeared, though we've no idea how you managed to get past everyone and smuggle him on to the plane."

Is that admiration in his voice?

"Cats are small and agile," Harry said. "We're also good at hiding when we need to and can fit in small spaces."

"Do you feel the same as Ted?"

Ted turned to face Harry and reached out his hands. Harry took them and met his gaze.

"Yes. I love him. I wouldn't have travelled halfway around the world to be with him if I didn't. I know I'm leaving my old life behind, but when you know, you know. Please don't make me leave. We'll follow the rules as long as we can be together. And you can call me anything."

Ralph puled a chair from under the small table and sat. "I don't know about you two, but I could do with a large mug of tea and some toast. I didn't get chance to have breakfast this morning."

"I'll do the honours," Harry said. "You sit."

Ted took the other chair. He was small next to Ralph, but determined to fight for Harry, whatever the cost.

"So, what are you going to do?"

"Nothing," Ralph said.

Ted jumped when metal clanged against metal as Harry dropped a spoon into the sink. He wiped his hands on his jeans. It was a hot day, but he had other reasons to sweat.

"What d'you mean, nothing?"

"I mean exactly what I say. In fact, this works better for us. You'll have a job and a relationship to keep you on an even keel. We have other shifters on this estate and on others on both islands, also in hiding for one reason or another. New Zealand has a few native shifters among the birds, but no land mammals. However, up until now, all of those we've given protection to have been non-carnivores. You will be an exception, Harry, but there are many domestic cats here, so your existence would not be commented on."

"How many others are there on this estate?" Ted asked.

"Just under one hundred. Some families and couples with some singletons. You will meet them, and work with them. You, Harry, can continue in your current work or do something different, if you want."

Harry placed the tea and toast on the table then jumped up to perch on the work counter. "Are we allowed to leave the estate?" he asked.

"Within limits. There is a small town twenty-five miles away. As I said, pest control is an issue here too."

"I have no interest in continuing killing things for a living, but I would like to continue my education and do a degree in history, then maybe teach."

"Really?" Ted said turning his head to face Harry. "You've never said."

"No. It didn't fit in with my devil-may-care attitude to life. I thought I'd given myself away talking about that painting of Elizabeth after I'd managed not to look as if I was interested at the British Museum. And to be honest, I wasn't the best student in school."

"I could look into that for you," Ralph said. "In the meantime, I've brought some catalogues for clothes and furniture. If you let us know, we can order them for you."

"What about the internet?" Ted asked. "There's a TV."

"There's satellite connection for computers and the TV and radio. We'll get you documents with new surnames. You can keep your first names. This will take a while to set up." He picked up his bag and pulled out a few catalogues. "Food deliveries are done every week, but we keep the freezer well-stocked. Good tea, Harry. Is there anything else?"

Ted unfurled his fingers and glanced at Harry. "Probably hundreds of things, but just the one I can think of for now — will I be able to transform? I know I'll be allowed, but will my body cope?"

Ralph leant forward. "It's been many years since you did. You'll need some preparation. We have someone who can help, but there are limits."

"What sort of limits?"

"You can only take your beaver form within two miles of this cabin."

The brook is near enough. "Could you talk to this person who can help?"

Ralph pushed back the chair and stood. "I'll contact you on the radio and someone will be by tomorrow to pick up the list from you." He held out a hand to Harry.

"It's been interesting to meet you. We'll let your family know you are safe, but not where you are, and you can't contact them unless circumstances change."

"I understand," Harry said. "Thank you for letting me stay."

"You being here benefits Ted, but it benefits us too. We'll be in touch."

As soon as Ralph had left — Ted watched him wander off down the path — he turned to Harry.

"You are sure, aren't you?" Thousands of butterflies beat their wings in his stomach at the thought of what Harry might say. Nausea threatened to overwhelm him.

"Stop it," Harry said. "I smuggled myself onto a plane for you. I told you I wanted to be here, and I still do. Now, at least I can study." He looked down at what he was wearing. "And order some clothes. Should I worry about who is paying for all this?"

"I suspect Ralph is rich enough, if he owns this huge estate. The McStaggs have old money. Let's sit outside and do some shopping."

* * * *

Over the next week, they ordered clothes and selected furniture, Ted met his new boss, the estate manager, and began a crash course in New Zealand flora and fauna, and Harry chose a course he could do online — at least the pandemic had been useful in some ways. On the following Wednesday, they were visited by the person Ralph had mentioned could help Ted.

When the car pulled up in front of the house, Ted opened the door. He'd spoken to Dr Kauri online and now they were to meet in person. The most surprising thing about her was that she wasn't a shifter.

"This is a first for me," she said. "Meeting a were-beaver, but I've met lots of others. I'm one of those humans who has the ability to see your other form, even someone who hasn't transformed for many years, like you. My culture has many beliefs about animals and many stories."

"I'm glad you are able to help, Dr Kauri."

"Please, call me Maia. We're going to be spending a lot of time together. I will teach you ways to move your body and train your mind. It still won't be easy — I imagine Harry here hardly feels it when he changes."

Harry had sat himself on the sofa — to help, he said. Ted thought he was curious like the cat he was.

"No, not much, or rather not for long. It's hard to explain. But I still try to stretch before each transformation if I have time. Cats are flexible creatures as well."

"I suppose it helps if you have the ability to land on your feet."

Ted chuckled. "Not always. He landed on his arse when we first met."

"That's true, and once he'd saved my life, he had to look after me, or that's what I tell him. I hope you don't mind me staying. I'm interested in seeing what you do as well."

"And I'm interested in your experience, and you can tell me the meet-cute story over a coffee later. Now it's time to get on the floor and start to stretch."

* * * *

The lessons continued for weeks. Harry started his course, and Ted began mapping out the trees on the estate to see what needed to be felled and where more could be planted.

"This place is vast," he said. "I bet you could fit the Lake District in it and more."

"I know," Harry said. "I've been learning stuff online. Here is about the same size as the UK, but while there are nearly seventy million people back home, there are only four million or so here, and the population density is more than ten times less. My history and geography knowledge of New Zealand is improving every day."

"I spoke to Maia earlier. She reckons I could be ready for my first transformation."

"Do you?" Harry asked.

"I want to, but I have to admit I'm scared of how much it's going to hurt."

"We'll both be there to hold your hand. Why don't you contact her and set a date?"

Ted breathed in the way Maia had taught him. Harry enveloped him in his arms and the tension in his muscles and bones faded away. "Thank you. I'll call her. Let's go for a walk to the fairy glade. We could relive our first night but the other way around."

Harry took Ted's hand. "Sounds like a plan to me, but I'll grab a blanket this time."

* * * *

Two weeks later, Ted lay on the floor staring at the wooden ceiling, breathing slowly in through his nose and out through his mouth, with Maia on one side of him and Harry on the other.

"That's it," Maia said. "The drugs will help with the pain and muscle cramps. It's best to keep your limbs straight. You need to clear your mind and create an image of yourself as a beaver."

Ted had practiced this over and over. Harry had told him there was no magic word, phrase, or action, like saying open sesame or clicking his fingers, he only had to become his other half and let his beaver side embrace the rest.

"But what if I get halfway? What if I end up with a human head and a beaver body?"

Harry had assured him this didn't happen—ever. You were either one thing or another.

"Now, stretch every part of your body from your toes upwards like you've been taught."

Ted did as he had learnt to do, moving every part and every muscle. "Okay, I'm ready to try. Sorry, I was forgetting my Yoda advice. I'm ready to transform."

Harry squeezed his hand and shifted away from him to give him space. Maia patted his other hand and did the same. Once he had become a beaver, he wouldn't be able to talk, so they had worked out signals using his tail—*I'll have a tail*—one slap for yes and two for no.

"I love you, Harry."

"I love you as well, you daft idiot. Now go."

Ted breathed again, closed his eyes, and brought the image of his other self to mind. The air whooshed around him, his body moved without his direction, and pain shot through bones and sinews, making crunching and creaking sounds as they shifted. For a few moments, he lost himself before he found his other half, caught in limbo, then everything stopped and his body calmed. The pain had gone even when he moved.

"Has it worked?" he said, not daring to open his eyes. No answer came. *Of course, they won't understand me.*

He lifted his eyelids. The first thing he noticed was his view of the room had changed. *I'm shorter.* He lifted his hands and saw paws held close to his body. He touched himself to find he was covered in dense brown fur. Finally, he stood on two feet, shakily at first.

"Ted, are you all right?"

He understood. The human part of his brain kicked in but in his beaver body he could understand but not reply, and there was no other beaver in this country to talk to. He lifted his tail once.

"Thank goodness."

Ted waddled to the mirror. *At last, I'm my whole self, after all these years. I want to go to the river. I want to cut down a tree, though I hope I get my human teeth back. I want to swim.*

He scampered across the room and glanced back at Harry. He couldn't reach the handle. Harry opened the door and Ted set off, leaving the others to catch up with him.

He loved the warmth of the sun on his fur, and the feel of the earth under his paws as he scurried through the undergrowth until he reached the fairy glade.

I'm surrounded by wood. He wanted to cut one down—just a little one, but he didn't know each species well enough yet. He stood and sniffed the air. It smelt different. So many more scents reached his senses and he heard the trickle of water over rocks.

I need to... He set off to the stream and waited there until Harry and Maia caught up. He didn't want to disappear and worry them. Next to him lay a fallen branch. He picked it up and chewed, not knowing what it would taste like in this form. His teeth cut through the wood into the cellulous and he swallowed.

"We're here," Harry said, when they caught up. "I see you found lunch."

Ted lifted a paw and pointed to the water then waddled in. He dived and explored, working out where he would build the dam, meeting the other creatures who lived there, who were perfectly safe from him and whom he was perfectly safe from. He slapped his tail on the water. It was glorious.

This is who I am meant to be, who I was always meant to be.

He wasn't sure how long he was in the water. He dragged himself to the riverbank and shook the water from his fur. It was time to go back to being Ted. He sat back on his haunches.

"We need to return to the house," Maia said.

He slapped his tail once and followed them back to the cabin to face another shift back to his human self.

This time it hurt slightly less and once more, he had no pain once he was back in human form, just a sense of loss. Then he remembered he was naked and that Maia was still in the room. Heat rushed into his face and he grabbed for the sheet they'd left over the chair.

Maia chuckled. "I've seen it all before," she said.

"Yes, but you haven't seen mine."

"Don't concern yourself, you've nothing to worry about."

Harry burst out laughing. "Hands off, he's mine."

Ted sat up, now covered, "I'm still in the room, you two."

"Sorry, I couldn't resist. You seem to be all right and recovered well. Are you?"

Ted stretched each limb. "I'm fine now. The pain could have been worse and was less the second time. Being my other self-answered so many questions, but left me with a sense of longing to transform again. Everything I did as a beaver was instinctive. I knew what to do, and I wanted to do more, though it was frustrating not being able to talk to you. I wonder if we could learn sign language."

"It's a thought."

Maia stood. "I'll leave you both now. Remember you still need to take care. It'll be some time until you can transform without preparation. I'm here for you as long as you need me."

"I would hug you, but I'm conscious of being naked under here. I couldn't have done this without you."

Harry stood and hugged her. "I'll do it instead, then cuddle him."

"Any excuse. It's been a pleasure. This is one of the joys of my job, helping people be who they are." She opened the door and stepped out. Harry closed it behind her and they were alone again.

"Are you really all right?" Harry asked.

Ted nodded. "Yes. I am. More than all right. I understand so much more now of what I've missed. I know we've both given up so much to be here..." He left the sentence hanging.

"It was my choice, Ted. I wanted to be with you. My family will understand. Rich will hold things together. Here we can both be who we are in more ways than one. You make me happy, Ted. We've so much to look forward to, meeting other shifters on the estate, and being ourselves knowing this place is set up to protect us and allow us to simply be."

"I'd better get dressed. We've got the Christmas decorations to put up and I need to cut down a tree."

"Really?" Harry said. "As much as I love your lumberjack look..." He clasped Ted's hand and dragged him across the room. "I can think of something much more exciting to do with a naked man."

Ted grinned and leapt onto the bed. "You'll get no argument from me."

E p i l o g u e

Ten months later

"I can't believe it's over a year since we first met." Harry sat next to Ted on a log in the fairy glade. Ted spent time there whenever he could.

"Aye, a year since I let my lips touch yours and never wanted to stop kissing you again."

Harry grinned and nudged him. "You soppy old romantic, you. Who'd realise under that hairy exterior there was a big expanse of mushiness?"

"You, thank goodness."

Harry kissed him and wanted to do more but today they had plans. The glade was laid out with a few chairs and a table.

"Are you dry enough to get dressed now?" he asked.

"You know the water falls off."

"Because you're so hairy." Harry stroked Ted's face.

"You can talk. Your face is almost as hairy as mine now."

"It makes me feel all rugged and outdoorsy, even in this suit. Come on, we'd better get you dressed or the others will get here and find you naked." Harry brushed down his suit and helped Ted into his.

"I'm sorry your family can't be here," Ted said as Harry created a proper knot in his tie.

"Me too, but we won't be alone, and somehow I can feel Thom and Rich — maybe it's a triplets thing."

Voices drifted through the trees. "They're here," Ted said. "Are you still sure you want to do this? It's not too quick or anything?"

"No. I can't wait to be your husband and I can't believe we get to say our vows here, in our glade, next to the dam and pond you've created. I hope Ralph picked up the celebrant."

"You've not run away and changed your minds, either of you, then." Ralph's voice boomed across the space. Next to him stood a woman who was clearly a doe, and also Ralph's partner, Alice. It turned out she was a certified celebrant and had married many of the pairs on the estate. They were followed by Maia and their nearest neighbours, Mary and Bo, a pair of wallaby shifters, who'd been rescued from a fire in Australia a few years before.

"No, Ralph, we're here."

"You're doing a great job with the stream," Alice said. "I love this place. I'm glad you chose it for today. Oh, come here the both of you, looking so handsome. I need to cuddle you."

Harry and Ted stepped forward and let Alice and the others surround them in warmth and friendship as they all had from the first. Harry wiped a tear away from his eye and did the same for the one rolling down Ted's cheek into his beard.

"Right, could the groom and groom take their places. I have to do the formal bits."

Harry held Ted's hand and they strolled to the centre of the glade where the sun streamed down on a warm spring day. They listened to Alice's words and made their vows then signed the papers with the witnesses. And it was over.

"Too late to change your mind now," Maia said.

Harry gazed at Ted. "Why would I want to? He makes me the happiest person alive, and every day when I wake up next to him is a good day."

"Now who's soppy," Ted said.

"Both of us. Let's go back to the house and open that champagne then it's time for the wedding breakfast in town, or more accurately the wedding lunch. That'll be a first, too."

The town was just inside the boundaries of the estate. It was a quaint little place with shops of every kind and places to eat which reminded Harry of somewhere out of a Hallmark movie, the sort of place the cynical businessperson would return to and fall in love with the Christmas tree salesman or the woman who owned the rather shabby hotel. Harry loved it. He lifted his left hand.

"I'm not sure I'm ever going to stop staring at this ring."

Ted squeezed his thigh under the table. "It does look beautiful on your finger."

"Bloody hell, are you two going to be like this forever?" Mary asked.

"Probably," Harry replied, nudging a fork across the table to the edge.

"Did I hear right?" the owner said, placing the tray of drinks on the table. "Did you get hitched today?"

"We did," Ted replied.

She turned to face the room. "Hey everyone, this is Harry and Ted and they just got married."

People clapped and whistled. Despite this being their first visit, they knew most of the customers. Many were shifters brought there for various reasons, but some were visitors who'd stumbled on the place.

Nancy spun on her heel. "These drinks are on us," she said.

They ate their meal and chatted about future plans until only a few visitors remained in the dining area. Harry and Ted said goodbye to everyone then sat at the bar to drink their last round. Another of the customers waited to pay his bill and was chatting to Nancy.

"We've a motorhome and we're doing a tour of both islands. This place isn't on the map, which is weird, so we found it by accident. It's so quaint with all these little shops selling all sorts of things, and not a supermarket or big name in sight. It's like something out of a film. We have to say the food is excellent and this place is beautiful."

"Well, thank you."

Ted and Harry sat on stools and listened to the chat until the man turned to them. "Congratulations on your nuptials. Me and my partner have been married…" He paused as if trying to remember something… "We've been married for forty-six years. It's a great thing being with someone you love." He turned and waved at his wife.

Harry smiled and took hold of Ted's hand. "I couldn't help hearing you're on a road trip. Where are you off to next?"

"We're going to this place about fifty miles away — we don't like to travel far in one go. I doubt you know anything of it, but it does have an interesting story. It's called Cowbridge. Apparently the founder emigrated from somewhere in Wales and kept cattle which were herded over the river on a bridge that now needs to be replaced. Anyway, that's not the interesting bit."

"Oh," Ted said.

"No, it has another name. The locals call it Beaverton."

Ted tensed beside Harry. "Really? Is there a reason?"

"Just a local story about how there were once beavers living locally, though some people think they were otters brought here by settlers. As you probably know, we don't have any native land mammals. Anyway, there are little wooden statues of the beavers all over the place. The story even got on the news recently. Imagine that—beavers living here. In a way it's sad there aren't any." He stood and turned when his wife called his name. "It would be amazing to think they might exist somewhere in secret, building dams and making ponds. Oh well."

As he wandered away. Harry gazed at Ted. "Well, he'd be happy to know there's a beaver here now, isn't there, my love?"

Nancy placed the round of drinks on the table and winked at them. Ted picked up a tray. "There most certainly is."

Sign up for our newsletter and find out about all our romance book releases, eBook sales and promotions, sneak peeks and FREE romance books!

Want to see more from this author?
Here's a taster for you to enjoy!

Sporting Chance
Alexa Milne

Excerpt

Oh hell!

His arse hit the ice.

This was going to be so embarrassing.

He really should have looked where he was going and taken more care. It wasn't that he meant to show off in front of the kids when they'd goaded him into demonstrating how he could skate backward. But that was how he found himself crashing into another body, a rather large male body, then scrabbling, unsuccessfully, to try to get himself up as he apologized. Iestyn heard the kids laughing. How the hell was he going to get up and retain some sort of dignity? Whose bloody idea had it been to come on this skating trip from school, and why had he volunteered to go? He heard a voice—a rather gorgeous lyrical voice—say something, but he wasn't sure what. He found himself looking up into the face of the most handsome man he'd ever seen.

"Would you like some help getting up?" the vision said, holding out a hand.

Iestyn took the help offered and let the good-looking stranger pull him to his feet. He was shocked to find, when he'd stood up, that the man appeared to be significantly taller than his own nearly six feet.

"Thanks," he said, brushing the ice from his trousers. He glanced over to find the kids staring at him. "What? You've seen a man fall over before, haven't you? Even a teacher."

But they just kept on staring at the man who had helped him up.

"Sorry about that lot. Honestly, you can't take them anywhere, and thanks for hauling me up. I'm not very good at this lark, really." He didn't want to stare but he couldn't resist looking the man up and down. His rescuer was impressively built with blue eyes and blond hair that seemed determined to defy any sort of styling.

"Yeah, that much is obvious but don't worry. I can cope with men falling at my feet. I get it a lot, though usually it's because they've just missed tackling me. The blond, godlike creature held out his hand. "Sorry. It's not often that I have to introduce myself. My name is Dan Morgan."

"Ah, judging from the reaction of the kids, I should have heard of you."

A smaller man, who was standing behind them, sniggered at his comment.

One of the boys rushed forward. "Can I have your autograph, Dan?" he asked.

The other kids came forward too, offering whatever they could find for him to sign.

"You don't have any idea who I am, do you?" the younger man said as he signed the autographs.

"No, sorry. I don't, but obviously the kids do, so you're either some sort of pop star or, from what you've said, a sportsman. I'm guessing rugby."

Josh, a character in Iestyn's form, stepped forward. "Take no notice of Mr Jones. The only game he plays is chess. He wouldn't know one end of a rugby ball from the other."

"Well, to be fair, they are actually pretty similar," Dan replied.

Iestyn frowned at Josh, not for the first time, then looked back at Dan. "So you play rugby then, and I should know this because?"

"Bloody hell, sir. Sorry, but he's Dan Morgan." Now it was Josh's turn to frown. "He plays for Glamorgan Giants and Wales. Most experts reckon that he's going to be Welsh captain for the Six Nations. Call yourself Welsh, sir!"

"Actually, that's rather a moot point. I may be called Jones but I wasn't born in Wales, despite my father's best efforts. I was born in the Highlands of Scotland, because we were on holiday and I came earlier than expected. My dad was gutted, I can tell you."

"Sounds like an interesting story," Dan said. "Perhaps you'd like to tell it to me sometime soon, maybe over dinner."

Iestyn Jones blinked a few times and wondered if he'd heard right. Had this guy just asked him out? Dan had to be at least ten years younger than him, not to mention six inches taller.

Dan passed him a card that said "Ring me" and gave a number. He smiled and walked back to greet his friend who had been standing some distance away. Watching him go, Iestyn held onto the card and twirled it in his fingers, not sure how to react to this strange development.

"You're in there, sir," he heard a familiar voice say.

"Shut up, Josh. Come on. I see Miss Jenkins over there tapping her watch. It's time we weren't here."

"But, sir, he's gay and you're gay," Josh persisted.

"Really?" He shouldn't have been surprised. His gaydar was normally useless. "Never mind that. I don't need a matchmaker, thank you." That he was gay was no secret to the kids or to any of the other staff.

His best friend Julie Jenkins came toward him. "Is it right what the kids have just told me? Have you just been asked out by Dan Morgan? My God, he's gorgeous. I can't tell you how many women would like a piece of him."

"Well," Iestyn said, grinning widely. "It seems that Dan Morgan wants a piece of me."

About the Author

Originally from South Wales, Alexa has lived for over forty years in the North West of England. Now retired, after a long career in teaching, she devotes her time to her obsessions.

Alexa began writing when her favourite character was killed in her favourite show. After producing a lot of fanfiction she ventured into original writing.

She is currently owned by a mad cat and spends her time writing about the men in her head, watching her favourite television programmes and usually crying over her favourite football team.

Alexa loves to hear from readers. You can find her contact information, website details and author profile page at https://www.firstforromance.com

ENTWINED PUBLISHING